CREATURES
OF
HABIT

Pat Mullan

CREATURES OF HABIT

By Pat Mullan

An ATHRY HOUSE book

Copyright © 2014 Pat Mullan

ISBN-13:   978-0983865209
ISBN-10:   0983865205

Cover design by BEAUTeBOOK
Original photography by Stefano Corso at Wikimedia

Praise for Pat Mullan's CREATURES OF HABIT

"Creatures of Habit, the shimmer of evil..."

"There are shades of Chesterton, Dorothy L. Sayers, and even Tom Clancy in Creatures of Habit, Pat Mullan's powerful new novel. Set mainly in "Celtic Tiger" Ireland, the punning title displays the shimmer of evil that the novel's hero, the all-too-human Ed Burke, senses throughout. Pederasty, madness, and murder abide in this complex and fascinating story; a story stolen by humanity's seemingly bottomless capacity for corruption. Ed Burke is just the man to smoke it out. This is certainly one of the most exciting, and powerful, thrillers I've ever read—the complex art of the thinker's mystery. Great stuff!"   **E. M. Schorb**
E.M.Schorb, award winning author and poet: winner of The Frankfurt Grand Prize in fiction for his novel, Paradise Square; 1973 International Keats Poetry Prize; Verna Emery Poetry Prize for Murderer's Day, his fourth collection of poetry (Purdue University Press). E. M. Schorb's new novel, Fortune Island, was published in 2009.

More praise for PAT MULLAN

"Pat Mullan is a natural born storyteller with a gripping, engaging style. He may just be the next big thing in Irish crime fiction." **Jason Starr, author of LIGHTS OUT**

"Pat Mullan's latest, **LAST DAYS OF THE TIGER**, is a razor blade down the spine. So fast-paced, expect whiplash. This is Irish noir with a hero whom you'll want at your back in any gunfight. Grab a copy and clear your schedule!" **James Rollins, New York Times bestselling author of BLACK ORDER.**

"**LAST DAYS OF THE TIGER** bristles with ingenuity and a plot to kill for ...this is a thriller of such high caliber that it transcends all genres...has all the Irish gifts: dizzy narrative, sly humour, and marvelous readability. It rocks!" **Ken Bruen, Edgar and Macavity Award winning author of THE GUARDS.**

"A high-powered legal thriller chocked full of betrayal, deceit, corruption, and murder. Mullan is Ireland's answer to John Grisham, with a smattering of Ross MacDonald thrown in. **LAST DAYS OF THE TIGER** will make your head spin." **JA Konrath, author of RUSTY NAIL.**

3

"LAST DAYS OF THE TIGER is a tight, intelligent thriller. Author Pat Mullan blends political intrigue and murder with a unique Irish flavor that goes down smooth. His hero, Ed Burke, is striking—almost an anti-hero in some respects. To unravel the deception and save himself, Burke must test old friendships, and determine who to trust in an Ireland changed by the Celtic Tiger. Mullan writes suspense with an edge reminiscent of Bob Ludlum. An author to watch." **Cerri Ellis - MOSTLY MYSTERY REVIEWS**

But who so shall offend one of these little ones which believe in me, it were better for him that a millstone were hanged about his neck, and that he were drowned in the depth of the sea. **Matthew 18:6**

1

Ireland

The two boys, breathless, reached the west corner of the big study hall and flattened themselves against the granite wall. Night had fallen and the wind had reached gale force. Sleety rain sliced the air like sheets of broken glass. The trees bent and groaned. Wearing short trousers, their legs were scorched red from knees to ankles,

They could see the flashlight coming towards them and they knew they'd have to run again. So they left the shelter of the wall and dashed past the handball court as the lightning illuminated everything. Exposed, they cut across the front lawn and ran towards the outer wall. They could hear the loud squelch of running feet behind them.

A line of ancient oak trees stood like sentries inside the outer wall. They hid between the trees, hoping their pursuers would bypass them. But that was a false hope. The flashlight reached the trees, weaving in and out, getting closer and closer. Panicked, Patrick, the older boy, started to climb the nearest tree. Terry, the younger boy, tried to follow but couldn't. So he ran, blindly, out of the shelter of the trees.   Patrick sat on a branch as the flashlight passed beneath him. He had stopped breathing and his heart thumped so loudly he imagined they must hear it.   But they moved on, following Terry as he fled.

Now alone and terrified, Terry ran into the blinding rain, his lungs seared from the effort. Lightning flashed again, silhouetting the old ruined tower that stood inside the north-east boundary of the school.   He stumbled over the uneven lumpy ground and, as the lightning flashed again, he saw the scaffolding clinging to the side of the tower. Erected recently by workmen hired to halt the deterioration, it seemed to offer him hope. Reaching the bottom of the scaffolding, he saw a wooden ladder the workmen used to get up to the first level. He started to climb as the lightning ended and the tower once again became pitch-black like the night above. On the first level he crawled over the rough wooden planks that bridged the gap between the metal scaffolding rods until he could feel the tower wall. Standing up he grabbed the next horizontal rod and, bracing himself between it and the wall, leveraged himself to the top level. Now he could hear voices nearby and streaks of light from a flashlight threw ribbons of white across the scaffolding. Trapped now, he realized he had nowhere to go. If he went back down he knew they'd get him. Backing up he found himself on a ledge near the door. He squeezed into the door frame, hoping to somehow disappear.

"We've got him! He's in the tower!" The first priest with the flashlight looked back at his companion, triumph in his voice.

"There he is!" he cried, shining his flashlight upwards until the boy stood transfixed in the glare, like a rabbit caught in a car's headlights.

"Don't! Take the light off his eyes!" The second priest, cautious, held the first priest's arm, "Let me talk to him."

The first priest hesitated and then moved the light away from the boy's face, "All right, we'll try it your way."

"Terry, can you hear me?

No answer.

The boy stood, fixed like a gargoyle, urine dripping down his bare legs and running into his socks.

"Terry, we are not going to hurt you. We only want you to give us your camera phone. The one you took the photos with."

No answer.

"Terry, you know we can't let you keep the photos, don't you?"

No answer.

"Terry, give us the phone and we'll say no more about it. Don't you want to go back to your room? You could catch your death out here on a night like this. You don't want to die over a few photos, do you Terry?"

No answer.

The first priest, *'I told you so'* in his tone of voice, cut in, "OK, we tried it your way. It didn't work, did it? Now we'll do it my way."

With the flashlight carving a path ahead of him, he moved to the foot of the ladder and started to climb. The boy saw him coming but he was cornered, nowhere to go. The priest, agile and sure footed, soon reached the top level of scaffolding, within easy reach of the boy.

"Give it to me! Now!"

8

The boy squeezed even further into the door opening. Sobs gurgled somewhere deep in his throat.

The priest, patience exhausted, reached for the boy. But the boy, terrified, tried to squeeze further into the door, lost his balance and fell. Seconds later, they heard the thump of his body on the rocks below.

"Oh, dear God, he's dead!" The words, almost a wail, escaped from the second priest as they stood over the boy's body.

The first priest took the boy's pulse and said, "Yes, he's dead." He knelt down beside the boy and searched the pockets of his school blazer. Then he searched the pockets of his trousers.

"Nothing!"

"Maybe he lost it somewhere tonight. Or maybe it's lying around here. Could have fallen out of his pocket."

They started to search, lighting arcs around the body, guessing how far a phone could have landed away from the tower. After fifteen minutes they abandoned the search.

"What will we do about him?" asked the second priest.

"Nothing! Leave him here! When he's missing tomorrow, the prefects will search for him. Someone will find him."

"There'll be an investigation."

"No, there will be no investigation. It's an accident. Another dare gone wrong. Climbing the tower on a stormy night."

The second priest couldn't disagree. He knew that some of the boys got up to daredevil antics, climbing the walls after lights out, things like that. But Terry was never one of them.

9

"What will we do about the phone?   What if it's lost and somebody finds it?"

"I don't think he lost the phone. He hid it. Or he gave it to someone."

They had almost reached the priests' residence hall and the storm had abated. The first priest stopped, turned to the second and said, with conviction: "That's it! He gave the phone to someone. We followed two of them tonight. And we lost one of them. Who was he?"

"We don't know."

"Well, who was young Terry friendly with? Who was he close to? "

"That's it, he wasn't close to anyone. He was quiet. A loner. Kept to himself. I tried to get him to participate. But he always held back, stayed on the fringes."

"Well, he must have a friend somewhere. He wasn't alone out there tonight. We've got to find that other boy. Soon!"

2

Patrick stayed in the tree for almost an hour. It was nearing midnight, the rain had stopped and the wind had eased. He climbed down and walked, then ran, back towards the junior dormitory. He shared a room on the top floor with Terry and Dermot, a farmer's son from the country.

Wide marble stairs swept upwards from the entrance hallway. He took off his shoes and soggy wet socks and climbed the stairs in his bare feet. The dormitory was silent. Lights out at ten pm was usually followed by a prefect inspection a half hour later. On some nights the Dean would sneak around about eleven, even as late as midnight, hoping to catch someone in the toilet. He'd relish meting out six on each hand with a leather strap the next morning. Luckily, he encountered no-one and, once on the top floor, he made his way to his room, the fourth door down the hallway.

He turned the door handle gently and entered. As his eyes adjusted to the dark, he could see Dermot bundled up in his blankets, asleep. But the other two beds, his own and Terry's, were as neat and well made as they'd left them. Terry had not returned. *They'd found him!* He feared the worst. *What would they do to him?* As these thoughts overwhelmed him, he shrugged his arms out of his wet blazer, emptying

11

the pockets as he usually did, and saw the phone. *Oh, Jesus! I forgot! He gave it to me, to keep it safe for him.* He felt afraid, very afraid. *Did they catch him? What did they do to him? Maybe they killed him!* And he immediately chastised himself for having such outrageous fears. *He's probably still hiding somewhere. He'll be back in the morning. I'll hide the phone and give it back to him tomorrow.* Although not convinced of his own reasoning, he accepted it. To do otherwise seemed unthinkable to him.

3

Terry was reported missing when he didn't show up for Mass next morning. A search of the grounds soon found him.   John Heaney, the tall geeky senior prefect, was the first to see Terry's body lying on the ground near the old round tower.   The two boys accompanying him ran towards Terry.

"No! Don't touch him!"

"He's not moving."

John Heaney knelt down beside Terry. From the pallor of his skin it was obvious that Terry had been dead for some time.

"Both of you – stay here. Don't let anyone near him. I'll tell the Dean."

The Dean called the Gardai and they notified the State Pathologist, Dr. Mona Kennedy. Luckily she was available and she reached the school by noon.   Her preliminary examination showed that death had resulted from internal injuries, most likely caused by an uncontrolled fall from the nearby tower. However, final cause could only be confirmed by autopsy.

In the meantime, the Dean and the President had insisted that the school day continue as normal. But nothing was normal.   Classes were subdued, priests taught from textbooks, students sat quietly and sombre.   Patrick had Latin and Maths that morning. Latin with Father McGinty, known by his nickname 'the goat'; English with one of the few lay teachers in the school, Mr. Galligan, a small five foot tall sadist who liked to walk on the top of the students' desks and pull them up by their ears. Patrick's darker thoughts often revolved around the most painful way to torture and kill Mr. Galligan. This morning Mr. Galligan was subdued in class, just like everyone else.

Patrick sat in fear all morning. He knew that Terry was dead. Everybody knew. There'd been no announcement. There didn't need to be. Everybody just knew. And Patrick was afraid. He knew that Terry had been murdered. He just knew. But he couldn't tell anyone. He didn't know who to trust. He'd hidden Terry's camera inside a pair of dirty socks that he'd stuffed in the bottom of his sports bag. What if they searched his room? What if they found it? He couldn't wait until lunch so that he could go back to his room and move the phone to a safer place.

4

Emmet Joyce got the tearful call from his wife, Claire, in his office at his car dealership, *Joyce Motors*, at ten a.m.

"Emmet, you need to come home. Now!"

"My God, Claire.   What's the matter? Are you alright?"

"Oh, Emmet ..."   and she started sobbing uncontrollably.

Emmet, his heart thumping, bracing himself for bad news of some kind, said, "It's OK, Claire. Take it easy."

After a minute, her sobbing subsided and she   tried   again,   "It's   Terry.   Something happened..."

"What?   Is he sick, is he hurt?   What happened?"

"Oh, dear God, he's dead!   Our son is dead!" and she started bawling again, this time her piercing cries shattering his ear.

"How? What happened?

"They said it was an accident."

"Who said …"

"The school. They called me. Said that Terry had been climbing that old tower. Fell out of it."

"When?"

"Last night, they said."

"Last night? In that wind and rain! Naw! Terry wouldn't do that! I don't believe it!"

"That's what they said, Emmet", and she burst out crying, unable to continue.

Emmet Joyce had been bracing himself for bad news of some kind. But not this! His own Terry. His son. Dead! He couldn't believe it. He could feel the anguish deep inside and the howl that erupted from his throat, a howl of madness. He put his head between his hands and the tears ran freely down his cheeks and through his fingers.

He drove home in a daze, eyes bleary with tears. Claire lay curled on the living room couch, almost catatonic. The blinds were closed. Shutting out the world. He knelt down beside here, laid his head in her lap, and hugged her. After a long time, their crying exhausted, he helped her to her feet and gently walked her into the kitchen. He sat her at the table and made a large pot of tea, her comfort drink. But there would be no comfort today, he knew. They sat there, wordless, for the longest time.

Finally, Emmet said, "We'll need to go and see him."

"There'll be an inquest."

"I know, I know. But we have to see him. I'll call the school."

16

"We have to tell our family.   But I can't, not this morning. I just can't."

"Claire, we'll see him first. Then we'll call them."

5

The dorms were off-limits at lunch time but Patrick took a chance. He had to get that phone. The junior dormitory was empty, not a soul in sight, especially not a prefect. So Patrick took the stairs two at a time and rushed, breathless, into his room. A quick look told him that nothing had been disturbed. *But they'd make it look like that, wouldn't they?* He dug out the dirty socks from the bottom of his sports bag and took a deep breath when he felt the phone still inside.

He had to see why Terry died. So he turned on the phone and selected 'pictures'. There were twelve pictures and, starting with the first one, he selected 'view'. The first was a goofy self-portrait, the second a snap of the College, and the next three quick shots of fellow students. But it was picture number six that stunned Patrick – and seven, eight, nine, ten, eleven, and twelve. The details showed that all had been taken last night, an hour before he and Terry had made a run for it. He went back to number six and looked at each of them again. Each picture showed the same two people, a priest and a student. The priest in the photos was Father Roland Cormack. And he recognized the student too. John Carty! Patrick was shocked. He had never seen anything like this before. And he was frightened. He knew that these photos were very dangerous.

They'll search this room! But they don't know I've got the camera. They don't know who was with Terry last night. Unless Terry told them! No, Terry would never do that! So I have time. Time to do what?

He didn't know. He only knew that he'd have to hide the camera somewhere else, somewhere he'd be certain they wouldn't look. *But where?* Then it struck him. Hide it right under their noses, in the sacristy beside the chapel. The place where he and all the altar boys got ready to serve mass. *The sacristy? Yes!* There was a locked cabinet where old cruet sets, extra candle holders, and other paraphernalia were stored. The stuff in it hadn't been used in months. So it would be unlikely that anyone would look there. He knew where the key was kept. He'd stash the camera way down under all this old junk and he'd hang on to the key himself. *That's it! I'll hide the camera there now!*

6

Miami, Florida, USA.

Ed Burke felt the water massage his chest as he sat deep in the Jacuzzi on his patio. He watched the golfers tee off in the distance and the geckos blowing out their necks as they climbed the mosquito screen, and he felt that all was well in his world. Closing his eyes, he lay back and enjoyed the warm sunshine bathing his face.

Somewhere between sleep and wakefulness, he heard the inviting tinkle of glasses and opened his eyes to see Maria standing over him holding two glasses.

"It's happy hour! Thought you'd like a gin and tonic."

"What service! You're spoiling me!"

"You're my hero! Or don't you remember?"

"Stop it! I don't feel like a hero. Just a survivor."

"Ease up! Remember why we're here."

Ed was now halfway out of the Jacuzzi. Maria put down the glasses and held his hand as he climbed out. They kissed and then clinked their glasses.

"Ah, this is the life," said Ed as they stretched out on the lounge chairs.

"Kevin made his flight OK?"

"No problem. 836 wasn't too busy, LeJeune was practically empty, and I made it into the airport in good time."

"He'll miss you."

"I know. And I'll miss him. But he's had a good two weeks here and his mother expects him back on time. Besides, he has to be back in school next week."

"I know all that. But still ..."

"We'll be back in New York in a month and he can come to the apartment on the weekend."

"He's a great kid."

"He likes you. You know that, don't you? Listen, I could be dead now and he wouldn't have me at all."

He fingered the scar on his chest as he talked. Maria noticed that it seemed involuntary, as though he didn't realize he was doing it. She thought it better not to mention it because he did it less frequently now. No point in making him feel self-conscious. The past six months had been good. He had healed, gained his strength again. Taking up the karate where he'd left off a few years ago, running every day, made him look in better condition now than before the shooting in Shannon.

One of the golfers clipped a shot and the ball splashed into the small man-made lake that functioned almost like a moat, separating their house from the fairway. They sipped their drinks and enjoyed the vista. Contrary to Maria's thinking, Ed knew well that he was fingering the surgical scar on his chest. He did do it less frequently and he supposed, as time passed, he'd stop it altogether. The nightmares had ended. He no longer woke up in a

21

sweaty terror in the middle of the night after re-living his near-death experience in Ireland.

"You've turned to gold!"

"Isn't it great? I thought I'd burn to death in this heat. But I'm lucky. I don't have that fair Irish skin."

"Well, you wouldn't be getting any tan in Ireland right now."

"Oh, I'm not here for the tan!"

"And what else would you be here for? Surely not the alligators. Or the lovely palmetto bugs?"

"You're so bad ..."

She pulled him off the lounger and dragged him onto the beach towels at their feet. Pinning him to the ground, she kissed his nipples and then gently traced his scar with the tip of her tongue. Then she pulled him to his feet and led him through the French windows upstairs to their large king-size bed that sat facing the window, now framed by the bougainvillea that climbed high on the patio and gently entwined itself around.

7

Sweat poured in rivulets down Ed Burke's chest as he bowed to George Kim, ending his weekly karate session.

"Very good, Ed. Very good."

"That's great praise, coming from you, George."

"Three months, Ed. Only three months and you're in fighting shape."

"*Komapsumnida*, George. Let's hope I won't need to do any real fighting."

George Kim smiled, without comment this time.

Ten minutes later Ed Burke drove west on 41st street till he reached the entrance to the Doral Saturnia spa. It was eleven a.m. He'd pamper himself for an hour before meeting Maria for lunch. He'd been coming here regularly for the past six months, yet every time he came he felt that he'd been magically transported to Italy. Parking effortlessly in front, he had the surreal sense of having arrived at a gracious Etruscan villa.

Not having enough time today for his regular massage, he settled into the outdoor tub and sat under the constant gentle rainfall and let it massage his shoulders. Soon he found himself suspended in that place between sleep and consciousness, that place where reverie and daydreams held sway, that place where unseen wounds found a healing balm.

He drifted back twelve months again to find himself in shock, on the ground, blood seeping through his fingers, Kevin standing somewhere above him, white-faced and crying, sirens loud in the distance, the sound of running feet, the pain, the wheezing and coughing, , the blackness, the dying of the light ...and then complete oblivion...

...to remember waking up again and slowly realizing that he was in a hospital bed hooked up to many machines. He drifted off again and the next time he woke to find a doctor and two nurses standing by his bedside. The doctor was examining him, checking his vital signs, smiling at him, reassuring him...

...and somewhere he lost time, his memory failed him, and the next clear memory he had was one of the nurse bolstering him up in bed as he sipped his first food...and Kevin sitting at his bedside, smiles fighting through the tears ...

...and later, much later that he learned that the bullet had torn his lung and that the air had flowed down his windpipe, out through the torn lung, and into his chest. His lung had collapsed, his heart couldn't pump enough blood, and the oxygen had stopped flowing to his body. Blood had seeped into the pericardial sac and had commenced to squeeze

24

*his heart.   Only the fast action of a paramedic saved
his life. The medic had inserted a big needle between
his ribs, near the breastbone, and aspirated the
blood...*

The gentle rainfall invaded his mind and
brought him back from the traumatic memory. He
grasped the sides of the tub to ground himself in the
present. In the beginning these memories had lasted
much longer and had left him drained. But they
happened infrequently now. *Time heals everything,*
he thought, as he climbed out of the tub and headed
for the changing room.

As he climbed behind the wheel of his car, he
looked at his watch: 11.45 am. Lunch with Maria at
Bennigans at 12 noon. No problem. He exited onto
41st street and headed east, past the Doral Country
Club and Cisco's, the place they'd visit on occasion for
their Tex/Mex fix. He knew he was almost there
when he passed Miami International Airport on his
right.

Right on time, Maria waited inside the door as
he entered Bennigans. Early enough to beat the
regular lunch-time crowd, they ordered their usual:
spinach salad with hot bacon, mustard and honey
dressing.

Maria seemed tense and Ed asked, "Is there
something wrong?"

She reached across and took Ed's hand
between hers, which only confirmed that something
was wrong, "Some bad news from Galway. Your
cousin Emmet called. His son, Terry, is dead."

"Oh my God! What happened?"

"An accident at his school. Fell out of one of
those round towers."

25

"Jesus!   I've got to go. I should be at the funeral."

"Emmet said they weren't going to bother you."

"Bother me! What the hell does that mean?"

"Well, you know. You were almost killed and they're worried about you."

"Damn it, Emmet's called me from time to time. He knows I'm OK. Didn't you tell him I'm in great shape again?"

"Yes, I did. But I'm not sure he believed me."

"I should be there."

"Well, they want you now. They don't think it was an accident."

"What do you mean?   What did Emmet say exactly?"

"He said they don't think that Terry fell out of that tower. They think that somebody killed him. But they can't prove it. And they believe that you could get to the bottom of it."

"I'm not exactly welcome in some places in Ireland these days. Doesn't he know that?"

"I think you should call him as soon as we get home. And I think you should go. I got the call from him about eleven, that's five in the morning in Ireland. I think they've been up half the night. They can't sleep. "

Ed pushed his half-eaten spinach salad away and stood up, "You're right. I have to go back. Book us flights to New York. We'll stop at the apartment and fly out to Shannon tomorrow."

"No, Ed. I've thought about this. You don't need me there now. I'd only be in the way. Until you find out what's going on. I'll stay in New York for a while.   I can take Kevin out bowling, movies, whatever. He and I got along well."

26

"Yeah, again you're right.   You're always right!   But I'll miss you."

Maria broke the sombre atmosphere with one of her deep throaty laughs, "It'll do you good! Get you to appreciate me more!"

Ed took a mock swing at her chin with his right and then held her close before they turned to leave.

8

Monsignor Thomas Fallon, President Emeritus of St. Curnan's, still retained an office and a position as faculty advisor at the school. Now seventy-three, his power and influence remained undiminished. A lesser man would have been moved to one of the Church's retirement homes to spend the rest of his days in anonymity. But not Monsignor Fallon, who was politically connected all the way to the College of Cardinals in Rome. Plump and effete in manner, he sat in utter disbelief as Father Roland Cormack finished talking.

"Roland, this is a disaster!"

"I know! I wish I could turn the clock back forty-eight hours."

"They'll say that you killed this boy!"

"But I didn't. He fell. It was an accident."

"Listen to yourself. If it's discovered that you followed this boy up into that tower and caused his death, they'll charge you. Murder or manslaughter, what's the difference? It'll be a show trial. They're out to get us now. Here, in the US, everywhere! This is a disaster!"

"No, no! There's nothing to suggest I was there when the boy fell. Only Father Nugent knows. And he won't say anything."

"How can you be so sure?"

"He's a wimp! You know him. He wouldn't say 'boo to a fly'."

"And why was he out there with you if he's such a wimp?"

"He knew about the photos. He thought he could talk to Terry. Get the phone from him. He liked the boy and he wanted to protect him."

"Father Nugent knows too much, that's what I think. And I think he's a risk."

"No, our big risk is that phone. The photos. We don't know what Terry Joyce did with it, or who he might have given it to."

"It's *your* big risk, not *our* big risk. Find that phone. Search everywhere. Find the boy who was with him last night."

"And if I don't find the phone?"

"Well, then you'd better hope it's lost, buried somewhere forever!"

After Father Cormack had left, Monsignor Fallon sat for a long time in contemplation. Then he picked up the phone and called Rome.

A few days later, Father Roland Cormack departed Dublin Airport on *Alitalia Flight AZ 3581* at 2:15 pm. With a stopover in Paris, he arrived at Leonardo Da Vinci Airport in Rome at 9 pm, fifteen minutes late. Craving privacy, he avoided the express train and took one of the white cabs instead. Cardinal Volpe was expecting him at the Vatican.

9

Shannon Airport, 7:30 am

Emmet Joyce waited in the arrivals area. The video screen stated that the Aer Lingus flight from New York had landed at 7:15 am, ten minutes early.

People began to emerge in one and twos, then in small clusters. Then Ed appeared, dragging a small suitcase.

Emmet waved and Ed moved towards him, looking healthy and tanned from the Florida sun. He dropped the case, put his arms around Emmet and told him how sorry he was. Emmet's eyes, red and dark-rimmed, watered as he said thanks. They didn't speak again until Ed was sitting in Emmet's car and they were about to exit the parking lot.

"I'm really glad you're here," said Emmet.

"You know I'd come right away."

"Ah, sure we're in shock. We don't know what to do."

"Tell me what happened. Take it from the beginning. As much as you know."

Emmet drove out of Shannon and took the exit to Ennis and Galway. On the way he brought Ed up to date on everything, .

"Terry died falling from that old tower. Accidental death, they claim."

"But you don't think it was an accident."

"It was no accident! What was Terry doing out at midnight on a stormy night like that? He didn't even like going out in the sun in the middle of the day, much less in a storm at midnight. And he didn't like heights. He suffered from acrophobia. He'd never have climbed up into that old tower. Never! Unless he was scared enough that he had no choice."

"What's the Gardai doing about it?"

"They're interviewing people. And you know where that'll get them. Nowhere! Especially with the priests. They only talk to God, not to us lesser mortals!"

"But what else can they do?"

"I don't know. Honest to God, I don't know. That's why we need you. If anybody can find out what happened, you can."

"You have too much faith in me."

They'd entered Ennis and they sat quietly for the fifteen minutes it took to negotiate the long sprawling streets of the town.

Finally, back on the main road with the speedometer nudging seventy, Emmet said, "Claire will be happy you're here."

"How is she taking this?"

"Badly! Almost lost her mind. The doctor gave her something. But you know Claire. She's stronger than me. My eyes are red from crying, hers just swim in sadness."

The tears were running freely down Emmet's cheeks and he blurted out. "I'm sorry!"

"Jesus Christ!   Sorry for what?   For feeling the pain?"

"You're staying with us.   You know that, don't you?"

"I never really thought about it."

"Claire wouldn't have it otherwise."

They didn't say much for the rest of the trip to Galway.   Emmet called Claire on his mobile when they reached the outskirts of the city and she was waiting at the door when they arrived. Holding Ed in the longest and tightest hug, he could feel her body shudder against him. Too sad to speak, she finally released him and took him upstairs and showed him his room.

As he came back downstairs, Ed could smell an Irish cooked breakfast, the bacon, the sausages, the mushrooms, all blending into the same appetizing aroma of his childhood.   Claire seemed to have bounced back.   Her face belied that but her voice carried her usual banter.

"I'm sure they didn't give you this on the plane. Sure they give you nothing these days."

"Oh, this is too much Claire.   You shouldn't have."

"Ed Burke, are you telling me that you're going to pass up my special breakfast?"

"Oh, no, no, no!   I love it!"

"And coffee for you, now that you're an American."

"Sure tea's fine too.   I'm not in the States now. I'd never drink tea over there.   They don't know how to make it."

For the next hour they tried to put the tragedy out of their minds.   Ed relished Claire's Irish breakfast.   He told them all about his last few months in Florida, about his road back to health, about his son Kevin, and about Maria Lane.

"You must bring Maria to see us."

"Oh, I will. She's staying at my apartment in New York for a while. Until I get a sense of things here. Kevin likes her. She'll be able to take him to the movies and stuff."

The Joyces' home looked out over Galway Bay and, at noon, the sun's rays sparkled on the water, as though conspiring to lift their sorrow until darker clouds appeared. But they knew they were only postponing the inevitable. Without preamble, Claire said, "I think somebody killed Terry."

"Why do you say that?" asked Ed.

"So many reasons. We've talked about them all before. He would never have climbed up into that tower unless he was afraid."

"But there's no evidence to prove that it wasn't an accident. Isn't that right?"

"That's because they left no evidence. They think they've gotten away with it."

"By 'they', do you mean the priests?"

"God forgive me, I do."

"Why do you think they had something to do with Terry's death?"

"And why not? Do you trust them any more? How many of them have been arrested lately for interfering with young boys? Perverts! And they're supposed to be men of God! Setting a moral example for us. The Church is full of them. I hate to think of any of them putting their filthy hands on Terry! It makes my skin crawl!"

"Did Terry ever say anything to you?"

"No, never. But he could have been afraid to say anything, couldn't he?"

"Have any of the priests at the school been accused of anything?"

"No, but there's been rumours.   There're always rumours. Most people   dismiss them, saying that everybody in the Church is getting tarred with the same brush these days.   We were seriously thinking of moving Terry to another school.   But he did like it there. And he was getting a good education.   So we didn't.   Now we'll regret that forever."

The conversation had reached a dead end. Emmet excused himself and left. *Joyce Motors* was a hands-on business and he couldn't afford to be away from it for too long.

After he left, Ed turned to Claire and said, "There's a priest at the school I'd like to talk to.   I went to secondary school with him. Haven't seen him since.   Used to chase the girls when I knew him. Never'd thought he'd become a priest.   Name's Michael Nugent. Do you know him?"

"No.   I've only met the Dean and the President.   It was all very formal. And, oh yes, that nice Father Cormack who teaches religion."

"Maybe I'll ask if I can see him too."

"You should do that."

Ed gave her a parting hug before leaving the room.

10

Detective Tom Buckley was a member of the Garda team investigating the death of Terry Joyce. He was surprised to learn that Ed Burke was back in Ireland. He knew Ed well, had grown up with him on the same street, knew the family, he'd played football with Ed after school. And he'd worked closely with Ed a year and a half ago after the Tanaiste's wife, Pia, had been found dead in Ed's bed. After Ed had been shot at Shannon he visited him in the hospital every day and he was there to see Ed and Maria fly out to the States. He never expected to see Ed back in Ireland again. But he understood. Terry Joyce was family and who better that Ed for the family to call on for help at such a time.

Tom knew that Ed was staying with Terry's parents, Emmet and Claire. So he picked up the phone and called him.

They met at the promenade in Salthill. At midday the sun shone brightly and the waters sparkled in Galway Bay. It seemed that a cross-section of humanity paraded up and down the promenade: elderly couples, hand in hand; young lovers; driven young women walking briskly with their dogs; intense young men on their mobile phones; tourists of every nationality meandering at their leisure.

Ed parked his car and as he walked on to the promenade he saw Tom standing there, arms folded, looking out across Galway Bay. Tom spun around when he heard Ed's voice, shook hands vigorously and instinctively gave him a hug.

"You look great! That Florida sunshine's been good for you."

"And Maria's been good medicine as well."

"You know, I never expected to see you back here again."

"I hadn't planned to come back. But when Emmet called and told me about Terry's death, I had to come. They don't believe it was an accident."

"That's why I wanted to talk to you. As I told you, I'm on the investigating team. Normally we wouldn't be involved unless there was clear evidence or suspicion that a crime had been committed."

"And you're saying this is being treated differently."

"Garda Superintendent Tim Quigley is a close friend of Emmet and Claire. He has no intention of indicting St. Curnan's for something they didn't do. But he wants to make sure that we do a thorough investigation. That we don't miss anything."

"And ...?"

"I hate to disappoint Emmet and Claire. But, so far, it looks like an accident. Mind you, we've started and that's only our first opinion. We'll check out every single thing, every forensic detail before we reach any conclusion. That'll take a while."

"Will you keep me informed?"

"Why do you think I'm here? I'm not supposed to discuss it with anyone outside the team but there's a lot of water under the bridge with you and me. I think you have a right to know what's going on. And if we find any evidence that it wasn't an accident, I'll let you know."

They walked the promenade for a while, reminiscing about the past, the good and the bad, and wondering if they might have run into bad times again.

11

With the inquest and autopsy completed, Terry's body was released to the family a week later. Dr. Mona Kennedy confirmed her initial findings. Death resulted from massive head injury, torn liver and lungs, caused by an uncontrolled fall from the tower. No evidence was uncovered showing any injuries other than those caused by the fall. It would be up to the gardai to support a verdict of accidental death once their investigation had concluded.

The requiem mass for Terry was con-celebrated by the Dean, the President, and three other priests. Usually only two altar-boys served mass but all ten were on the altar for this one. Not all of them played active roles but they sat there, in their surpluses and soutanes, as a mark of respect to their deceased fellow student and altar-boy.

Terry's coffin sat at the head of the centre aisle, directly in front of the altar. His family and close relatives occupied the first three pews. Ed Burke sat unobtrusively and unobserved, he hoped,

at the end of the third pew.   Close friends squeezed
into the next three or four pews.   All the boarding
students filled the remaining pews to overflowing,
and many stood solemnly at the rear of the chapel
and on the side aisles.

Patrick was chosen to hold the paten for the
Dean at communion time. The Dean stood at the
bottom of the altar, positioned to give communion to
Terry's family. Patrick had never met Terry's family
but he could see the resemblance to his dad, who
gently ushered Terry's mother out of the pew. They
approached the Dean who lifted a communion wafer
over the paten held by Patrick and said, *The body of
Christ.* Terry's mother took time to compose herself
and get the lump from her throat. Then she offered
her tongue for the host and Patrick looked directly
into her eyes. She must have seen something there
because she stopped, host on tongue, almost as
though she'd been paused like a frame from a video.
Then she moved on. Patrick was startled by this and
held the paten under Terry's father's chin, who was
red-eyed from crying and seemingly oblivious to
everything.

The rest of the mass passed in ritual fashion
for Patrick. He sat near the front steps of the altar
and imagined that Terry's mother was looking right
through him. *Just my imagination*, he told himself.

The cortege reached the family plot in the city
cemetery.   High   on   a   hill,   it   commanded   a
magnificent   view   of   the   city   and   surrounding
countryside. Almost created the illusion that all the
souls resting here were somehow observing every
move of the living. A feeling both comforting and
unsettling, thought Patrick.

Patrick stood uncomfortably as the coffin was lowered into the grave and the Dean said the final prayers and sprinkled holy water on the coffin. At the end, relatives placed the wooden cover holding the floral wreaths over the grave. Then the Dean turned to the family to offer his condolences.

Mrs. Joyce accepted with thanks and then suddenly turned to Patrick , "Did you know my son? Did you know Terry well?"

Taken aback, Patrick stumbled over his words, "Yes. He was my room mate."

"I knew it. What's your name?"

"Patrick. Patrick Clarke."

"Well, Patrick, one day I'd like to talk to you about Terry. You wouldn't mind that, would you?"

"No, Mrs. Joyce."

Ed gave her a hug as they left the graveside. As he did so, Claire said, "Did you see the boy that I was speaking to? I think you should see him."

"Who?"

"Patrick Clarke. He's a student, a boarder. He was Terry's roommate."

"And how do you think he can help?"

"That's just it. I don't know. He looked at me, stared at me, at the funeral mass. There was something about that look. Like he knew something that nobody else did. That boy is afraid of something."

"Could be your imagination. If he was Terry's room-mate then I'm sure it would be very natural for him to be upset by Terry's death. That could explain it."

"No, I don't think so. I felt that he couldn't wait to get away from me. And it seemed like he wanted to say something but couldn't. I can't explain it."

    "OK. I'll see if he'll talk to me."

After they had all dispersed Patrick sat in the car on the way back to the school and had the feeling of being cornered again. The same feeling he had when he and Terry were being chased by the two priests. Only this time he felt cornered by Terry's mother.

12

Garda Superintendent Tim Quigley pulled into the Joyce's driveway around seven pm. Terry Joyce's parents were close friends. He had come to reassure Emmet and Claire Joyce that the gardai were conducting a thorough investigation into their son's death.

Ed Burke stayed away. His last encounter with Superintendent Quigley was still fresh in his mind. When the Tanaiste's wife, Pia, has been murdered in Ed's bed in St.Cleran's, Special Branch detectives had held him for questioning. Ed still remembered Tim Quigley, the tall, good looking, well groomed senior Garda officer who had entered the interview room. So he decided that it was best that he stay in the background for the present.

Claire Joyce opened the door, "Tim, thanks for coming."

He reached out and hugged her, "Oh, Claire ...," but words failed him and he said no more.

Emmet Joyce stood in the hallway, sombre and sad. His eyes were still red-rimmed, evidence of continuous fits of crying. He shook Tim Quigley's hand. Then they both ushered him into the front sitting room and Claire excused herself to get tea and biscuits.

Emmet looked at the Superintendent, "We know you can't bring Terry back to us. But we want answers."

"That's why I'm here."

Claire returned with a tray of tea and biscuits and busied herself pouring three cups. The Superintendent added milk and his usual teaspoon of sugar. Taking a sip and finding it to his taste, he put down the cup and turned towards them.

"I know you want answers. I know you want an explanation for your son's death. I know that. I want answers too."

"Did you know that Terry suffered from a fear of heights? He'd never have climbed that tower, not even in broad daylight! Never!" said Claire.

"That's right. He was quiet, liked the books and the reading. He wasn't into physical things. God, I tried often enough to get him to go fishing with me, get him to go to the rugby with me. But he wasn't interested," added Emmet.

"That's what's troubling us," said Tim, "It seemed totally out of character for him to be missing from his room and outside on a terrible night like that. Never mind about climbing up scaffolding into that tower."

"So what are you saying?" asked Emmet.

"I don't know. It doesn't add up. He died in a fall from that tower. Of that we're certain. But what was he doing up there? What made him fall? Was he pushed?"

"You think somebody killed him? " asked Claire.

"No, I didn't mean it to come out like that. If he'd been out there on a dare with some other boys, he could have been pushed. But it could still have been an accident."

"But he'd never have been out there doing things like that. I know he wouldn't," insisted Emmet.

"And if we don't think he'd have done that, where does it leave us?" asked Claire.

"God, I dunno. I just dunno. I believe Terry was frightened that night. I can't prove it. I just have a sense of it."

"Frightened of what? Of who?" Claire's voice now had a pronounced tremor.

"Again, I don't know. We're examining everything. I have people going over that tower with a fine tooth comb. Looking for any scrap that might help us. We'll also be talking to all the teachers and many of the students. That'll take days, probably weeks."

"You don't seem very hopeful," said Emmet.

"Emmet, I won't promise you anything. There's no evidence that your son died from anything other than the fall from that tower. No evidence at all. If we can't prove that he was not alone on the night, then 'no', I won't be hopeful. And his death will remain a mystery. That's not very satisfactory. For you or for me."

"Somebody must know something," said Claire.

"That's where my hope lies. That we'll discover something during the interviews. Or that somebody will come forward and tell us something. And I'll make you a promise here tonight. I won't give up!"

He rose to leave, shook Emmet's hand, and gave Claire another hug.

They thanked him and then stood at the door and watched him drive away. Then they returned to the sitting room and sat quietly togetheruntil Emmet broke the silence.

"There's something wrong at that school. I know Tim is good at his job. But when the Church clams up, he'll get nowhere!"

"You don't think the priests had anything to do with Terry's death, do you?"

"I don't know what I think. Why shouldn't I suspect them?"

They sat, side by side, in silence for the longest time. Finally, Emmet put his arm around Claire and said, almost in a whisper. " Ed'll know what to do."

"But, Emmet, he almost died when he got shot at Shannon. And that's only nine months ago. He can't be well enough, can he?"

"You've seen him. He's never looked better. That girl, what's her name? Maria Lane. She's been with him in Florida. And I think she's good for him."

Emmet held her even closer and kissed her. They sat again in silence.

13

Patrick Clarke did not sleep well. He tossed and turned, his mind in turmoil. Violent dreams invaded his mind every time he dozed off: Terry's dead body, broken and bloody, lay in bed looking at him accusingly. A dream so real that when it woke him, he sat up and looked over at Terry's bed to convince himself that the bed was empty. At four thirty in the morning, he'd had enough. He couldn't sleep any more. In the next bed Dermot was sleeping, oblivious. So Patrick turned on his bedside lamp and tried to read. But he couldn't concentrate. Too tired and too distraught.

The gardai were interviewing everyone about Terry and his appointment was scheduled for ten am. Four days since Terry's funeral and his fear was still as strong. Terry's camera remained hidden in the sacristy. He didn't know what to do with it. He couldn't turn it over to the school. He didn't trust anyone, even the President. He'd thought about turning it over to the gardai in the morning but realized that he didn't trust them either. He didn't want to get involved. If he turned over the camera to the gardai, he'd have to tell them that he was with

Terry the night he died. Maybe he'd get blamed for Terry's death. He was too afraid.

But he had already made one decision. He had decided not to destroy the photos in the camera.

14

John Carty couldn't live with himself.   And he couldn't face the world.   He'd been with Father Roland Cormack the night that Terry Joyce took the photos with his mobile phone.   Terry ran away and Father Roland ran after him. He'd been living in fear ever since. Now Terry was dead and he knew they'd find the photos. He couldn't live with that.   He'd never be able to go home again.

He had made his decision, accepted his fate, and now went numbly through the motions.

It was dark outside.   He sneaked out after supper and made his way to the groundskeeper's shed. Old Tom, the groundskeeper, had invited him into the shed one day because he'd seen John always looking at him when he was mowing the lawn or clipping a hedge.

So John knew where things were kept.   The door was always left unlocked.   He pushed it open and edged inside.   He tripped over a lawnmower as he felt his way to the back wall where the various tools and equipment hung. It didn't take him long to find the rope.

He straddled the big thick branch, the one overlooking the path close to the school entrance. Taking the rope from around his body, he looped it three times around the branch and double knotted it. Then he looped the other end around his neck and knotted it tightly. Since he'd made his decision, he didn't hesitate. It was the only way out. He convinced himself that it would be quick. He swung his left leg back over the branch so that he sat facing the college. He could see lights in some of the windows, the brightest in the President's office which looked out over the front lawn and the trees where he sat.

He imagined the President watching him. He felt nothing, only emptiness. He slid to the edge of the branch and let go.

15

Even at sixty, Father Flaherty, the Irish teacher, was athletic and virile with the body of a man twenty years younger. While others read their morning breviary in their rooms, he donned a pair of runners and read his as he fast walked around the perimeter of the college grounds.

The light morning mist began to lift as he reached the stand of oak trees. He lifted his head to enjoy the beginning of a new day. But the sight ahead brought him to a sudden stop.

He stood, transfixed, clenching his breviary until his knuckles started to hurt. Shaking himself, he took the final few steps until he stood directly under the body that hung from the tree: a boy in the school blazer, short grey trousers, socks, no shoes. His neck twisted grotesquely out of the make-shift noose and his swollen tongue protruded from his mouth, gobs of saliva and mucous forming a trail down the front of his blazer.

Father Flaherty blessed himself and sank to his knees. He couldn't reach the boy so he recited the Act of Contrition where he knelt and asked God for forgiveness.

Then he got up, turned and ran towards the College.

He bounded through the front door, almost colliding with a group of students emerging from their breakfast in the refectory. He took the stairs two at a time, catching President McCafferty as he was about to enter his office. Sliding to a halt, he startled the President who turned around to see a red-faced Father Flaherty gasping for breath with sweat trickling down his cheeks.

"Father, what's wrong?"

"It's terrible, the boy ... he's dead!"

"Come in, come in ..." President McCafferty, now alarmed, gripped Father Flaherty by the arm, pulled him inside the office, and closed the door.

"What're you talking about? Who's dead?"

"John Carty. He's hanging – from that tree – look out your window!"

Father Flaherty had gained control again. His face was still red but now from anger. He steered the President to the large office window the overlooked the front portico and commanded a view of the lawns that swept down to the main gate and the line of oak trees, now majestic in the morning sun.

"He's hanging from that tree! And we're responsible. We took that boy's life."

President McCafferty stood transfixed before the window. He couldn't see the boy. His eyes were blurry with emotion. Somewhere deep inside he managed to get a grip on himself and turned to face Father Flaherty.

"Bernard, I'm as shocked as you. But I reject your accusation that we're to blame." With that, he strode to his desk, sat down and pulled the phone towards him.

51

But Father Bernard Flaherty would not be dissuaded, "I warned you! I knew this would happen. First that Joyce boy, now young Carty. Somebody has to pay. We have to take responsibility for this!"

"Bernard, Bernard, I've listened to you rant and rave like this so many times. You've alienated most of our faculty with your wild accusations."

"Wild accusations! Have you not been reading the newspapers? People have spat on me as I walked down the street. Spat on me! Do you hear me? Me, a priest, and they spat on me! I warned all of you that we must do something about this. Now it's too late!"

"Father Bernard, you're not helping. I do not want you charging around the school like this. Go to your room and pray for the soul of this unfortunate boy. I'm going to call the Gardai now. Then I'm going to call an assembly. I want the faculty and the students to hear this news from me. And I want the impact contained. Contained! Do you understand?"

But Father Bernard Flaherty was already on his way out, banging the large oak door behind him as he left.

A different Father Bernard Flaherty emerged from President McCafferty's office. He was no longer the light-hearted person who'd been out for his morning run. With the loose easy-going stride gone, the body had stiffened, the arms swung threateningly, the gait now one of an automaton, even the open face now closed into a bleak impenetrable visage. His hair, naturally tousled, sleeked back with sweat, now seemed designed for more serious purpose.

Once inside his own room, he put down his breviary and went to his bureau, pulled out the top drawer, retrieved a bottle of pills prescribed to him and clearly marked *prozac*. He opened the bottle and tipped one into the palm of his hand. Then he reached into the drawer again and squeezed two paracetamol tablets from a sheet of tinfoil. At the sink, he filled a glass with water and washed all three down his throat.

He sat down on the floor, in the lotus position, and started to chant in Latin ...

At twelve noon exactly Father Bernard Flaherty stepped onto the handball court. A tall three-sided concrete built court, it served as a whipping boy for him. On evenings and weekends, when he wasn't jogging, he was on the court, usually with an attentive, hypnotized audience. Boys would silently line both sides of the court, hands in pockets, watching every move he made, every time his hand whacked the ball with definite malice up against that wall. Every time he hit the ball, the boys' hands would strike in unison, punching inside the pockets of their trousers. This action was called *hinching*. Seemingly unaware of their involuntary complicity they would stand transfixed until he finished, *hinching* every time he struck the ball. But today he had no audience. He held the ball firmly in his hand, bounced it off the ground, and struck it hard with his right hand.

He kept this up until he collapsed, red-faced and breathless.

16

Father Michael Nugent had swapped his clerical attire for civilian clothes. He sat sipping a diet coke at a small table in the Italian restaurant where he'd chosen to meet Ed Burke for dinner.

Ed walked right past him.

"Ed, Ed ! " Father Nugent called after him and Ed turned back as Father Nugent rose to greet him.

"Michael! I didn't recognize you."

"It's been twenty-five years, you know! You don't look a day older but time hasn't been as kind to me." He ran his hand over his completely bald head in emphasis.

Ed laughed and, thinking that Michael Nugent was indeed a very different person from the testosterone fuelled young man who had pursued every girl in that last year in High school, said, "I never thought you'd become a priest, Michael!"

"Yeah, I'll bet you thought I'd be married with a bunch of kids, didn't you?"

"Yeah, I did."

"You never knew it but I was always drawn to the priesthood. I think I chased girls to try and find out if my vocation could stand the test."

"Obviously, it did."

"Yes, it did. But it's still a struggle every day."

"Well, I'll be honest with you. I think the Church should let people like yourself marry. Many of you are walking away from it all. And the Church is losing some of their best people."

The waitress arrived, ready to take their order.

"I know what I want. The pasta with pesto sauce. And some Ballygowan, not sparkling. But you haven't had time to examine the menu."

"No problem. Eating Italian is an easy decision for me. Spaghetti bolognese! I love it. And a glass of your best Chianti, please."

As the waitress left, Father Michael added, "I became addicted to Italian food during the three years I spent in Rome."

"Something else I didn't know about you. But why would I? We've lived in such different worlds."

"I suppose I know more about you. Couldn't help it after the events of a year ago. And the shooting at Shannon. Everybody thought you'd died. They did! They really did!"

"Do I look dead to you?"

Father Michael started to laugh, almost convulsively, totally disconcerting the waitress who'd arrived at the table with their orders. He recovered and, looking at her concerned face, said, "I'm sorry. I'm OK. Shouldn't laugh and drink at the same time."

"You went to Rome, you said?"

"Oh yes, after Maynooth I went on to College in Rome for further study. It was a prized assignment. There were only a couple of positions and I was one of the lucky ones. I loved Rome. And being so close to St. Peters. Life couldn't get any better."

They said nothing for a while, enjoying their food, but the silence of the unspoken became awkward.   Until Ed broke it, "I'm sure you know why I wanted to see you."

"About your nephew, I suppose."

"That's right. What really happened to him?"

"He fell out of the old tower."

"Look, we – his mother and father and me. We don't believe it!"

"What do you mean?"

"Come on!   We don't believe it was an accident. He wouldn't have been out there climbing up that tower even on a good night. Didn't you know that he feared heights?   Did you know him?"

"I knew him."

"And ...?"

Father Michael had stopped eating entirely when Ed had started to talk about Terry Joyce. Now he sat with his head in his hands. He started to massage his baldness before speaking again. Clearing his throat, he looked up at Ed, "You're right. He wouldn't have been out there on any night."

"If you know something, you've got to tell me."

"St. Curnan's is my life."

"You do know something and you can't tell me. Is that it?"

"Yes."

"Well, if I ask you some questions, can you answer them?"

"Alright, I'll try."

"Was somebody with Terry when he fell?"

"Yes."

"Another boy?"

"No.   There was another boy but they got separated earlier."

"One of your fellow priests?"

"Yes."

"And you saw this?"

"Yes."

"You were there too!   And you let this happen!"

"You have to believe me!   I only tried to help. I wanted to protect Terry. I tried to prevent it!   I've been in agony ever since."

"Did you tell this to the police?"

"No."

"Why not?"

"I can't."

"What do you mean, you can't?"

"The   *pontifical secret.* It prevents me from talking to anyone, even law enforcement.   The Church must conduct its own investigation before anyone else.   I can be excommunicated if I don't obey."

"You have got to be kidding!"

"No. Believe me, I am not."

"So where did this come from?"

"From the Vatican.   From Cardinal Joseph Ratzinger, prefect for the *Congregation for the Doctrine of the Faith."*

"You mean Pope Benedict!"

"Yes."

"When did he issue this?"

"Not very long ago. 2001, I think."

"Has this got anything to do with the scandals in the Church? The child sex abuse?"

"Yes."

"Oh my God!   Was Terry being abused?"

"No, no, no!"

"How can you say that?   How would you know?"

"I know."

"So why did he die?"

"It was really an accident."

"I'd like to believe you. But I can't. You say there was a priest there the night he fell out of that tower. And you were there too. Why? What did Terry know? What threat did he pose?"

Father Michael sunk his head into his hands and Ed could see that he was trying hard to hold back the sobs.

"Was Terry running away from something that night? Did that other priest climb up into that tower after him? That's what happened, isn't it? And, if that's not murder, then it's manslaughter. Who was that other priest?"

"I can't tell you that."

"You mean you won't! Is the school investigating any of this?"

"I don't know."

"I'm sorry. We have to know what happened that night. Terry deserves justice. You're a priest. Surely to God, you must see that. Otherwise what do you stand for?"

Ed Burke's anger got the best of him. He stood up, without saying goodbye, and stormed out of the restaurant.

17

George O'Hara had returned home from England and made money collecting people's garbage. Waste disposal he called it. With the money he made he started *Hara Homes*, a new construction company. Soon he had put the *Hara Homes* stamp on many of the new residential housing developments. He then branched into hotels and banking and insurance. A prominent backer of Irish charities, a weekly mass goer, and a major contributor to the Roman Catholic Archdiocese of Dublin, George O'Hara had become a pillar of the community.

He was in the middle of a meeting with three close colleagues, T.P. McGrady, Jack Simpson, and Shane Braddock when his secretary interrupted. She had strict instructions to hold all calls. Unless it was an urgent family matter or ... He looked around the table at his two colleagues, "I'll have to see what this is. Hopefully I'll be right back."

T.P McGrady looked irritated, Jack Simpson shrugged, and Shane Braddock sat impassively. These four men accounted for a major percentage of Ireland's GDP and significantly influenced the rest. From industrial conglomerates in five continents to prize racehorses, five-star hotels and prestigious country clubs, billions sat at this table today. They had built their empire on an equal measure of shrewdness and ruthlessness.

Twenty-five years earlier, TP McGrady had been an IRA prisoner, on hunger strike, in the notorious Long Kesh prison. Rumour had it that it was IRA money, the ill gotten gains of criminal activity, that McGrady had used to fund his first business venture. But no-one doubted that it had been McGrady's innate acumen and brilliance that was behind the phenomenal growth of his empire. An empire that stretched, nationally and internationally, from agriculture to food, from pubs to hotels, and from real estate to banking. Wealth and good living hadn't softened him. He remained as ruthless as he'd been in his early days with the IRA.

Shane Braddock, a geologist, and the youngest member of the group at forty-three, had leveraged his knowledge of the oil industry, and of greedy dictators in oil-rich third world nations, into lucrative drilling rights around the world. He had amassed an immense personal fortune along the way. He knew that control of governments and politicians was the key to power.

Jack Simpson was the odd man out. Born in the extreme loyalist Shankill in Belfast, he should not be here. Instead he should still be living in the north, a stalwart Unionist and an ardent member of his local LOL, Loyal Orange Lodge; a Brit to the core, to whom it would be anathema to sit at the table with these Catholic Irish. But Simpson, at only twelve years of age, had already rejected the entire Protestant vs. Catholic sectarian climate that he was growing up in. He couldn't believe in a God that Christians fought over so he rejected it and became an atheist. At fifteen he discovered that his only God was money. And when he looked south across the border he saw the new energy and the new money.

So he crossed the border to a new birth, a new future. With his Scots-Irish genes and his Presbyterian work ethic, it didn't take him long to make his first million.

At about the time that Jack Simpson made his first million,

As George O'Hara suspected, his secretary would only interrupt him for family or the Archbishop, "Yes, your Eminence, I can be there in twenty minutes."

Archbishop McCready paced up and down in front of the window, stopping frequently to look out at the rain as it pelted the glass. He barely acknowledged O'Hara's presence, seemed totally preoccupied, far away in some bleak world of his own.

Finally O'Hara said, "You wanted to see me?"

The Archbishop stopped pacing, turned around and walked slowly past his desk until he reached O'Hara. He took a seat facing him. His fingers drummed on his knees as he spoke, "The Church is in a lot of trouble again."

"What do you mean?"

"You helped us close that deal with the government. The one that capped our liability at €140 million. The child abuse."

"I did. And I think it was a good deal. It'll cost the Irish taxpayers a lot more than that. You got away lightly."

"I know. We're in your debt. And, now, just when the matter was fading with the public, we have that death at St. Curnan's."

"Death at St. Curnan's?"

"The boy who fell out of that old round tower — and died ..."

"But I don't see the connection ..."

"There's a lot more to it than what you read in the papers. President McCafferty spent an hour with me on the phone last night. We're headed for a lot of trouble if we don't do something about it."

"What happened?"

"It seems that boy wasn't alone when he died. And it may not have been an accident. Two of St. Curnan's priests were there. One of them's in Rome. Until this blows over. But I'm afraid it may not blow over."

"There's something you're not telling me, isn't there?"

"Yes, there is. President McCafferty believes that some of his priests may have been involved with the boys, the boarders ..."

"When you say 'involved', do you mean ..."

"Yes, yes ...I mean exactly that! There've been rumours for some time, he says. But he could never prove anything."

"And do you mean that now he can?"

"No! But he knows the names of the two priests who were with that Joyce boy on the night he died. And one of them was Father Roland Cormack!"

"You don't mean of '*The Cormacks*'?"

"The same. And it was Monsignor Fallon, a first cousin of Lord Desmond Cormack, who got Father Roland out of there, sent him off to Rome. Without even consulting President McCafferty!"

"I thought the monsignor had retired. And that his family had taken care of him a long time ago."

"No, they didn't. I think they'd rather not acknowledge that the monsignor is a member of their family."

"Wasn't the Vatican prepared to laicise him one time? Over his extreme views. On sex, on everything."

"Yes, indeed. But, blood's thicker than water, or in this case 'thicker than the Holy See'. Lord Desmond Cormack intervened and the monsignor was quietly moved out of the limelight. And they've done the same this time by sending Father Roland off to Rome. "

"But that's good, isn't it? He'll be out of here till this blows over."

"But will it blow over? The church is already in trouble. Mass attendance is falling. Young men are not coming into the priesthood. We are reorganizing parishes into clusters because we don't have enough priests. One priest will have to serve more than one parish. He'll have to cover a cluster. If this matter at St. Colamn's gets any more publicity it can only make things worse."

"But what can we do?"

"I can't do anything. But you can."

"I'm not sure what you mean."

"The second priest there when that boy died is Father Michael Nugent. He's sworn to say nothing and he understands that the matter is being investigated by the church. But President McCafferty is worried about him."

"Worried that he won't keep quiet, you mean?"

"Exactly. I think he needs some encouragement, some reassurance. And it would be better if it didn't come from the church. It would be better if it came from someone respected by the community. Someone like yourself. You're an alumnus of St. Curnan's. You could talk with him. Empathize with him. Show him how much we need to protect the church from this."

"I think there's an alumni event coming up. Maybe that could provide me with an opportunity to talk with him."

"And, George, our understanding as usual. We never had this conversation."

George O'Hara thought that he'd never seen the Archbishop so unsure of himself. He looked like the Chairman of a company under threat from so much risk that it was afraid it might have to seek protection from its creditors. Well, at least he'd capped the financial risk at €140 million. The risk to goodwill was another matter entirely. Not to mention the risk of a very visible blemish on the Archbishop's image, especially with the rumour mill having his name on the next list of cardinals. And what if this Father Nugent failed to cooperate. He might be forced to use more than empathy.

18

The St. Curnan's alumni association dinner was a grand affair, much more ostentatious than previous dinners, because the college was publishing a history volume to celebrate its one hundredth birthday. Many famous alumni attended; neurosurgeons to writers to politicians returned from Chicago, Sydney, Toronto, Paris and elsewhere. Bios of former presidents and memories of illustrious alumni alleviated the regimented photographs and academic descriptions of life at St. Curnan's.

George O'Hara, being one of the *Alumni Illustrissimi*, had his own bio page in the book and, being an excellent after-dinner speaker, entertained everyone over dessert. Mingling later after the dinner had ended, photographs taken, and formal events over, he singled out Father Nugent. Father Michael, feeling privileged to have been approached by George O'Hara, easily agreed to follow him to a quiet corner of the bar. Not a drinker himself, he could see that George's tongue had been loosened by the amount of wine he'd consumed. Dispensing with any preamble, O'Hara went directly to the reason he wanted to talk. Very soon, Father Michael could see the political pressure that was being applied. If

George O'Hara had singled him out to ensure that he kept his mouth shut, how could O'Hara have known.

"Mr. O'Hara ..."

"Call me George, Father Michael."

"How do you know all this? The only person I confided in was President McCafferty."

"Oh, you must know how worried President McCafferty has been about all of this. And I am family here. Who do you talk with when you have a problem? Your family, of course. He wasn't breaking a confidence with you. And I am not breaking a confidence either. Can't you understand that?"

"All I know is that this is an inappropriate conversation. You've laid out your position. Very eloquently, I'll admit."

"We are concerned, that's all. You realize the damage this can cause the church if it's not handled properly."

"And it's obvious that you consider me a risk."

"No, no. I felt that it couldn't hurt to have this little conversation, if you know what I mean."

"You're wrong. It hurts. I'm disappointed. And this little conversation is over."

Father Michael got up from the table and walked away, leaving no doubt at all in George O'Hara's mind that he had failed.

19

Every Saturday night, Father Michael Nugent celebrated midnight mass at the local parish church. With young men no longer choosing the priesthood, the ranks were becoming thin.   Older priests predominated, many infirm, most unable to carry the demanding work-load. So Father Michael helped out every Saturday. He often thought that the shortage could be solved easily by permitting a married priesthood, and by allowing women priests as well.

The night sky was pitch black, no moon and no stars, and the streets were empty as he crossed the roundabout half-way between the college and the church.

Engrossed in his own thoughts, he failed to see the car, lights off, engine purring, sitting at the corner of the intersection.

Until dazzled by the high beams. Startled like a rabbit caught in the headlights, he stood transfixed. Too late, he tried to jump to safety. The car hit him head-on, flung him up against the windscreen, and dumped him on the road. Brakes screeching, it sped away.

Porch lights in two nearby homes illuminated Father Michael as people rushed out to see what had happened.   They knew that he was unconscious, maybe even dead.   They didn't move or touch him. Some stood guard while one called for the police and an ambulance.

On the critical list for twenty-four hours, Father Michael was moved to the serious but stable list: broken leg, broken arm, fractured collarbone, broken ribs, concussion. Painful but not life-threatening. No fractured skull, no punctured lungs, no internal injury or bleeding.

"Your guardian angel must have been looking after you."

Father Michael opened his eyes and saw Ed Burke standing over him. He tried a weak smile.

"Well, I suppose the Lord wasn't ready for me. Or, more likely, I'm not ready for the Lord."

"I'm glad. You could have been killed."

"I know."

"That was the intent, don't you think?"

Father Michael's face now looked deeply troubled.

"The police think it was deliberate."

"They're right. The car was found, burnt out, the next morning."

"But why would anyone want to kill me.   I don't have any enemies."

"Ah, but you have secrets."

Father Michael looked alarmed. That thought had never crossed his mind. Until now. Yes, he had secrets.

"You don't think ..."

"Yes, I do.   You were there the night that Terry died. There was another priest with you. You wouldn't tell me who that was. Said your lips were

sealed by some ridiculous *pontifical* secret!   You're
the only one who knows.   If you had died, that
knowledge would have died with you.   No secret, no
scandal!   Isn't that a tidy solution?"

"Oh, my God!"

"I'm afraid he won't help you.   He almost let
you get killed!"

"But surely they wouldn't commit murder?"

"But their friends would!"

Father Michael's right arm and leg were in
casts and he was immobilized in the bed.   But he still
had his left arm and now he sank his head into the
crook of that arm and stifled a sob.   Ed waited until
he had composed himself again.

"You said there was another boy with Terry
the night he died.   You lost that boy, didn't you?"

"We never discovered who he was. ”

"Why were you chasing them?"

"Terry had a phone that he'd taken photos
with.   We didn't find it.   He might have given it to the
other boy."

"And the priest with you wanted those photos
badly!   Isn't that right?"

"Yes, yes, yes!"

"Can't you see?   You can't protect these kids.
You can't stop these people.   You must give them up!"

"How can it get any worse?"

"It's already worse.   You must know that
another boy is dead.   Hanged himself.   From one of
your precious oak trees.   Young man called John
Carty."

"Dear God!   Yes I know."

"Lamenting it won't help.   Neither will your
prayers.   I know you mean well.   But you have to
open your eyes. These people are evil."

Tears flowed freely down Father Michael's
cheeks.   Ed reached for a face cloth from the side

table and gently dried the tears away.   Afterwards, Father Michael seemed to have made a decision.

"Sit down.   I have a story to tell you.   It'll take a while.   I have to start back in the Penal Days in Ireland.   Back in 1772."

Ed Burke knew all about the Penal Days in Ireland. His illustrious namesake, Edmund Burke, described the laws as '*a machine of wise and elaborate contrivance, as well fitted for the oppression, impoverishment, and degradation of a people, and the debasement in them of human nature itself, as ever proceeded from the perverted ingenuity of man'*. Under these laws, Irish Catholics were forbidden the right to exercise their religion, the right to receive education, the right to enter a profession, the right to hold public office, the right to engage in trade or commerce, the right to live in a corporate town or within five miles thereof, the right to own a horse of greater value than five pounds, the right to purchase land, the right to lease land, the right to vote, the right to keep arms, the right to educate their children.   Priests and school teachers were banned and hunted with bloodhounds.   Schoolteachers hid and taught behind a hedge on a remote mountain while someone kept a lookout for the English soldiers.   These were known as the 'hedge schools'. On Sundays, the hunted priests celebrated mass in open fields or on the mountains, using altars of earth and stone, while people watched for the English soldiers.   Ed recalled that the French jurist Montesquieu said that this Penal code was '*conceived by demons, written in blood, and registered in Hell.'*

"One family played on both sides back then. The Cormacks of Castle Cormack," and seeing the look on Burke's face, exclaimed, "You look surprised!"

"Yes, I am! But I suppose I shouldn't be!"

"The Cormacks switched religion to save their lands. They became Protestants and the Crown gave them the titles that they have until this very day. But it was a clever ruse. In secret they remained Catholic. The Archbishop was a Cormack. He dressed in rough homespun clothes, walked among the people, and hid and slept in holes in the ground. He organized hedge schools, said mass in secret places, and kept education and religion alive. The Cormacks publicly disowned him and privately supported him."

"All this history is very interesting but what has it got to do with the deaths of these boys?"

"The priest with me the night that Terry Joyce died was Father Roland Cormack!"

"Jesus!"

"That's why I have to tell you the history of the Cormacks. You need to know what you are up against. The Cormacks have been the staunchest supporters of Rome through the past 700 years. They can trace their influence back to the great Irish saints and scholars of the Middle Ages. They believe they have a right to the throne of St. Peters. Oh yes, they firmly believe there should have been a Cormack Pope. And they still believe that. Father Ted's path through the hierarchy was already bought and paid for. That's why you need to know all of this. You need to know who you are up against."

"Would they kill you to protect him?"

"The Cormacks? No, I doubt they'd go that far."

"Well, somebody wants you silenced! Where is Father Roland now? I want to talk with him."

"Then you'll have to go to Rome!   He was reassigned there a few days after Terry's death. Part of his career path."

"That's far too convenient for me!"

Father Michael's face had turned ashen and he seemed short of breath. Burke could see that this had taken a heavy toll so he stood up, "I think you've told me enough. You need to relax and get some rest."

"Agh! I'll be alright."

"You know I'm going to have to follow up on all of this. And I'll have to name you."

"I know, I know. I did go to see to President McCafferty in the beginning.   I thought it was in confidence.   Then George O'Hara came after me. Said they were concerned about the church's reputation. Worried about me! "

" *The* George O'Hara?"

"The very same ..."

"Ah, God, now all the pieces of this jigsaw are beginning to fall into place."

"You don't mean he had something to do with the attempt on my life. I can't believe that."

"I'm not saying he did. But he has a lot of power and a lot of unscrupulous friends. His friends were behind the attempt on my life a year ago. But I can't prove that."

Father Michael's face had drained of what little colour it had. He summoned up his last ounce of energy and indignation, "I don't want to be part of any cover-up, any *pontifical secret.* No more!"

Ed handed him a glass of water from the side-table and told him to get well. He left as the nurse approached.

20

The Irish Daily News,
Dublin

"Jesus Christ! Look at you! There's no fire in your gut anymore. Ever since you went back to live with your mother ..."

"Come on, that's a low blow. If my mother didn't have Alzheimer's... I'm always on time. Never miss a deadline. You don't have to go around, in a blind rage, wanting to know where the hell I am ..."

"OK! OK! But maybe I liked the fire in the old Sean Coyne. I don't see that these days."

"That's because you give me rotten assignments. Ambulance chasing. Petty crime ..."

"That's not my fault. It's quiet out there. Too quiet. Not even a good rumour. Until now."

"What do you mean?"

"When did you last see your friend, Ed Burke?"

"Hell, you know the answer to that yourself! After he was almost killed, he left the country. Went back to the States. I doubt if you'll ever see him on this side of the pond again!"

Sam McDevitt's burly look was topped by an ungainly mop of white hair that seemed to be in constant battle with itself, as indeed McDevitt seemed to be with himself. He had to admit to himself that he missed the verbal jousting that he used to engage in with Sean Coyne.

Sean had been, was, is the best investigative reporter in Dublin, he had to remind himself. But he'd lost it lately. Ever since he and Burke took on that corrupt Tanaiste and his gang a year ago. He used to be a free spirit, another girl every month, until his mother came down with Alzheimers and he had to move back to the family home. A blue-eyed, dark haired, good lookin' kid that all the girls went for and everybody wanted to tell him their secrets. But now he looked bedraggled, tired, worn out.

Maybe I can resurrect him, he thought, as he said, "Well, that's where you're wrong! He's back!"

"You're kidding! I don't believe it!"

"You remember the story about that boy who got killed in St. Curnan's. Fell out of an old round tower. It didn't make page one. Maybe you missed it."

"Naw, I read it. A terrible accident? What's that got to do with Ed Burke?"

"The kid was his cousin."

As Sean tried to digest this information, Sam McDevitt followed with, "There's more. Another kid, at the same school, hanged himself."

"Jesus! I never heard about that."

"It's been well buried. Lost among all the other young people who are killing themselves these days. Didn't you read about the two who met over the internet and made a pact to kill themselves? Met a week or two later and did it. So it's not surprising that this boy's suicide never surfaced."

"You think there's something going on at the school?"

"You're damn right! Two boys dead. Ed Burke nosing around. Don't you think that's very odd?"

"But it might be a coincidence. And if that boy's Ed's nephew, there's nothing odd about him being there."

"Ah, but there's more. One of the priests at the school got run over by a car. He's lucky, he's still alive."

"Yeah, but a car accident. What's that ..."

"It was no damn accident! The car was found, burnt out, a couple of hours later. It'd been stolen. That's a planned 'hit and run', if you ask me!"

"But why would anyone want to knock off a priest?"

"Damn good question! And you're going to find the answer for me. As of right now, you're on the case. I want you in Galway as soon as you can get your ass over there!"

"I'll have to contact Social Services. My mother ..."

"You take care of that. But I want you on the case now. I'll keep page one of the weekend edition open for you."

As Sean turned to leave, Sam McDevitt yelled after him, "And I want to see that fire in your gut again!"

21

President McCafferty answered the phone himself when Ed Burke called.   After the introductions, the President said, "Mr. Burke, we are very saddened by the death of Terry Joyce. He was a good student and his conduct was excellent. We are praying for him and his family. And our family here too. All our boys are family to us, Mr. Burke."

"That's what makes it so hard to understand. May I come and see you?"

"Of course, Mr. Burke.   My door is always open to family.   How about this afternoon? Would three be suitable?"

"Yes, that's fine, thank you. I'll be there."

Without wheels, Ed Burke was lost. He blamed it on his years in America.   But, as he looked around Galway, it seemed to him that people here would also be lost without wheels. *The Americanisation of Ireland. Blame it all on the Celtic Tiger.* He went to Budget car rentals and got a brand new shiny black car, a Toyota RAV4.   Perfect for the Irish roads, the good ones and the bad ones.

At noon, he negotiated the *roundabout from hell* at the Galway Shopping Centre. Mid-day traffic was building and soon this roundabout would indeed be *hell.* Some smart planner had installed a series of traffic lights at each entry and exit point in the roundabout, in an attempt to prevent gridlock. Most people didn't have a clue about how to use these lights. Tourists who normally drove on the right side of the road in their own countries not only had to re-orient themselves to driving on the left but they had to contend with the mystery of this roundabout with lights. Put simply, the problem was traffic congestion. Galway had become the fastest growing town of its size in Europe and had outgrown its infrastructure. A bypass was the only solution for this *roundabout from hell,* thought Ed as he exited the roundabout and headed for the Dublin motorway.

St. Curnan's was near Ballinasloe, the town on the extreme eastern edge of the county, a town famous for its annual horse show. A show so ancient that rumour had it that the Emperor Charlemagne had sent emissaries to Ballinasloe to buy Irish horses.

He stopped in Ballinasloe, bought *The Irish Times* and had lunch in a small café that appealed to him: smoked salmon on brown soda bread, followed by a large mug of Bewley's dark coffee, his favourite. *Best lunch in the world,* he thought, as he scanned the news. Usual stuff: Bush sneaked into Iraq to pretend that his surge was working while the Brits pulled out of Basra, leaving it all to the Shiite militia. Kilkenny beat Limerick in the hurling final. Flipping through the pages, he was captured by a headline: *Vatican investigates 'suicide' of elite officer.* A member of the Vatican Gendarmes had been found dead with a gunshot wound to the head. The Vatican offered no explanation as to why a young elite member of the Gendarmes would have committed suicide. The article went on to talk about a recent case involving the Swiss Guards where one of the Guards had killed the guard commandant and his wife before shooting himself. In this case the Vatican had attributed it to '*ratus di follia*', a moment of total madness. But the guard's mother had insisted that her son had been the victim of a plot. *Mystery and intrigue! Makes the Vatican a perfect refuge for Father Roland Cormack,* thought Burke.

At a quarter to three, Burke drove through the imposing front gate pillars of St. Curnan's and drove leisurely up the driveway that circled the sweeping expanse of front lawn and led to the gravelled parking area directly across from the front entrance. Only a few cars were parked so he had plenty of spaces to choose from. The morning mackerel clouds had disappeared and the skies were a bright optimistic blue as he left his car and walked the few yards to the front entrance.

Terrazzo tiled floor, patterned in the shield of St. Curnan's, greeted his entry. He turned the corner into the main hallway, almost bumping into a young priest who directed him to the President's office on the second floor.

At exactly three, Ed Burke knocked on the large oak door of President McCafferty's office and was greeted with a very loud "Come on in!".

"Mr. Burke? You're a punctual man." President McCafferty's voice came from behind his large desk and an even larger stack of documents that almost dwarfed him.

"Thank you for taking the time to see me."

"Not at all. As I told you on the phone, I am always available to family. And, in this tragic case, my time is yours. I've already met with Terry's mother and father and I'll do my best to answer any questions you may have.   Please, please, take a seat."

Ed Burke sat down on the large black leather sofa and President McCafferty left his desk and came around to sit beside him. A large man with a broad ruddy friendly face topped by a shining bald head and tufts of white hair at his temples, he seemed totally approachable.

"Now, Mr. Burke, how can I help?"

"Terry's death was no accident!"

At this President McCafferty sucked his breath in and seemed to gird himself for what was to come, "But surely the boy was out there climbing that old tower on a very stormy night and lost his balance. Tragic, but boys are always into risks like that."

"Terry wasn't that kind of boy. I'm sure you know that and I'm also sure you must have been troubled by the way he died."

When the President said nothing, Ed decided to jump right in, "Two of your priests were with him when he died. Did you not know that?"

President McCafferty, now tight-lipped and grim faced, protested, "What's your proof of that, Mr. Burke? Who told you that?   There are many people who spread false rumours."

"No false rumour. Comes directly from one of the priests who were there that night.   Father Michael Nugent."

"But Father Nugent's in hospital after that terrible accident."

"Again, no accident.   The gardai believe that somebody tried to kill him. I believe that too. And now Father Michael does as well. That's why he talked to me. He's afraid but he's not going to keep silent any more."

"Oh, Lord!"

"Father Michael said that the other priest with him that night was Father Roland Cormack. Father Cormack was trying to get a mobile phone from Terry that night. A phone that contained incriminating photos. Terry was fleeing in terror that night. Father Michael blames Father Cormack for Terry's death. Do you know what is going on at your school?"

President McCafferty's grim face now looked slack and he seemed to have aged instantly. His lip trembled as he spoke, "Father Michael did come to see me?"

"But he didn't come to you soon enough, did he? He was afraid. Afraid of the church, I think. He seemed to feel he was bound by some ridiculous *pontifical secrecy* edict of the Pope. And I understand that Father Roland is no longer here. In Rome, I believe. Isn't that convenient?"

"But, Mr. Burke, he was only here on temporary assignment after he returned from Boston. Rome was always his next appointment."

"The fast track to the Vatican! Greased by the Cormacks, with collusion from Rome!"

"Now look here, Mr. Burke, you can't come in here and attack the church. The Cormacks have always been true to the faith. They have died for it. Our church owes its very survival to them. Father Michael must be mistaken. Perhaps the car injury has affected his mind."

"Oh, come on! You know very well that Father Michael is the least devious person you know. And there is nothing wrong with his mind. He's telling the truth. You know that and you can't accept it. Because, if you do, it will rock your faith to its very core! And I don't think you could survive that. Surely you must have been aware of things that went on within these walls, evil things that the church wanted to keep in the closet with their *pontifical secrets!*"

Burke realized that he'd had to let off steam and he stopped.   He almost felt sorry for the President who had sunk deep into the black leather, head in hands.   They sat, side by side, saying nothing, for a while.

Then President McCafferty composed himself, "You're right, Mr. Burke. Perhaps I've been naïve. I will see Father Michael again and I will ask the Gardai to commence an investigation immediately. I don't believe this matter can be contained within these walls."

"There's something you can do for me.   There was a second boy who fled the night that Terry was killed and there's a possibility that it may have been his roommate, Patrick Clarke.   I'd like to speak to him."

"We really should leave all of this to the Gardai now.   But maybe you've earned the right to ask some questions, Mr. Burke.   I will make arrangements to have you meet the boy."

With that, he shook Burke's hand, got up and headed back to his desk without even a good-bye. Ed attributed the lack of grace to some kind of post-traumatic shock that President McCafferty might be suffering.   So he also left without saying goodbye.

22

Ed Burke picked up the last crumbs of black pudding from his breakfast plate and licked them off the end of his fork. Refilling his coffee mug, he browsed the last issue of the *Galway Independent*, open on the table beside him.

Absorbed in the paper and glowing inwardly from his hearty breakfast, he was barely aware of the persistent ringing of the phone, somewhere in the background. Until Claire's voice cut through, "It's for you. I think he said '*Sean Coyne*.'"

"Sean, how'd you know I was here?"

"Are you kidding, Ed? The whole country probably knows! This is not the US of A. Here everybody knows what everybody else is doing!"

"God, it's great to hear your voice! Where are you?"

"I'm here. In Galway. And I need to see you."

"OK. How about Jury's? Meet you there. Noontime."

By noon traffic-free Shop Street teemed with people, locals and tourists. Crowded tables on both sides forced people to squeeze through the middle. Ed

Burke, head down against the bright sunshine, edged his way towards Jury's Inn. Sitting at the bottom of Shop Street, it faced the Spanish Arch and bordered the River Corrib. He'd picked Jury's because the bar was always quiet and empty, in complete contrast to the madding crowd on Quay Street.

Sean Coyne stood on the front steps of Jury's as Ed approached. Breaking into a huge grin, he launched himself off the steps and caught Ed in a massive hug. Ed, momentarily taken aback, hugged him in return. People looked at them with amusement and curiosity.

Breaking apart, Sean said, "Jaysus, Ed, you look great! The Florida good life, hah! We'd never know you'd died a year ago!"

"Living well is the best revenge, my friend!"

As they walked into the lobby and turned right into the bar, Sean looked at Ed and said, "It's obvious you've been living well. But revenge! What happened to that?"

"I walked away from it, Sean. The Tanaiste's dead, Tucker's dead, the Beetle's behind bars for the rest of his life. I think that's enough revenge for Pia."

"But McGrady, O'Hara, Braddock ... the bastards behind it all ..."

"Yeah, I know. They still have their millions. And their freedom. But they're like eunuchs in a harem now. And that's the worst life sentence for people like them."

"I wouldn't be so sure of that."

At the bar Ed ordered a cappuccino and Sean a Ballygowan. They decided to save the adult beverages for another time. It was a big open place, not a soul at the bar and only an elderly couple at a distant corner table. Which suited them fine.

They carried their drinks to a table and, as they sat down, Sean said, "But I didn't come here to talk about all of that."

"And I thought it was because you missed me!" Ed laughed.

Sean smiled at that and then got serious, "McDevitt's holding the front page on the weekend edition for me."

"And ..."

"Oh, come on! You know why I'm here. Those two dead boys at St. Curnan's. And one of them's your cousin's boy. That's why you came back, isn't it? And you didn't come back for a wake, did you?"

Ed said nothing. Just stared at him.

"So don't say anything then! Your cousin's son falls out of an old tower at midnight in the middle of a gale. And another boy hangs himself. Don't tell me that fall was an accident! And what about the boy who hanged himself? Is there some connection?"

"Listen to me. I don't want Terry's name, and mine, splashed all over your front page! It might act like Viagra on those eunuchs we talked about."

"But there's something going on at St. Curnan's. Something stinks!"

"Maybe. But I don't know ..."

"And what about the priest? The one that got run over and almost killed. Hardly your run-of-the-mill hit and run!   Not with a burned out car. You know I'm going to run with that, don't you? It's my job. And I smell a damn good story here. And there's probably no way you can keep your cousin's name out of it. So why don't we team up like we did the last time?"

Ed Burke had been considering all of this as Sean pleaded his case. They'd been a good team a year ago. Sean's investigative journalism and his use of the media had been crucial in exposing the corruption and abuse of power in the highest ranks of government. But this was different. Or was it? Maybe this was also a case of the corruption and abuse of power.

"OK. But what I'm going to tell you is strictly off the record. No front page. Not even in small print on your back page. You agree?"

Sean sat for a moment sipping the dregs of his cappuccino, thinking that he'd have to agree. So he said, "I'm on board. You know that. But I want the scoop on all of this."

"I don't know what the scoop is! It may lead to nowhere. Then again, if you lived in the States, you might have a Pulitzer Prize winning story here."

"That's good enough for me!"

"Tell me about the Cormacks ..."

"The Cormacks?"

"The Cormacks of Castle Cormack."

"You mean the Medicis of Ireland!"

"That's exactly what Father Nugent called them."

"The priest that was run over?"

"Yes. I managed to convince him that his life was in danger. That somebody intended to kill him. So he talked."

"Why would somebody want to kill him?"

Ed realized that he'd dropped Sean into the middle of the story and knew that he'd have to start at the beginning. And that's what he did. When he finished, he held Sean's arm in a tight grip and said, "All of this is off the record!"

"My God! What a story! McDevitt would salivate to get his hands on this. This Father Cormack killed young Terry, didn't he?"

"Yes. The same as if he'd put his hands around his neck and strangled him!"

"But you have no proof."

"That's right. I can't prove any of it. The only witness is Father Nugent. At first he wouldn't talk. Told me he was under strict orders from the Church. *The pontifical secret.*"

"*Pontifical secret ...*"

"An edict from Cardinal Ratzinger. Stops him talking to anybody, even law enforcement before the Church conducts its own investigation. Perfect cover for a cover-up, don't you think!"

"Ratzinger? You mean the Pope!"

A rhetorical question that Ed felt little need to answer. Instead he said, "It's the Cormacks we're up against."

"Aw, Christ! Forget it!"

"You mean I can't take on a Cormack."

"That's exactly what I mean!"

"Roland Cormack killed Terry and I'm going to get him if it's the last thing I do! That's why I want to know everything about the Cormacks. Every damn thing!"

"Where's Roland Cormack now?"

"Don't know. He's gone. Father Nugent thinks he's in Rome."

"In Rome! Surely not at the Vatican!"

"Exactly at the Vatican!"

"So the family wielded their power."

"Have you heard of a Monsignor Fallon?"

"Fallon? Fallon? Yes, yes, of course. Isn't he a member of the Cormack clan too? There was a scandal. Long time ago. The Cormacks covered it up and the monsignor disappeared."

"Well, he didn't disappear. He's at St. Curnan's."

"He can't be. That's impossible!"

"He's there alright. And Father Nugent is sure that the monsignor arranged the Vatican assignment for Father Cormack."

"Just like that!"

"Yeah, just like that!"

Exhausted from the intensity of their exchange, they both sat back in their chairs to take a deep breath and try and gain some perspective.

Finally Sean said, "The Cormacks may have gotten Father Roland out of the country. But I don't think they'd have tried to kill Father Nugent."

"You don't?"

"I don't. That's beneath them. No, they'd have silenced him in some other way. Religion is a powerful weapon. And, when you're a believer, you can be convinced of anything. That's the weapon they'd have used to control Father Nugent. Religion!"

"I agree. So who would have wanted to silence Father Nugent?"

"Somebody who wanted to nip this in the bud. Prevent another scandal."

"And another scandal would mean more lawsuits, more millions in payouts. They have a sweetheart deal on that from the government. That could be it. And maybe somebody became too zealous, decided to exceed their mission and take out Father Nugent."

"And, maybe St. Curnan's is only the tip of the iceberg!"

23

Ed Burke met Patrick Clarke, on neutral ground, beside the old walls that served as a handball court; a place as far away from spying eyes and the main school buildings as one could get.

At eleven am the morning mist was beginning to lift and the sun peeked out, promising a good day. Ed arrived first, found a good spot to sit and waited. At exactly eleven, Patrick Clarke emerged from the mist, walking slowly.

Ed waved to him and, as he approached, stood up and stretched out his hand in greeting, "Patrick, I'm Ed Burke, Terry Joyce's cousin.   Thank you for coming. Sit here."

Patrick Clarke, neat dark hair, deep blue eyes, wore a school blazer, grey slacks, and well-shined shoes, a tribute to the order and discipline expected of a boarder at St. Curnan's.

"It's not my idea to meet with you, Mr. Burke. The President insisted."

"Well, I'm glad you're here. I want to talk about Terry. You were his roommate and I believe you were good friends."

"Yes."

"Did President McCafferty tell you anything?"

"No, he said that he wanted me to meet you first. Then he wanted me to see him after we'd met"

"I know that Terry was chased by two priests that night.   And I know that his death was no accident!"

Patrick Clarke's face turned red, his eyes bleary, and he struggled to breathe.   Ed gave him time to compose himself.

"One of those priests confessed. That's how I know. I've told President McCafferty and there will be a criminal investigation. The Gardai will be all over this school. Do you understand?"

Patrick nodded but said nothing,

"I also know that Terry was not alone that night. Another boy who was with him fled."

Patrick continued to sit, immobile.

"Patrick, I think you were that other boy. The Gardai will find out, that's for sure.   And their methods won't be pleasant. It's best that you tell me what I need to know. Were you there that night?"

"Yes."

An answer so feeble that Ed had to watch his lips move to confirm it.

"But you know why Terry was afraid that night, don't you?   He had a mobile phone and they wanted the photos he'd taken. Isn't that right?"

Patrick had stood up, clenching his hands.

"Isn't that right?"

Patrick nodded.

"And he gave that phone to you, didn't he?"

Patrick now looked afraid and backed away.

"Patrick, if you have that phone you should turn it over to the Gardai."

Patrick still said nothing.

"If you won't do that, then give it to me.   If there's something on that phone that you don't want to talk about, something you're afraid of, why don't you tell me about it?   I can help you. You can talk to me.   You know you can't cover this up.   Don't you want to get the person who killed Terry? "

Patrick Clarke continued to back away. Now he turned and started to run, faster and faster.

24

Castle Cormack stood majestically overlooking Lough Corrib, the Mweelrea mountains picture perfect in the distance.

Ed Burke stopped his car at the crest of the hill. He'd driven through the main gates minutes earlier, unaware of what lay ahead. The road down to the castle undulated through a magical green carpet, enriched by trees and shrubs, planted centuries past by experts.

He eased the car into first and coasted at about five miles per hour down towards the castle. Crossing the bridge over the river that flowed into the lough, he found himself in the rear courtyard. He parked there, got out and walked around the side of the castle.

Unprepared for the view that greeted him, his eyes found it impossible to capture the labyrinth of flower beds, lawns, gravelled paths, hedgerows, fountains, and sculpture that covered the expanse between the castle entrance and the boundary wall bordering the crystal clear waters of the lough. The power of the Cormacks emanated from every inch of the place.

Huge lions, carved out of Connemara marble, guarded the entrance. He climbed the steps to the open front door and was immediately greeted upon entry by a young lady who seemed to have materialized from nowhere.

"Mr. Burke?"

"Yes."

"He's expecting you. I'll show you to the study."

"Thank you."

She led him through an oak-lined hallway hung with ancestral paintings. Stopping at a closed door, she knocked and, in response to a muffled voice, opened the door, ushered him inside, and closed it behind him.

It was going to take a while for his eyes to adjust to the dim light.

"The eyes, the eyes. I must keep the drapes closed."

The voice came from a high-backed chair, under a reading lamp, close to the bookshelves that lined one wall of the room.

"Thank you for seeing me."

"I was intrigued when you called. How could I refuse to see you!" the voice answered with a note of mirth, even an undertone of mischievousness. *Maybe I'm reading too much into it,* Ed told himself.

Ed's eyes had now adjusted to the light and he saw the man behind the voice rise from the high-backed chair and stretch out his hand in welcome. A firm and confident grip belied the frailty of the tall eighty-one year old Lord Desmond Cormack, Earl of Dunvegan.   Wrapped in a long purple robe, pyjamas peeked out near ankles that disappeared into dark green slippers. A crown of white hair topped a once-handsome face, cheeks now hollow from age. But the

92

eyes sparkled like the crystal clear waters of the lough outside.

Looking at his watch, he continued, "It's eleven a.m. Coffee time for me. Will you join me?"

"Thank you. I'd love to."

As though by prearranged signal, the door opened and the same young lady arrived with a pot of tea, two fine china cups enscribed with the Cormack coat of arms, milk and sugar, and an assortment of biscuits, all well distributed on a large silver tray. She left as unobtrusively as she'd entered and Lord Desmond busied himself putting sugar and milk in his tea as he commented, "Flora, my niece. Wonderful girl. Don't know what I'd do without her."

"You're a lucky man, your Lordship. Living in this beautiful home ..."

But Lord Desmond, after deciding quickly that Burke wasn't taking the mickey out of him, interrupted with, "Lucky! Hah! A heavy legacy comes with all of this!" as he waved his arms expansively around him and continued, "That's what brought you here, isn't it? At least you intimated that when you called. You didn't come to walk through the gardens and smell my roses, did you? And call me Desmond. Please! "

"No, you're right. I didn't."

His Lordship nibbled on the end of a biscuit, sipped his tea and waited for Ed Burke to compose what he wanted to say.

"They call your family the Medicis of Ireland. Your links with the Church, with Rome, with the Crusades. But you never got that Papal Crown. The smoke from the Sistine Chapel never announced a Cormack Pope."

That fired Lord Desmond, "Yes, we failed. And look what we've had. A Pole and a German! Even an Englishman in the past, Nicholas

Breakspear, Adrian IV. I'm sure you know that. But never an Irishman. Don't you think we're long overdue an Irish Pope?"

"So you haven't given up the hope?"

"We'll never give it up."

"And you've had big disappointments, haven't you?"

"What do you mean?"

"The Monsignor for one. Monsignor Fallon."

"Agh, the Monsignor, yes. Would have made a fine Pope. Well on his way when he was crucified over those indiscretions!"

"Indiscretions!"

"Yes, indiscretions! The Monsignor had no victims. Only a case of unspoken love. The love that's been part of our human nature for all time. Would you reject our Easter 1916 leader Patrick Pearse, the man who founded this state? Would you have him vilified because he delighted in the physical beauty of boys or boyish young men?"

"But innocent young boys need to be protected from predator priests!"

"And who in our family is such a person? Not the Monsignor! Never!"

"Then you're naïve or out of touch. You have a nephew, your youngest brother's son, in the priesthood. You have high ambitions for him, haven't you?"

"Father Roland. A fine young man. And what do you mean by bringing him into this conversation? What do you mean 'I'm out of touch'?"

"I'll give you the benefit of the doubt and assume you haven't heard."

Ed Burke then started back with the two boys being chased through the grounds of St. Curnan's on that stormy night, ending with the death of one of them, his cousin Terry Joyce. Lord Desmond sat mute as Ed continued to tell of the attempted murder of Father Nugent and Father Nugent's confession that it had been Father Roland Cormack who was responsible for Terry's fall from the old round tower on that stormy night.

Lord Desmond said, "This Nugent. One man's story. Covering up for himself, probably."

"No. I believe Father Nugent's telling the truth. So I think that Father Roland should come forward."

"Well, why come to see me? Haven't you talked with him? I'm sure he's denied the whole thing."

"That's it. I can't find him. That's why I'm here. I assumed that you would know. And I also assumed that it would be in your interest to clear the family name."

"Clear the family name! What impudence! You're saying one is guilty until proven innocent! Well, Edmund Burke, I do not know where Father Roland is and, if I did, I wouldn't be inclined to turn him over to a lynch mob!"

"My cousin's boy was murdered in St. Curnan's. And another boy has hung himself in the school grounds. And I believe that Father Roland knows about it. And, yes, as far as I'm concerned, he's responsible for the death of young Terry. So – let him come forward and prove his innocence. If you believe in him that much, then you must believe it would be in you family's interest to clear this up. I'm sure the house of Cormack doesn't need another scandal."

Lord Desmond had had enough. What he'd hoped to have been an interesting social visit had turned into something darker, more sinister. He stood, expecting Ed to stand at the same time. Ed followed and rose to his feet.

"Mr. Burke, I'm sorry for the untimely death of your young cousin. Which I'm sure was an accident. My family has many enemies. And some would love any opportunity to smear us. Understand that!"

He ushered Ed to the door, turned and headed back to his chair in the study.

When Ed had departed, he rang for Flora, "Flora, please get Monsignor Fallon on the phone. Right away, thank you."

25

His foot slipped but he hung on. Suspended twenty feet above the ground, he hung on to a small tree that grew stubbornly out of the rock fissure. Winded, with muscles that hurt from disuse, sheer willpower and revenge drove him on. Finding sounder footing, he rested and looked around.

Everything looked ghostly in the dusk. The lights of the town glimmered in the distance. Looking up, he could see the top of the college walls five or six feet above his head. He started to climb again.

Almost there.

The luminous dial of his watch read 10 pm. Stars decorated the sky above. He sat in a sheltered cove behind the wall. He'd been here for over an hour. When he reached here, there'd been enough light left to show the hundreds of cigarette butts that now carpeted the ground beneath his feet.   Students' secret smoke hole.   Well hidden but holding a good view of the college and its grounds,   perfect for keeping a look-out for the prefects or even the Dean.

Clothed totally in black, he wore a black ski cap that could easily convert to a balaclava.   A rope hung, lariat style, over his left shoulder.

It's time, he said to himself.

The school grounds were deserted. All the students were now in their dorm rooms, in bed with the lights out. Four or five windows shone like beacons on the second floor of the faculty residence hall.   One light shone out of the large French windows overlooking the roof of the main building's entrance porch.   The President's office.

Rested after his climb, he ran across the sloping front lawn until he reached the shelter of the main building.   Out of breath, he stopped for a minute   and then moved cautiously, close to the building, until he reached the entrance porch.

Taking the rope from his shoulder, he threw it up and lassoed one of the marble stanchions mounted on top of the porch.   He hooked the end to his belt and rappelled himself to the roof of the porch.   Light from the French windows suffused out in a circle, leaving the edges of the porch in darkness.   He looped the rope around the stanchion and, carrying one end, crawled across the porch to the edge of the French doors.   Slightly ajar to let in some fresh air, he could see President McCafferty sitting erect at his desk, reading from a stack of papers.   In his late sixties, his bald held alleviated by clumps of white hair at his temples, his ruddy face testimony to the outdoor athletic life he led as a young man, as a star of the local Gaelic football club, he seemed preoccupied and totally unaware that he was about to have a visitor.

Vengeance is mine. Good enough for the Lord, good enough for me.

26

President Sam McCafferty dropped his papers and stood up in shock.

The black clad man had entered his office through the French windows and was now standing holding the end of a rope. He said nothing, just stood there, fully intent on unnerving him. President McCaffrey thought fast. Too late to call anyone to help. Besides they didn't live in a high risk place so they had never felt the need for their own security force. *No, I'm on my own,* he thought, *I'll have to talk my way through this.*

"Who are you?"

No answer.

"What do you want?"

No answer.

"I have no money or valuables here. If you came to rob me, you've wasted your time."

No answer.

"If you talk to me, maybe I can help you."

No answer. The man took a couple of steps into the office and looked around, as though searching for something.

"Won't you tell me what you want? Maybe I can help you."

No answer. President McCaffrey realized he was getting nowhere and wondered if he could make a run for it. If he could move out from behind his desk and edge his way towards the door, maybe he could do it. So he came out from behind his desk and stood to the side, saying,

"If you're in some kind of trouble, maybe I can help you. You can talk to me."

No answer. The man's eyes seemed angry. The rest of his face was covered in a black balaclava.

"I won't tell anybody. No need to involve the police. Whatever trouble you're in, you need to talk to someone."

No answer. The President decided to take the first step towards the door. But, as he did so, the man took some things out of his pocket and threw them at him. They hit his chest and dropped on the floor at his feet.

"Pick them up!"

The voice, loud and angry, showed no sign of weakness. The President found himself thrown off-balance, his plan of escape unattainable. Nothing to do but obey, play this thing out, and hope for the best.

He bent down and picked up the items from the floor. Students' caps with the school emblems pinned on the front.

"Look inside. Read the names!"

President McCaffrey read the names and his ruddy face suddenly lost all its colour. Now he knew the visitor's purpose. His legs started to tremble,

Fuelled by fear, the President made a dash for the door. Too late. The man rushed him, grabbed his soutane so fiercely that it ripped from the neck to the waist. The President had never been a fighter and

101

had lived a life of non-violence, but now he kicked out at his assailant and landed a blow to the man's thigh. Which only infuriated the man who swung his fist and connected with the President's jaw, stunning him and knocking him to the ground. Vulnerable now, the President could feel the rope around his neck and hear the man's voice, a voice vaguely familiar.

"An eye for an eye. A tooth for a tooth. Isn't that what the bible says? Well, isn't it? A life for a life!"

The man tightened the noose around the President's neck and, with almost superhuman strength, began to drag him across the floor towards the French windows. The President tried to dig his heels in, tried to resist, but the man tightened the noose. Once out through the French windows, the man grabbed the other end of the rope, already looped around the stanchion, and commenced to tug, just like a tug-of-war game. The President, unable to resist, slid inexorably towards the edge of the roof. Finally the man kicked him over the edge and braced himself as the President's body jerked the rope taut.

Vengeance is mine. Good enough for the Lord, good enough for me.

27

The Carty farm lay in poor land about fifteen miles from St. Curnan's. Reached by a rutted country road, the land could barely sustain sheep and the few Connemara ponies. Ten miles from the main road, the Carty's were isolated. Not served by any bus route, they rarely saw another human being. They did have electricity and a phone line.

Ed Burke had called ahead and was surprised that Mrs. Carty had agreed to see him. He had expected to encounter some reluctance and was prepared to use whatever persuasion necessary.

He switched on the windscreen wipers as misty rain closed in. Mrs. Carty had given him good directions and he saw the rusty metal gateposts up ahead. He negotiated the pot-holes and edged his car between the gateposts. With hedges brushing him on either side, he squeezed his way through. A large old farmhouse faced him, half of the roof thatched and the other half slated as though it dated from two different periods. Outhouses and barns with rusty zinc roofs crowded together behind the farmhouse.

A few chickens scattered out of his way as he swung the car around and parked near the front door. The rain had stopped but the sky remained dull and overcast. The smell of burning turf captured his nose and he could see the wisp of smoke trailing languidly from the chimney. The front door opened and Mrs. Carty stood there as he approached.

"Mrs. Carty, I want to say how sorry I am. Thank you for seeing me today."

A tall woman, she stood with hands sunk in the pockets of her apron. Her bedraggled greying hair framed a big-boned weather-beaten face. Unsmiling, she stood back and ushered him inside.

Fire blazed in the grate of a large stone fireplace. A wicker basket, filled with turf, stood at the ready. Huge iron hooks over the mantelpiece supported a shot-gun, a working gun, a hunter's essential. A big pine table occupied the centre of the room and a willow-pattern tea-set sat waiting. Red geraniums on the window-sill added the only colour to the room.

Two tall-backed chairs sat on either side of the fire and she guided Ed to one of them. He sat and she turned on the kettle saying, "I'll make tea."

"Please don't go to any bother, Mrs. Carty."

"No bother. We usually have tea at this time of day. John loves his tea," she said, talking about her son in the present tense as though he was still alive.

Ed's eyes wandered as she buried herself preparing the tea. Six or seven framed photos competed for space on the side-board tucked against the wall under the window.

Mrs. Carty carried the teapot to the table and invited Ed to join her. Passing the sideboard he paused at the photos, confirming to himself that they were all of her son. One photo showed him standing in his football outfit on the school pitch while, in another, he was dressed in his surplus and soutane obviously taken before or after he'd served mass.

"Your son was a fine young man."

She didn't say anything right away, instead busied herself pouring two cups of tea and offering Ed the biscuit tray.

"He was our only son. All that we had," and she slumped into her chair, seeming to shrink before his eyes. Ed waited.

"Did he ever talk about the school? About the priests? About anything that was troubling him?"

"John was a good boy. A good student. He wrote a letter home often. He was doing so well. We were so proud of him."

"But, Mrs. Carty, what made him end his life? What drove him to it?"

"We don't know. His father .... " She immediately stopped talking.

Ed waited but she seemed lost, gone somewhere else.

"Mrs. Carty, you were about to say something about John's father."

She pulled herself out of it and said, "His father lived for John. He admired him so much. John was going to be – going to do – the things he never could. John's death killed him inside."

"I'd like to see him."

She seemed unprepared for his request. Her resolve suddenly collapsed and she dropped her head into her hands. Tears trickled down her cheeks. Ed's first impulse was to reach across to her, touch her hands, comfort her. But he knew that that would have been a bad move. Accustomed to the stoicism of farmers who depended on no-one but themselves, she had to find her own inner emotional strength.

She gained control again, looked Ed directly in the eyes, and said, "I haven't seen Joe since the day after John's funeral. I don't know where he is."

"Did he not say anything?"

"No."

"Have you called anyone?"

"Only his brother up in Mayo. But he hasn't seen or heard from him."

"Did he take anything? A suitcase? Anything?"

"Only the clothes he was wearing. Nothing else."

"Did you tell the gardai?"

"Sure, why would I do that? He's away somewhere. Somewhere to be alone. To get away. Even from me. You see, he couldn't handle John's death. And this house reminds him of John. Every minute. It gives me comfort. But not Joe."

"But aren't you worried?"

"I am. I am. But what can I do. Only hope that he'll come back soon. There's things to be done around here. And only he can do them."

She got up and began to tidy away the dishes. On her way back to the table she reached under the sideboard, pulled out a shoebox and handed it to Ed, "I lived for his letters."

Ed felt awkward. He didn't want to read her son's letters. Didn't believe he'd learn anything from them. But he felt he should make some gesture. So he lifted the lid and thumbed through the letters. They were all neatly inserted in their envelopes, except the two top ones, the most recent ones. Looked like they'd been read again and again. He scanned the top letter. Just as he suspected: a simple, uncomplicated story of his last week's activity at St. Curnan's, ending with his love and how much he looked forward to coming home for the holidays. Not

the last letter of a boy who was about to commit
suicide.

After a time, Ed felt that he should leave. He
couldn't do anything to lessen Mrs. Carty's sorrow
and he hadn't learned anything about her son's
problems. He only learned that his father was
missing.

28

Ed Burke decided that he had availed enough of his cousin's hospitality. He knew that Claire would encourage him to stay but he needed his own place, a base to operate out of, a place to retreat to when needed: his cottage at Claddaghduff on Connemara's west coast.

He hadn't been to the family cottage since he fled to Florida, at least eighteen months ago. The cottage, overlooking the beach in Claddaghduff, hadn't changed in twenty years. Oh, there was a new kitchen, microwave, oil fired central heating. But the rest remained the same. Even the thatched roof. Few of those left in Ireland. The cottage had been in his mother's family for ages. When he was a little boy, he remembered coming here in the summer time with his mother and father. A cheap holiday that let his mother escape her hated Dublin. How she loved it here. Totally at home. She became a changed woman after a week. A spring to her step, a glow in her cheeks, a sparkle in her eyes. His father hated it here. Hated the isolation, the barren Connemara landscape, the people. Couldn't wait to get back to his Dublin. But Ed always had a good time. Running on the beach, taking riding lessons on the Connemara ponies, learning to swim. It had been a playground for him. A vast playground with no people. He imagined that he was a great Irish king and ruled as far as he could see ...

These memories always came back to him as he neared Claddaghduff, the place which connected him with his past.

He paid a local man to keep an eye on the cottage, to open the windows and air the place. So it smelled fresh when he entered. Turf and wood stood piled up in the fireplace. He struck a match and lit the kindling.   Soon the leaping flames brought warmth and life.

But Ed couldn't relax and get cosy. President McCafferty's funeral was scheduled the day after tomorrow at Galway Cathedral. He would attend.

Two days later Ed drove into an already crowded parking lot at the rear of Galway Cathedral. He got lucky and squeezed into one of the last places available. It was windy and blustery but not rainy. Sean Coyne would be here and they planned to meet after the funeral mass. Ed closed his car door and, head down against the wind, strode towards the Cathedral.

Sean Coyne waited inside the main entrance. Ed joined him and they found seats near the centre aisle, mid-way to the altar, as the funeral mass commenced.

President McCafferty's coffin already lay on a catafalque at the head of the centre aisle, directly in front of the altar. Organ music reverberated around the perfectly acoustic space and Ed looked over his shoulder as the first of many priests walked, two by two, up the centre aisle towards the altar. He counted at least forty of them as they passed. Once they reached the altar, they sat in pre-arranged semi-circles. Ed had already counted those on the altar: ten priests and three bishops would con-celebrate the requiem mass.

The requiem mass lasted about an hour with a fine homily/eulogy from one of the bishops. *A most impressive service*, thought Ed, *fit for a head of state.* It was obvious that President McCafferty had been held in high esteem.

Ed Burke and Sean Coyne did not follow the cortege to the cemetery. Sean had seen enough. Besides he wasn't covering the event for the press. He was here to brief Ed on the Cormacks. They left their cars in the church parking lot and walked across the bridge into town and found a quiet corner table for lunch upstairs in *Ard Bia* on Quay Street.   They both settled for sparkling *Ballygowan*; a sober lunch, as befitting the day and the topic they met to discuss.

"Ed, tell me what you think. Who did it?"

"You mean, who killed President McCafferty?"

Sean made a face to show what else could he possibly mean and answered with a "Yeah!".

"You're the investigative reporter. I'd expect you to know before me."

"Hey, that's not fair!"

Sean's voice had risen and the waitress looked at them disapprovingly, letting them know that tranquillity was the expected ambience at *Ard Bia*.

"Easy. I was only kidding. The gardai think that John Carty's father did it."

"The boy who killed himself?"

"Yip. But I'm not so sure."

"Why?"

"I went to see Mrs. Carty and I didn't get the feeling that her husband was a killer."

"Did you talk with him?"

"No. That's the problem. He was missing. Been gone since the day after his son's funeral. The boy was his life. He couldn't handle it."

"So there's the motive."

"I know that. That's why the gardai think he did it."

"And you don't."

"I liked Mrs. Carty. Strong woman. She hadn't reported her missing husband to the gardai. Not the thing to do. Still thought that he'd be back. After he'd cried out his days and nights."

"But he's still missing?"

"Yes."

"So, he could be the killer."

"He could. He has the motive. But I have an uncomfortable feeling about it."

"This has been in all the headlines for the past few days. And this funeral will keep it alive. I'll have to write about it. And I'll have to talk about the gardai's suspicions. If Carty is reading all of this and, if he's an innocent man, this should flush him out."

"Maybe."

"On the other hand, if he's guilty ..."

"Or dead!"

"You really think he might be?"

"No, I don't know. Nobody knows. Maybe Mrs. Carty is right and he'll turn up at her front door at any minute. But I wouldn't bet on it!"

"Alright, I'll go along with you. Let's say you're right and Carty didn't kill the President. Who did it? Who do you think did it?"

"I don't know. But we can't assume anything. Maybe his killing had nothing to do with Carty's death. Or young Terry's death either. Maybe it has to do with somebody else entirely. Maybe it's been simmering for a long time."

"Look, Ed. I'm supposed to be a damn good investigative reporter and I'm confused. There's more than one party playing in this killing field. Whoever tried to kill your Father Michael was not the same person who killed President McCafferty. Different agenda. Different motives. One's a cover up. And the other's an act of revenge. Retribution!"

They'd ordered already and the waitress arrived with their lunch. Their table was tiny so she busied herself rearranging everything to make it all fit. Finally, with a well practised '*enjoy your meal*', she left.

They ate in silence for a while until Ed asked, "Did you find out anything about Father Roland Cormack?"

"I did, I did. And it wasn't too difficult. He's being groomed alright. Fast track to the Vatican."

"Sean, I know that."

"Wait, wait. There's a lot more!"

"Yeah, sorry, go on ..."

"Father Roland went straight to the States after ordination. Plum assignment in Boston. Assistant to the Private Secretary to Archbishop Volpe, a powerful man in his own right within the church."

"Being groomed, hmph ..."

"In more ways than one."

"What do you mean?"

112

"I've been doing some research. I need to know what we're dealing with. I mean, I never liked getting all that church liturgy beaten into me in school. Turned me off. If I'm going to write about what's happening here, what happened to Terry Joyce, and why, I need to go back to basics. So I did some digging. I've got a cousin in Boston, ex-priest, couldn't take the whole routine, left after ten years, so I figured he'd be a good place to start."

Sean took a deep breath before continuing, "You've heard of Father Andrew Greeley?"

"You mean the American priest who writes all those novels?"

"Yes, he coined the phrase *The Lavender Mafia*. The man knows what he's talking about. According to my cousin Joe in Boston, Joe Brosnan by the way, there's a subculture in the priesthood that promotes a gay agenda. They have ensured that their sexual orientation and ethos has dominated seminary life for years. You can imagine the power they control as they climbed through the hierarchy. They are *The Lavender Mafia!*"

"And you think that Father Roland was involved in this subculture when he was in the States?"

"Absolutely! My cousin Joe will swear to it. He says that Archbishop Volpe was the head man in this network in the States. And Joe should know. He worked in the chancery when Father Roland was Assistant to Volpe's Secretary."

"I need to talk with your cousin. Will he see me?"

"I'm sure he will. He knows why I called. He knows about the boys who died at St. Curnan's. I told him about you."

"I have to go to New York anyway. See Maria.
And Kevin. Maria's coming back with me.   I'll make
a detour up to Boston."

They finished lunch and left. Sean had a deadline to
meet and, as they parted on the street outside, Sean
said, "Volpe's now a Cardinal. He's at the Vatican.
Isn't that where Father Cormack went?"

29

An angry Monsignor Thomas Fallon bounded down the stairs of St. Curnan's, rushed out the front door, and headed for his car. He'd been summoned to Castle Cormack. *Summoned!* That's the only word that came to mind. Lord Desmond had been furious after the visit from that man, Burke. Insisted on seeing him immediately. He knew it'd be a good two hour drive and two hours back again. Desmond would invite him to stay the night but he'd deny him that pleasure.

In twenty minutes he was on the main road heading west. Checked the clock on the dashboard: almost four thirty. He turned on the radio. Music wasn't his thing, certainly not the pop tunes that filled the airwaves from Radio2. Then he realized that *The Last Word* talk-show was due to commence on TodayFM. That'll do nicely, he thought. Let me listen to the latest discourse and help to kill the next hour or so. Leaning over to turn on the radio, the car behind annoyed him. Even though it wasn't dark, its headlights were on full. Maybe he'll turn off and I'll lose him soon. Cautioning himself to relax, he turned up the volume and drove at a steady sixty miles an hour.

The Avenger had been waiting for this opportunity for days. The monsignor was evil. He knew that. And no-one had done anything about it. Now the monsignor had covered up a crime and moved the guilty one out of the country. Moved him to Rome where he'd get protection. The Church had failed. Failed to purge itself of this evil. The Church had lost its way. These evil people were no better than the Templars who used to reject Christ and spit on the cross. But God found a way to make them pay. We burned them at the stake. Well, I am doing God's work. I will make these evil ones pay. I will teach this church to change its ways.

An eye for an eye, a tooth for a tooth. He pressed down on the accelerator and closed the gap between his own car and the monsignor's. Let him experience fear. Yes, that's what I intend for the monsignor. Fear!

Nearing Galway, the traffic had increased and Monsignor Fallon no longer felt intimidated by the car that seemed to ride directly behind him. Other cars moved in and out and passed him as he stayed at his consistent sixty miles an hour. He negotiated the roundabouts and turned right on the Headford road. Fifteen minutes later, the traffic had lessened and now another car rode close behind. Could it be the same one, he thought, and immediately dismissed that thought and accused himself of getting paranoid.

Putting it out of his mind, he concentrated on the radio where Matt Cooper of *The Last Word* was attempting to moderate a heated debate about the US Presidential election between a liberal democrat and a conservative Republican. A struggle for power, he contemplated. Well, being a member of the Cormack clan, I know all about a power struggle.

With his mind engaged by the debate, the car seemed to run on automatic and he had to bring himself back when he reached the gates of Castle Cormack. All the staff had left for the day; only the caretaker, a maid, and his Lordship's personal chef remained. A side entrance had been left unlocked for him and he made his way through a maze of hallways until he reached Lord Desmond's office. But it was empty. He called out but got no answer. But he had a sense about where he might find him. He retraced his steps, went down a short staircase, turned the corner and turned the handle on a large door that opened into the snooker room. The light was dim, barely enough to illuminate the balls on the table. And sure enough, Lord Desmond stood there, leaning on a cue stick, contemplating his next move.

"Ah, Thomas, there you are. Take a cue stick and join me."

"I'm afraid not. You know I've never played this game."

"No misspent youth in the pool-halls of Dublin for you. You marched to the beat of a different drum, didn't you?"

"Did you bring me all the way here, just to harass me?"

"Don't be so damned sensitive, Thomas!"

"I don't appreciate being summoned here at a moment's notice, Your Lordship."

"Your Lordship! I remember when you used to call me Desmond."

117

"And you're probably going to lecture me that blood is thicker than water, aren't you?"

"In our family, it is!   That means that, as head of the family, I need to be informed immediately when there's a crisis.   It shouldn't be left to an arrogant stranger like this Edmund Burke to tell me what I need to know."

"Who is this Burke? I don't know him."

"No, you don't.   But he's the cousin of that young boy, Terry Joyce, who died in your college.   He seems to think that Father Roland had something to do with this.   Father Nugent, do you know him, told all this to Burke. Is that true?"

"The boy's death was an accident."

"Then why would Burke come here and blame Father Roland?"

"Father Roland was there when the boy fell out of that tower."

"So you confirm what Burke told me."

"No, I do not.   I don't know what Father Nugent told him. If he said that Father Roland killed that boy, then he's lying. Probably trying to protect himself. Roland followed the boy because the boy had done something wrong and he needed to stop him from making things worse."

"You're talking in riddles. Don't give me that cleric-speak. You're not in the pulpit now."

"The boy had taken some photos. Photos of Father Roland, photos that could have been misunderstood. Father Roland needed to get them. Now you know."

Lord Desmond sagged at this.   He moved away from the pool table, set the cue against the wall, and sank into a tall wing-backed chair in the corner.   He propped his elbows on the arms of the chair, clasped his hands together and used that to support his chin. He said nothing.

118

Monsignor Fallon continued, "Father Roland came to me. I decided that he needed to be as far away as possible until this whole thing blew over. The boy's death was an accident. That's what the autopsy has shown. He was due to be in Rome in three months time anyway. I called Cardinal Volpe and he was happy to take him sooner. Cardinal Volpe has great respect for Father Roland. He impressed him greatly when he worked with him in Boston."

Lord Desmond had regained some of his composure and, looking directly at the monsignor, he said, "But it hasn't blown over, has it Thomas. If Burke knows, other people know. And Burke is a determined man. He believes the boy was driven to his death. And he's looking for justice. This was always too big for you. Why didn't you let me know? I would have stopped this before it went any further. You have ignored the power of this family. What the hell were you thinking of?"

"I didn't see the need to bother you. Besides, it was embarrassing for Father Roland. He preferred that you didn't know."

Lord Desmond was now on his feet. He ushered the monsignor out of the snooker room and walked him to the large front drawing room, saying nothing on the way. Once there, he poured two small glasses of Jamieson's and offered one to the monsignor.

"We need to spend some time on this, Thomas. You'll stay the night. I've already ordered dinner for two."

But Monsignor Thomas Fallon was too old and too tired to spend the night on family intrigue. He still simmered with resentment from the imperious way

119

that he felt he'd been treated. So, to his Lordship's amazement, he took only one sip of the whisky, put down the glass, and brusquely walked out.

30

The Avenger saw him leave and watched as his car moved slowly out of the main gates and turned left onto the road that would take him past Lough Corrib and onwards to Galway. He had parked on the verge of the road opposite the castle's main gates. As the monsignor passed he put on his headlights, high beams this time, pulled out and drove after him. He soon caught up and immediately began to close behind the monsignor's car, knowing that his high beams would torture the monsignor.

Monsignor Fallon almost swore out loud. If he'd been accustomed to using swear words when angry, he'd have done so. He pounded the steering wheel and screamed *damn! damn! damn!.* The high beams penetrated his car, reflecting off his mirrors and distracting him. He knew that this could not be a coincidence. It had to be the same person. He was very afraid. Why would someone follow him? He had no enemies. And he had no money. They'd get nothing if they robbed him. Maybe I can lose him, he thought. He pushed down on the accelerator and watched the needle move from sixty to sixty-five to seventy. He didn't feel safe at this speed, especially now that it was dark, but he had to try and get away. It had started to rain and his windscreen fogged up. He strained to see as the high beams behind continued to drill into him. Maybe I should get off the road, he thought. The village of Cong lay a mile ahead and he decided to stop and seek refuge there.

Losing his concentration, he suddenly realized that the speedometer needle was nudging seventy-five as he entered the village of Cong. He hit the brakes and tried to slow down. But the rain had slicked the ground and he missed his turn-off into the main street of the village. The car spun out of control, almost hitting the dark limestone plinth of the Market Cross, and crossed the street at an angle narrowly missing the corner houses on each side until it finally slid into the old wall surrounding Cong Abbey. Steam rose out of the radiator and the bonnet had crumpled like a piece of cheap tin. The adrenalin was telling him to flee and the seat belts were cutting into his neck and shoulder telling him not to move. He released the seat belt and looked over his shoulder to see the street in darkness behind him. No sign of the car that had followed him. Maybe this is God's will that I should come to the Abbey on a night like this. Fumbling under the seat, he found a flashlight he'd stowed there. Hoping that the batteries still worked, he turned it on. It worked but dimly. The batteries were on their last legs. It wouldn't last long. The rain had lessened and he made a decision. He'd visit the Abbey and pray. Then he'd find somewhere to say for the night and get a garage to take care of his car in the morning.

Pulling the hood of his raincoat over his head, he had enough street light to let him see the entrance to the abbey, a few yards ahead. Founded by the last

High King of Ireland, Turlough O'Conor, in the early twelfth century for the Augustinians, its ruined walls still stood, a monument to its grandeur.   Passing through its very beautiful doorway, he turned the flashlight on and briefly illuminated the intricate carvings that framed it. Even though he'd been there many time before, he was still in awe of the artistry.

He stepped through the doorway and stood inside the great abbey church. The rain had stopped and the sky now served as a huge vaulted roof. He felt the majesty of God here and, using the flashlight, stepped over the tombstones that paved the floor until he reached the centre.   Kneeling then, he clasped his hands in silent prayer.

The sound of footsteps on gravel brought him out of his reverie of prayer in time to see the rays of a very powerful flashlight streak across the walls at the gable end. Painfully, he forced his arthritic hips to support his legs as he stood. But the flashlight, almost a searchlight had now found him and he stood there in its glow.

"Monsignor, so good of you to wait for me." The voice was strong, even theatrical, with a strong sense of threat.

"Who are you? What do you want with me?"

"It doesn't matter who I am.   It's God who wants you, wants a reckoning with you."

That was enough for the Monsignor.   This man sounded deranged. He'd have to get away from him. So he turned and ran, stumbling over the large flat tombstones. If he could make it to the forest at the end of the open cloisters, he might be able to hide. He knew the direction but he couldn't see and his flashlight was almost dead. But he could see more from the powerful light that his pursuer splayed back and forth. He dashed ahead, then tripped and fell, the flashlight clattering away from him.   Hurting badly, he got up again and finally made it though the church wall into the cloisters at the rear. He knew that if he followed the path straight ahead, it would lead him into the dense Ashford forest where he might be able to hide.

He could sense his pursuer closing in so he started to run, blindly, tripped and fell almost immediately. Stunned, he tried to get up but couldn't. Then he felt strong hands behind him, lifting him and holding him. He was powerless to fight back as he felt some kind of restraints tying his wrists together behind his back. His attacker said nothing. Monsignor Fallon fell back on the only defence he knew: prayer. He prayed as his attacker pulled and dragged him down the pathway between the trees until they reached the river. He couldn't see it clearly but he could hear the rush of its water.

The Avenger knew what he must do. But he wanted the monsignor to know why. He wanted to give him time to repent before he met his God. An old abandoned stone house, the walls still standing, stood out over the river. Used as a fish house by the friars, it was constructed over the river to trap the fish in a crib underneath. Swimming about they touched a wire that rang a bell to let the cook know. The Avenger thought that the old fish house would do nicely. Dragging the monsignor onto it, he looped a rope through the restraints on his wrist and pushed him over the edge until he was waist deep in the river. He tied the rope around a metal barrier that had been installed to protect the tourists and stood up. The monsignor had said nothing, only prayed all the time, and now prayed even louder. He took the bible out of his pocket, held the flashlight over it, and in his deep theatrical voice, started to read:

"Monsignor, you must already know why you are here.   You must know the crimes you have committed. No? You do not defend yourself. Yes, go on, pray. Maybe the Lord will forgive you. After all he is compassionate, we think.

But I will read from the bible so you can listen to his anger:

From Romans 1:27 : *"They wanted to have sex with one another. They did wrong things with other men. Their own bodies were punished because of the wrong things they did."*

From Romans 13:13 : "We must not do any kind of wrong thing with sex."

And in Jude 1:7, *the Lord says that "Sodom and Gomorrah and the surrounding towns gave themselves up to sexual immorality and perversion"*

Monsignor Fallon had stopped praying and was trying to speak. But only phlegm and grunts emitted from his mouth. He could not utter any words. His tongue failed him and he could feel his heart racing and then skipping and stopping and spluttering. He could hear his torturer's voice clearly and it seemed familiar to him. But he believed that he was only imagining that. He tried to speak again but his larynx had shut down.

"And, Monsignor, you and those like you are no better than the people of Sodom and Gomorrah! I see you trying to speak but the Lord won't let you defend yourself. No, there is no defence for you. You are guilty. And what punishment does the Lord dictate?   He says, 'If your right eye makes you do wrong, take it out and throw it away. It is better to lose a part of your body, than for your whole body to be thrown into hell. If your hand or your foot makes you do wrong, cut it off and throw it away!   It is

125

*better for you to enter into life without hands or feet
than to have two hands and two feet and be thrown
into the fire that burns for ever.'*

*"And what does he tell us to do? You must
know the answer. He tells us to " take the man or
woman who has done this evil deed to your city gate
and stone that person to death."*

*But I will leave you here like this and if the
Lord has compassion he will save you!*

The water now lapped over the monsignor's chest and
he no longer felt anything in his legs. Before he
lapsed into unconsciousness, something screamed in
his brain "I know that voice! I know who he is."

*The Avenger left Cong in a state of numbness. He
felt both exhilarated and depressed. He did not feel
any remorse. He never felt remorse. Driving with
his right hand he fingered his rosary beads in his left.
He wasn't saying the rosary. He mostly used the
beads as a touchstone, a comforter, a device to control
his emotions.   He knew that he was God's
instrument. God had asked him to clear out the
temple, to pluck out the eyes that offended, to cut off
the hands that scandalized. His work had only just
begun. He inserted the CD of* Biscantorat *and hit the
play button. Adjusting the volume, he almost closed
his eyes as* The Sound of The Spirit from Glenstal
Abbey *filled the air.*

The chapel appeared like a ship in the mist. A
triangular shape, beached on the mountainy
roadside, buffeted by the rain and wind, the

invitation *Stop and Pray* , black on white, glared at Father Bernard Flaherty in the headlights of his car.

He pulled into the small empty parking place in front of the church. One light shone inside through the large transparent front windows. He sat for a while, then got out, pulled the hood of his coat over his head, and strode through the rain to the front door. It was open. He entered and looked around. Empty, as though it had been reserved especially for him. For a brief moment, he wondered if this church really existed, wondered if it would really be here if he drove past in tomorrow's daylight.

He walked slowly up the centre aisle until he reached the altar rail. Without hesitation, he knelt and let his wet raincoat drop to the ground at his feet, puddles of rainwater soon accumulating on the tiles that surrounded him.

And he prayed.

Dear Lord, I did not ask for this. Just as you did not ask for the suffering you endured, for the brutal crucifixion, so I have not asked to be your instrument of vengeance. But your church on earth must be cleansed of its sins. Your people must see that the will of God is carried out. Your people will know the signs. They will know that these defilers have been punished by you. They will know the signs. Just as you prophesized against the Philistines when you promised that you would stretch out your hand against them, carry out great vengeance on them and punish them in your wrath. They knew that you were the Lord when you took vengeance on them.

Slowly he rose to his feet, raised the raincoat from the floor and pulled it around his shoulders. He genuflected, turned around and walked briskly out of the church. The rain had turned to a fine drizzle, peppering his face and filling him with renewed energy. He felt cleansed, refreshed, his soul blessed by God. He climbed into his car and headed towards Athlone. It was Easter holidays at St. Curnan's and he wasn't expected back for two weeks. Enough time to let the news about the monsignor get absorbed in his absence.   He headed for the monastery in Mullingar. They were expecting him and he would be able to find solace there. And await the word of the Lord.

He didn't know it then but he wouldn't have to wait very long.

31

At noon, Ed Burke's *Aer Lingus* flight lifted off into the dark and overcast Dublin sky and, seven hours later, descended into Boston sunshine.

He knew Boston well. In the early days in the States, as a young lawyer on the bottom rung of an aggressive criminal law firm, Ed was assigned every petty criminal defence in the book. That often took him to Boston to defend north-end petty criminals, some of whom would later become major clients of his own New York law firm. Long days spent toiling in the defence of the indefensible took their toll and they'd often end in long nights in the pub, sometimes in *Roisin Dubh*, the *Black Rose.* He promised that he'd treat himself to a pint there before he left. For old time's sake.

He gained five hours in time zone difference and sat in a taxi on his way out of Logan Airport by three pm.

Joe Brosnan was expecting him. Sean Coyne had made all the arrangements in advance, assuring Ed that his cousin would be only too happy to see him and that he had plenty of room in the old rambling house he owned in Cambridge.

With eyes glued to the window as they circled Harvard Square, he sucked in the essence of it all, remembering days long past when he'd hung out here after his gig as guest speaker to the graduating law students at Harvard.

In an instant they entered Massachusetts Avenue and left the Square behind. A few minutes later they took a right into a road, bordered by old Victorian style homes. The taxi pulled up outside a house on the right, halfway down the road. Ed paid the driver and retrieved his bag from the boot. As the taxi drove away he climbed the front steps to Joe Brosnan's door. He rang the doorbell and waited. And waited. Eventually he heard the lock turning and the door opening.

"Ed Burke, it's you, isn't it? I'd recognize you anywhere. Sean described you well."

Joe Brosnan was a tall, angular, affable man. Friendly eyes and a ready smile shone out of a face that looked toughened and well worn from the miles it had travelled. His fair hair was greying and thinning out on top.

"Joe, thank you for inviting me."

"Ed, Ed, no trouble. Besides, you're here to talk about my favourite subject. I should be thanking you."

He ushered Ed up the narrow stairs that clung to the wall until they reached a large open landing that lead into a warm, cosy living room. A bubbly lady put down a magazine and stood to greet Ed.

"Ed, this is Annie. "

"Good to meet you, Annie. And thanks for having me."

"It's nice to have you stay with us. We seldom get any visitors. You'll have tea. Or maybe you'd like coffee."

130

"No, tea will be fine. And, listen, I don't want you running after me while I'm here. I mean that now."

Annie laughed loudly, a sound of dismissal, and headed towards the kitchen. Joe invited Ed to sit down and took his bag upstairs to his bedroom. Ed glanced around the room, a TV and stereo in the corner and books lying everywhere. But no photographs or anything personal. Only a couple of landscapes on the wall that seemed to be the kind of pictures you got as a new home gift and didn't know what to do with them. Stuck with hanging them to avoid awkward feelings when the giver visited, you never took them down again. Ed didn't think that these two landscapes would be the kind of art that Joe and Annie would choose to hang on their wall.

Annie returned with a tray of tea and biscuits, "It's afternoon tea time for us. We like to keep up the old traditions. Of course it's about nine o'clock tonight by your internal clock. But you're better off forgetting about that."

"Oh, I do. I seem to be able to adjust my internal clock. Always. I've never suffered jet lag. And your tea is just what the doctor ordered."

Joe came back and Annie poured the tea.

"Sean didn't tell you about Annie, did he?"

"No, he didn't. But you're a nice surprise Annie."

"Annie and I are both former religious. Annie was in the Dominican Order when we met. At a time when I was disillusioned."

"And when I had decided that I should never have become a nun. It was the wrong choice for me", said Annie.

"You look like you've found each other, found a life. That's great. I'm happy for you both."

Ed spent the rest of the evening in their very enjoyable company. After a light pasta meal, they ushered him up to his room with a generous nightcap of his favourite *Drambuie.*

Annie did volunteer work and was conveniently gone early next morning, leaving the day to Ed and Joe.

Joe used one of the rooms in the large old house as an office and at nine am, fortified with a pot of strong coffee, they retired there. Books lay strewn everywhere, waiting for shelves or charity auctions. A stack of newspapers leant precariously against the side of Joe's big old wooden desk, the kind of desk one expected to see in the bishop's house. Joe dug through the papers, retrieved seven or eight without overturning the lot, and held up the headlines for Ed to see. Joe read them: " 'Cardinal Law under pressure to resign', 'Pope accepts Law's resignation', 'Bishop O'Malley pays $120 million in abuse claims', 'Portland Archdiocese settles 100 claims for $53 million' ,'Archbishop of Portland files for Chapter 11 bankruptcy', 'Diocese of Tucson files bankruptcy', 'Diocese of Spokane files bankruptcy' ".

"I thought this was a good place to start, Ed. It seemed to me that I was in an organization more interested in protecting its ass that kicking out the feckers that were destroying everything."

"Did you know this was going on?"

"Did I know? Are you kidding? We all knew! But we were indoctrinated. Taught to toe the line. Taught that the Pope was infallible. I know, I know. He's only supposed to be infallible in matters of faith. But it's very easy to be brain-washed into the concept that he and the Church are infallible in everything.

When you give yourself, your life, your heart, it's a hard, hard thing to believe you're living a lie."

He threw the papers back on the pile, "I know you came here to find out about Father Roland. But you won't understand what I'm telling you unless you know the history. Not just the history from today's headlines. I mean the history of the centuries."

He drained his coffee mug before he continued, "Have you heard the term *The Lavender Mafia?*"

"Not until your cousin Sean told me about it."

"Well, trust me. It's real. *Lavender Mafia* is the fancy name that Rev. Andrew Greeley gave to this secret and powerful network of gay clergy. There's speculation that more than twenty percent of the priesthood is gay. That can't be proven of course. But they've been the gatekeepers at many of our seminaries for years. Ensuring that only those who are sympathetic to them get in. It's been as blatant as that. And, they've moved up through the hierarchy. Imagine the power and influence that they have."

"Sounds like the kind of scurrilous stuff that people who hate the church would use to undermine it."

"Exactly! That's what those in the hierarchy say! Lies disseminated by the church's enemies! But they're not lies. And I am not an enemy of the church!"

"Well, those newspapers sure aren't lying."

"Absolutely! Do you know that the Church is facing lawsuits estimated at about $2 billion! Two billion! And they've deported an Irish priest, a Father Aloysius Smith, from California. Looks like his trail of abuse is going to cost the Church $23 million alone! Where did these people come from? From seminaries that were run by the *Lavender*

Mafia – that's exactly where! And this Irish priest came out of an Irish seminary run by them. So the network is worldwide. Reaches right into the Vatican!"

Now red-faced and angry, Joe got up from his desk and paced back and forth shaking his head.

"So they drove you out?"

He'd calmed down a bit so he wandered around the desk and sat down again before answering.

"No, they didn't drive me out. But they helped me make up my mind. Them and Annie. I'd been troubled for a long time. I think I probably shouldn't have gone through with the ordination. But you know what it's like back home when everybody in the family knows you're going to be a priest. When your mother tells you that she really wanted to be a nun when she was a little girl but she had to work at home and couldn't get away. And how she'd promised her first-born to God. That was me. How do you fight that when she drills that into you from the age when you begin to speak? Used to make up her dressing table in the bedroom like an altar and I'd play priest. Jasus, I was only six or seven at the time!"

"You didn't stand a chance."

"You're right. But it took me years to learn that. To learn that I was living my mother's vocation, not mine. Oh, I tried. I really did. You see I believed in everything the Church stood for. And when I learned that that was a lie, there was nothing else. Annie saved my life. She was getting out too. Not because of me. No, no, she'd already decided when we met."

"Well, I like Annie. I think you're a lucky man."

"Don't I know it?"

134

Joe was relaxed now and his laughter came from somewhere deep and pleasurable, carrying with it the sense of inner peace he felt when he talked about Annie.

"And Father Roland Cormack ..."

"Yes, Father Roland. Now you know the background. And you need to know the man. Firstly and most importantly, he came out of that same seminary in Ireland that produced the priest we deported. Secondly, he came to be groomed, to acquire the 'blue chips' he'd need to grease his way up the hierarchical ladder. Sure, Lord Desmond wants a Cormack in the Vatican but the *Lavender Mafia* want him there even more. And they are even more focused and ruthless than Lord Desmond!"

"And you know this ..."

"I was right there. In the centre of Archbishop Volpe's diocese. I saw everything. I suppose they thought that I was a mild mannered harmless little priest from Ireland, not someone with the pedigree of a Cormack. Father Roland is a quick study. He learned real fast. In six months he knew how to run this large diocese. Every aspect of it. The Archbishop loved him!"

"Loved him ...?"

"No, not that way. Although I'm sure he was tempted. Father Roland is a good looker alright. Hah, that kind of love was reserved for the young I'm afraid, and for the seminarians. Father Roland often taught at the seminary. I'm sure he found solace there."

"Seems like Archbishop Volpe treated Father Roland like a protégé."

"Yes, and he didn't hide the fact. He didn't care if it looked unseemly. The Archbishop had the power. Political power inside and outside the Church. And every dog, every priest, on the street

135

knew that he headed the *Lavender Mafia.*   Soon
after Father Roland returned to Ireland, Archbishop
Volpe got his red hat from the Pope and a plum
assignment at the Vatican."

"And now his world has crumbled here."

"Yes, when he left he had no successor, no-one
to put a leash on people, no-one to call in political
favours and cover-ups.   No-one to squash any
emergency scandal."

"And you think that those newspaper
headlines wouldn't have existed had he still been
here?"

"No, not really. I think too much damage had
been done. People were not going to keep silent. Like
they did in the past. But I believe that he could have
squashed a lot of it.   Damages might be in the
millions,   not   in   the   billions.   And   all   these
bankruptcies. I think he'd have managed that."

"So Father Roland left no dirty laundry behind
him here."

"Ah, hah! A clever operator! You won't find a
thing."

"You seem to have a bit of admiration for
him."

"No, no!   Dammit, I must be giving you the
wrong   impression.   I'd   say   fascination,   not
admiration. Father Roland was a ruthless, driven
man."

"Ruthless enough to kill?"

Joe looked hard at Ed as he thought about
that.   He went silent for a minute or so, to
contemplate the question.

"No, I'd never have thought that. But, still, if
something was going to block his way or undermine
his ambitious goals, I'd say he'd have to defeat it.
Yes, he'd have to.   And from what you've told me
about the death of Terry Joyce, it wouldn't be beyond

Father Roland to have pursued the boy to his death. He didn't shoot him and he didn't strangle him but he'd be capable of pushing him off that old tower. Make it look like an accident. If it got rid of the problem, he'd be callous enough to do it. Remember, he's a Cormack before he's a priest. And how did the Cormacks get where they are – and keep it – through the centuries? Not by being wimps, that's for sure!"

"He's in Rome now."

"Of course. At the Vatican with Cardinal Volpe. His safe haven."

"We'll see about that."

"Forget it! You'll never pin anything on Father Roland."

"I don't want to 'pin' anything on him. I want to bring him to justice for Terry's death. He's at least guilty of manslaughter."

"You'll never prove it."

"I think Father Nugent will sign a statement."

"But he's at the Vatican. No-one's ever been extradited from there. They have no extradition treaties with any country that I know of."

"I'll make it too hot for them to hold him."

"How? You think any legitimate press, other than the British scandal sheets – and nobody listens to them – will print your claims?"

"I think your cousin Sean will."

"Well, I wish you all luck. But I wouldn't give you much of a chance."

"Don't you want this entire *Lavender Mafia* thing brought down?"

"Of course I do. But how are you going to do that?"

"Good old business techniques. Declare the product bad for your health. The product that the Church sells. Drive the customers away. And those customers who stay will insist on quality control, on cleaning out the seminaries, on firing corrupt employees, on insisting on good governance. If the Vatican begins to lose its customers, its churches will close, it'll begin to lose its business. It won't be a case of one of your dioceses going bankrupt. They'll have to sell the Sistene Chapel!"

"Jaysus! You're mad!"

Ed knew he'd learned all he was going to from Joe Brosnan. He needed to get back to Ireland as soon as possible, see Sean Coyne, meet the Minister of Justice, confront the Archbishop. And go to the Vatican.

Next morning he took the Amtrak train out of South Station. As it rolled through the countryside his mind turned to Maria and Kevin and he felt excited about seeing them again.

32

RTE News

*The body found in Connemara this morning has been
identified as that of 49-year-old John Carty, missing
from his home since last month. His body was found
floating in the Ballynahinch river by two German
tourists out for an early morning walk. Mr. Carty, a
farmer from the Ballinasloe area has been missing
since his son, tragically, committed suicide.*

Tom Buckley, standing at the lunch counter in his
local deli, heard the news item over the radio and
knew he'd be needed on this one.   Luckily his
sandwich had arrived at the same time. He paid and
headed directly for his office.

   "He's looking for you, Tom,"   said Sergeant
Ford.

   "Thanks, Bill. I expected he would."

Tom knocked on Chief Inspector Flood's door, opened and entered. The Chief looked up from the papers on his desk. "Tom, have you heard the news?"

"Just heard it on RTE."

"Well, they didn't release the news until they'd notified his wife. And it seems we're the last to be told. But you can't expect the local gardai to be up to speed on every high profile investigation in the State."

"So, what do you think?"

"Tom, we're not paid to speculate. We need to find out if Carty had anything to do with these killings. Mind you, it's been our best guess that he might be our man. See, there I go, with the speculation. But, still, he's been the number one suspect. It's easy to think of him being deranged, blaming them all for the death of his only son."

"But what if he's not the one? What if he didn't do it?"

"That's what we need to find out. Dr. Mona Kennedy'll be examining the body. I want you there. She knows you're coming so I'd get over there right away. She's a busy lady and I know she'll be moving on this one right away."

"I'm on my way,"

Turning at the door, with a mouthful of sandwich, he said. "What if Carty's not our man?"

"God help us if he's not."

Dr. Mona Kennedy pulled on a pair of surgical gloves and walked to the examination table. She compared the access number and name on the tag tied to the big toe with the information on the chart she held in her hand. Satisfied, she started her external examination, speaking into the small attached microphone:

"... body is that of a middle-aged Caucasian male, blue eyes, brown hair; the body weighs 182 pounds and is 69 inches long. There are some abrasions and cuts on the face and forehead, most likely consistent with the body being dragged along the bottom of the river. There is no evidence of any significant cuts, injuries, or stab wounds on the body. Decomposition has commenced, with gas forming within the tissues. This is consistent with the body having been discovered floating on the surface of the water. Given the moderate temperature of the water at this time of year, I would estimate that the body has been in the water for at least two weeks. Preliminary examination is consistent with drowning but I will reserve judgment until a full autopsy is carried out ...

Tom Buckley had arrived thirty minutes earlier and turned to face Dr. Kennedy as she emerged. They knew each other from previous investigations so introductions were unnecessary.

"Hello Tom, nice to see you again."

"Yes, we should stop meeting like this."

Dr. Kennedy laughed heartily at that, her first laugh of the day, "Fresh coffee. Would you like some?"

"Absolutely"

They fixed two cups from the pot sitting in the small kitchenette in the corner of the room, usually reserved for staff.

"What can you tell me?"

"I only did a preliminary examination so I can't really be sure at this time. I can say that he was in the water for some time. But I'll need a full autopsy to be able to tell you more. That will be needed to confirm that he did indeed drown. I'd assume that that will be the assessment. There's no evidence of foul play, if you're looking for that.

There're only some abrasions on his face. But I'm sure he got that when his face scraped on the river bottom as the currents dragged him along."

"I understand. I really want to know how long you think he was in that river."

"That's easy. He's been there at least two weeks."

"OK. That rules him out."

"Rules him out?"

"As a suspect in our murder investigation. I know you have little time these days to keep abreast of everything outside of your own world."

"You can say that again!"

"John Carty was our prime suspect in the murder of President McCafferty. Right on the heels of the death of a couple of kids at the school. One was his only son. Suicide. Carty went missing right after his son's suicide so that gave him the motive. Revenge is always the strongest motive. Besides, we don't have any other suspects."

"So now you know it's not him."

"Right. President McCafferty was killed a week ago. That rules him out in my mind."

"OK. I'll let you know more after I get the results of the full autopsy. We'll be carrying that out tomorrow morning."

With that, Tom could see that she needed to move on. He thanked her, and as he left he turned around and said, "You're over-worked. You need a couple of assistants."

"Hah! Tell that to the people in the government!"

33

Sister Brigid walked briskly out of the front door of Dunfergal Abbey, stopped briefly and looked across at the sunny sparkling waters of the lough and the changing green and bronze colours of the hills that seemed to stand guard over it all. She never failed to thank God for letting her live in this most beautiful part of his world.

But today her heart felt heavy and sad. She stood for a while, then turned left and walked down the tree-covered lane towards the little cemetary. Despite leading a life she treasured, her body had not aged well. At sixty-one, her pasty transparent skin, thinning grey hair and stoop made her look seventy-five or older. In contrast to that image, she walked ahead smartly.

Before she was aware of it, her reverie had brought her to the incline that led up to the small graveyard that was neatly surrounded by a wrought iron railing. Pausing, she looked over the railing at the simple arrangement of graves, each one marked by a simple cross with the name inscribed on it.

She immediately knelt down and took out her rosary beads. Fingering them almost like touchstones, she started to form the words in her head. With lips moving, she soundlessly spoke to the Lord: *Oh dear Lord, you know that I never ask you for anything. You have given me everything I ever wanted. So I always come here to thank you. But, dear Lord, my heart is sad today and I come here to ask your intercession and your forgiveness for my brother and your servant, Bernard. Please hear me today. Please stop Father Bernard. Please let him see the error of his ways. Please tell him that you do not want him to avenge you. That's what they say he is doing. They say that he thinks that he is acting out your wrath. That he is your avenger. If you can't persuade him, please send him to me. And please give me the strength to save my brother's soul.*

The tears had begun to roll down her cheeks and she fished in her pocket for a handkerchief. As she was blowing her nose, she heard the sound of laughter and happy voices, immediately followed by Camilla and Lucia, two of the young novices. She realized that her time for solitude and prayer had ended.

The girls saw her as she stood up and they were about to leave when she called them. They turned and said, almost in unison, "Sorry, Sister Brigid."

"I'm going back. Won't you walk with me?"

And they did. Side by side, they chatted away they reached the front door to the Abbey, keeping her in company until they had almost dispelled the dark nightmare that had brought her down to the little graveyard.

34

When Ed reached Penn Station, Maria was waiting. She ran to him, he dropped his bag, and they held each other for the longest time. He held her head, gently rubbed away the tears from the corner of her eyes, and said, "God, I missed you so much."

"I know, I know. We can't do this any more. I'm going back with you."

They hugged and laughed as they ran outside for a taxi. The streets seemed to whiz by in a blur for Ed. Maria was an opiate for him and his favourite city could not compete. In no time it seemed, he stood paying the taxi driver and a minute later they were in the elevator on the way to his fourth floor apartment on East End Avenue.

An hour later, sated by their lovemaking, they lay side by side in serenity. Maria kissed him gently and looked at him with concern in her eyes.

"You seem troubled."

"I'm worried about you."

"Why?"

"You know why? You almost died the last time. And this is no longer about the death of Terry Joyce, is it?"

"No, you're right. But I can't walk away from this. I just can't."

"But it's too dangerous!"

"I don't think I'm in any danger. Nobody's trying to kill me. Why would they? I'm not a threat."

"But if you pursue this, you will be a threat. Can't you see that?"

"And you think they'd have me killed? Do you really believe they'd do that?"

"You're digging into something that's very rotten. And I believe totally immoral. Why should they stop at murder? Why?"

"But I have no choice. We have to confront these people, challenge them, stop them."

"And that's why I'm worried. They're very powerful. You'll become a huge threat to them."

"But they'll be too busy dealing with their own internal threats."

"And you think you can challenge this? You think you can overturn something that may have even been going on for centuries!"

"No, no! I don't. I'm not naïve. They can do it themselves. They can expel this evil from within. They can stop the coverup. They can start excommunicating every one that they find. They can begin working with the law in every nation. They can restore the belief of the faithful. Only they can do that. If there's any way that I can set that in motion, I will!"

Maria pulled him close to her and held him. Then she kissed his eyes and lingered at his lips before pulling back, "You're a stubborn man!"

Ed laughed, "Oh, well, you better get used to it. I can't change now."

146

And then, more soberly, he said, "I have to go where this takes me. You must know that. I've always believed in separation of Church and State. If, by exposing all of this, I can get Ireland to do that, then Terry's death will not have been bloody useless. And any risk I take will be well worth it."

Later, over lunch, Maria said, "Kevin's excited about seeing you. He's been here for a couple of overnight stays when you were away. We've done some fun things together. I don't think his mother is too happy about it but it was a convenient place to dump him when they did weekends in the Bahamas or whatever."

"Yeah, his mother's been pissed at me for a long time. And she'll never forgive me for almost getting killed in front of Kevin at Shannon. I know it took Kevin a long time to get over that. Sometimes I think his mother would have preferred if I'd died."

"You don't mean that."

"I do."

"But Kevin loves both of you."

"I know that. I never say a bad thing about his mother to him. I don't speak about her at all. I'm sure he has tons of things to ask me but he never does. Maybe we can talk when he's older."

"When he's older maybe he won't care."

"Yeah, I've already considered that. But I do the best I can. I'd sure love to spend more time with him. But I can't live here now. That's my loss."

"And Kevin's loss too."

"Yes."

"Well, he's going to meet you at five today. And he'll stay over for the weekend. It's all arranged."

Ed's face broke into a huge grin, almost knocking twenty years off him and transforming him into a teenage boy again. Which is exactly the way he often felt when he hung out with Kevin.

35

Ed Burke took a taxi across town to Mordy Stein's penthouse on Fifth Avenue. With a view over Central Park, he had to admit that it was one of the best locations in New York. Sue, his ex, was living in style and Mordy could afford it. Just hope they haven't screwed up Kevin, given him an elitist view of life. He felt the loss inside again, the emptiness at not being there for Kevin, the missed birthdays, and all the holidays especially Thanksgiving. *Stop it, stop it,* he told himself. *How many times have you played this record, over and over again? What's done is done. You can't live in the past. Let's move on.*

Kevin was waiting at the front door with a big smile on his face. Ed held the cab door open for him and he jumped across the pavement, almost colliding with people walking past. He jumped into the cab and put his arms around his father.

"You'd think I hadn't seen you for a year or more," joked Ed, "sure it's only a little over a month since you were with us in Florida."

Ed squeezed him tighter. Then he pushed him back, looked at him and said, "You're getting taller, skinnier. Growing up, huh?"

"Aw, dad, I'm twelve now. Soon be in my teens!"

"God help us!" laughed Ed and Kevin responded by throwing a punch at him.

The cab driver had been sitting patiently through all this until he saw and opening and asked," Where to, Sir?"

"Oh, sorry, didn't I say? Take us back to First Avenue where you picked me up."

Then turning to Kevin, he said, "Maria's making dinner for us. Your favorite. Can you guess?"

"Chicken Thai curry?"

"Right first time!"

"Then I thought the two of us would take in a movie. What do you think? Anything on you want to see?"

"Oh, I'd really like to see *I am Legend* with *Will Smith*. It's playing now."

"You know, that sounds like my kind of movie as well. Good choice!"

The movie was great and they both escaped into the frightening world of Will Smith. Kevin sat transfixed. He knew in his heart that no matter how bad things got, Will would come out on top and save the day. Just like his dad. So he was devastated when Will Smith died at the end of the story.

They walked back in silence until Ed asked, "You're very quiet. Didn't you like the movie."

"Yes, I did. "

"So what is it then?"

150

"I didn't want Will Smith to die at the end."

"But he sacrificed himself to save others. Isn't that a good way to die?"

The tears welled up in Kevin's eyes, a lump grew in his throat, and he couldn't speak. Ed could see the emotion that had overcome him so he didn't push the subject, just left him time to pull himself together.

"Dad, you nearly died too at Shannon. I can't forget it. Sometimes I have nightmares. Can't get it out of my mind."

Ed pulled Kevin to him right there on the street. Kevin felt a little self-conscious and tried to push away. Ed let him and said, "But you told me the nightmares had stopped."

"No, I used to get them every night for weeks after you were shot. I could see you falling and the blood spreading down the front of your shirt and I could feel the panic rise up inside. I used to wake up screaming."

"I know. Your mother has never forgiven me. Took a lot of persuasion to get you down to Florida."

"But I don't get nightmares like that any more. I only wake up in a bad dream sometimes. I don't scream any more."

"God, I'm so sorry to have put you through this Kevin."

"I'm afraid of losing you, Dad. I don't want you to die."

"Kevin, you're not going to lose me. I'm fine. Nobody's trying to kill me now."

Kevin didn't answer. Ed knew that he hadn't entirely convinced him. They walked back to the apartment, just enjoying being in each other's company.

36

The news media descended on the little village of Cong like a swarm of locusts: RTE, CNN, Sky, BBC, and other foreign networks. The killing of Monsignor Fallon was the story of the day. Coming on top of the murder of President McCafferty and the insidious rumour that another priest may be the killer was enough to propel this story to the front page.

The guards had cordoned off Cong Abbey and adjoining streets and were only permitting residents through. No-one was permitted onto the grounds of the abbey itself.

CNN, Sky, and the BBC were in the air as well as on the ground. Helicopters hovered overhead. Villagers stood in small clusters and in twos and threes outside of their houses watching in wonderment.

Charlie Crowe of RTE stood at the junction of the main street and the adjoining street that led to the abbey. With his back to the Market Cross, he stood facing the camera and started to speak, loudly enough to carry his voice over the sound of the other reporters' voices and the whirr of the helicopters overhead.

"The last time there was this much excitement in this picturesque little village was fifty years ago when John Ford brought Maureen O'Hara and John Wayne here to film *The Quiet Man*. That was innocent excitement and those were innocent times. And these are evil times. A priest, a monsignor was murdered here. This was the place where Roderick O'Conor, our last High King, spent the final years of his life. This is a peaceful place, revered by the people and respected by the thousands of tourists who come to visit. But, after this murder, nothing will be the same. Unfortunately it will be remembered as the place where a priest was murdered..."

In New York, the news reached Ed Burke in a breathless call on his mobile phone from Sean Coyne. Ed immediately called Aer Lingus and got lucky. He moved their return flight to the next day.

That evening, NBC carried the news on its broadcast. Maria Lane had turned on the news as she and Ed entered his apartment. Ed had already gone to the bathroom and rushed out as Maria's screeched, "Ed, Ed, now! On the news! Quick! Quick!"

Stunned, he watched Charlie Crowe reporting from Cong and then listened to Brian Williams try to give an American in-depth analysis of the story. But, as in all American news, even that of a respected broadcaster like Brian Williams, it turned into a sound-bite, another story dulled by the nightly news from Iraq and the crazies, loose with guns, shooting kids in schools and diners in places like McDonalds.

"You told Sean we're flying out tomorrow?," said Maria.

"Yes.   He'll come see us as soon as we get back?"

"And what about Tom Buckley."

"I sent him a text. He'll be up to his neck in this.   I should be there.   This is crazy.   First President McCafferty and now the monsignor."

"You can't beat yourself up. At least we'll be back tomorrow."

They turned off the news and Maria crossed to the bar where she made two large gin and tonics. They had no lime so they settled for lemon instead.

37

The day after he arrived in Mullingar, Father Bernard Flaherty received a phone call from an old friend, an admirer, who had often shared his views and his anger.

"Father Bernard. I'm glad I found you before the gardai."

"Peter, what's wrong?"

"The gardai are looking for you. They want to ask you some questions about the death of that monsignor in Cong. Haven't you been reading the papers? It's all over them. That fellow Sean Coyne's had it on the front page of *The Irish Daily News.*"

"We don't read the papers here. No papers, no radio, no television, no outside interference. It's a place for contemplation."

"Well, if I found where you are, I'm sure the gardai will not be far behind me. Get out of there right now. You'll be safe here."

Father Bernard didn't need a second warning. He knew they'd find out one day. He didn't expect it to happen so soon. But he also knew the Lord would provide for him. And Peter McDaid was the Lord's way of providing. Peter had been in the seminary with him but he'd left before ordination. *Disillusioned*, he said. In the years since, they often met to talk, discuss, and argue about the state of the church and about the evil ones who had infiltrated. In their darkest, and whiskey filled moments, they had even discussed the kind of torture and death that the Lord should mete out to these people. And he knew that Peter believed that to be wishful thinking, never once surmising that Father Bernard would one day act it all out. *But Peter knows now, doesn't he?*

Traveling light, he only carried an overnight bag. He walked into town and took a taxi to the railway station. He knew the gardai would have his car's description and licence plate so he couldn't take a chance on being picked up. He bought a ticket to Heuston Station in Dublin and saw that the next train was due within the hour.

He bought *The Irish Daily News*, a coffee to go, and sat down in the station. He'd already seen the headline on the newsstand, *Forgive me, Father.* He'd seen other tabloid headlines that screamed out various headlines: *Justice!, Vigilante Priest, Hang 'Em.* He was totally unprepared for that, for the angry sentiment in those headlines. So, as he sipped his coffee, he read the article by Sean Coyne in *The Irish Daily News.* It was a continuation of the previous day's reporting about the finding of the monsignor's body and the evidence that led them to him.

Stupid! Stupid! Stupid! He chastised himself when he learned that he'd given himself away when he lost his money clip among the graves stones at Cong Abbey. He'd missed it but assumed that he'd left it back in his room at St. Curnan's. Reading on, it seemed that many people regarded him as a hero, a priest who was enacting the kind of justice they'd like to have done themselves. He had tapped into a people suffering in silence for too long, a people who had always obeyed their priests, who had been taught that everything that happened in their lives, good and bad, was the will of God. The gardai issued a statement asking him to turn himself in, if not to them then at least to his own church authorities. No comment seemed to be forthcoming from Archbishop McCready's office. *That's not surprising*, thought Father Bernard, *as a Cardinal-to-be he's the church's political animal and will do anything to stay above it all.*

Interrupted by the arriving train, he folded the newspaper, put his coffee cup in the bin, and walked down the platform. He boarded about the middle of the train, ensuring that he found a seat pointing in the direction he was traveling. He never liked to feel that he was reversing in a moving train.

Peter McDaid, ruffled, ruddy, and a little overweight, was waiting in Heuston Station when he arrived. McDaid had followed his passion for architecture after he'd left the seminary and, with the growing demand in a very affluent Ireland, had built a successful practice. He'd never married.

They hugged and walked quickly out of the station to Peter's car, parked on the street nearby. In no time at all they weaved their way through the Dublin traffic and reached Peter's house in Rathgar, an upper middle-class neighbourhood of the city. Peter had a comfortable red brick townhouse, set back behind small hedges and wrought-iron railings on a peaceful tree-lined street. Inside, high ceilings and art captured the eyes, making the house seem even larger.

Peter took Father Bernard to an en-suite room on the second floor, and ushered him inside, saying, "This is yours. Stay as long as you need to. But we'd better talk when you're ready."

Father Bernard looked at him, his eyes moist, and said, "Bless you, Peter. You know, you would have made a very compassionate priest."

Father Bernard unpacked his bag, soaked a hand-towel in warm water in the bathroom sink and sank his face into it. Looking at himself in the mirror, he thought that he showed no signs of the pressure of recent days. *The Lord is good,* he thought.

The aroma of good coffee captured his nose as he made his way down the stairs.

"In here," he heard Peter call and followed the voice across the hallway, past the drawing-room, and through to the completely modern but perfectly homely kitchen. Coffee and croissants waited.

"They're the best. From my favourite bakery. Picked them up on the way to the station. Figured that you wouldn't get anything like this in that monastery in Mullingar."

"How can I thank you?"

"You're in a lot of trouble. If you've done what they claim, then I owe you. You remember the nights we agonized over the church. What was happening. The abuse. The lies. The cover-up. Even though I got out, I never truly left. Then to find out that my time had been sullied by these people. I'd have cheered the first person who'd have lined them all up against a wall and mowed them down. If you've mowed some of them down, than I cheer you. And I will help you in any way I can."

Father Bernard had a lump in his throat. Peter was probably the only friend he'd ever had, and Peter's emotional outburst had overcome him.

Peter waited until Father Bernard had pulled himself together and then asked, "Did you do it?"

Father Bernard put his hands together, as though in prayer, and leaned his face into them for a moment.

When he took them away, he looked Peter in the eye and said, "The Lord has used me as an instrument of his vengeance. You could say that I have acted as God's Avenger. But why ask me this question when you already know the answer. You hold the name of the disciple that our Lord held in most esteem. Peter. And yet He told Peter that, before the cock crowed three times, he would deny him. You won't deny me, will you Peter?"

"Bernard, why would I give you sanctuary here if I was about to deny you? But someone will deny you. Someone will turn you in to the Gardai. You know that, don't you?"

"I must carry out the work of the Lord."

"Well, if it's any consolation to you, the people are behind you. Have you seen the papers? They sympathize with you. They see you as a fellow sufferer who decided to act on their behalf."

"God threw the money changers out of the temple and he has asked me to make an example of those who are defiling his temple today. His people know that."

"At least you won't be crucified. We don't have a death penalty."

"I am not afraid to die."

"I know that. And it's doubtful if anyone could find a jury to convict you."

"What happens to me does not matter. It will be the Lord's will."

He got up from the table, raised his right hand and blessed Peter, and said, "I think I'll rest now." Then he walked across the hall and up the stairs to his room.

38

Ed Burke had kept his Dublin apartment in Ballsbridge Gardens when he was recuperating in Florida. He'd had a year's lease on the place so he held on to it. Besides, for that first six months of recovery, he was too weak and debilitated to think about it. Maria had given up her apartment when she moved with him to Florida so now it made good sense to have a Dublin base.

Their Aer Lingus flight from New York arrived on time at 7:30 am at Dublin airport. An hour later, loaded down with baggage and a dozen bagels that Maria had picked up at the airport, Ed paid the taxi driver and hauled the bags into the lift. Maria turned the key in the door, they pulled the bags inside, and collapsed in the living room.

Ed looked at his watch. Nine am. He knew that his body was still on New York time and that it was only four in the morning. But he wouldn't sleep. He never did.

"I'll make coffee. Toast the bagels," said Maria, as she rose and headed for the kitchen.

The phone startled them. Maria said, "I'll get it."

"It's for you. Sean Coyne."

He took the phone from Maria and said, "Sean, you must have a tracking device on us."

"I've got to see you. Can I come over now?"

Ed realized that Sean wasn't really asking permission. He was on his way.

He hung up the phone and said, "Better make coffee for three and put on another bagel."

Thirty minutes later Sean Coyne sat facing Ed with a chunk of bagel in his jaw and announced, "He trussed the monsignor up like a turkey and dunked him in the Corrib. At that old abbey in Cong. Must have followed him when he went to Castle Cormack."

"Do they have any suspects?"

"Well, it's not John Carty. That's for sure. They found his body. In the river. Looked like he'd been there for a while."

"I never thought it was Carty."

"I've asked Tom Buckley. He's on the case. Tells me they have no idea who it is. Unless he's keeping a lid on it and knows more than he's saying. But I didn't think so."

"Well, I have to see him anyway. I'll try and prise it out of him if he knows anything."

"Good luck!"

"This maniac is grabbing the headlines. He's diverting attention. This will suit some people just fine."

"What are you talking about?"

"I don't want the attention diverted from Father Roland Cormack. I want him to face justice for the killing of Terry. And I think he's also guilty of unleashing this monster. Don't you think that young Carty, President McCafferty and Monsignor Fallon would still be alive if he hadn't killed Terry?"

"Maybe. But you don't know that."

"No, I don't. But all the attention will focus on this killer. That's not what I want."

"What do you want? I don't understand."

"I'll explain. Your cousin Joe helped me to think this through. It's about more than Terry now. I want these people brought down."

"Hey, that's impossible. Just get justice for Terry and walk away. You can't win. Besides, nobody outside the church can bring them down. It has to be an inside job."

"That's exactly what I said to Joe. Drive the people away. If the Vatican begins to lose its customers, its churches will close, it'll begin to lose its business."

"And how do you expect to do that?"

"Not me. We. We're going to do that. Start a series of articles in your paper about it. Tie in with the other papers, nationally and internationally. Bring all the media on board."

"But we can't publish speculation. They'll sue us. They'll put us out of business."

"You're the best investigative reporter I know. And I can look under the rocks. The two of us can do this. And you've got the best starting point in the world. The deaths of Terry and young John Carty. Everybody wants to protect their kids."

"Sam McDevitt might buy it. Just might, mind you. There's no guarantees. He believes in the integrity of the press. But he's not afraid to take on the establishment. He's done it before. You know that. And, I thought of something. He's a member of that separation of Church and State group."

"That's perfect. When can you set up a meeting with him?"

"I'll ask him today and I'll let you know. Listen, I should get out of here and let you guys get some rest."

"Rest! We're up for the day," laughed Maria, "Ed is anyway. Just hope I can keep up with him."

Ed said nothing, just flexed his muscles, grinned and reached for Maria. They stood in a hug as Sean left the apartment.

39

Tom Buckley agreed to meet Ed at seven that evening. Even though he felt that the jet lag might get the better of him by then, he knew that he couldn't waste any time. He intended to meet the Minister of Justice and needed to know how the investigation was going before that.

They met at a nearby café. Tom hadn't seen Ed since that brief meeting a couple of days before Terry's funeral. Tom looked tired.

"Thanks for seeing me. And, if I don't look too alert, I hope you understand."

"Hey, look at the rings under my own eyes."

"Yeah, you look a little beat."

"Since this thing started, well since the suicide of young Carty, I've been running on about four hours sleep a night. And you bloody well know that I need eight, at least seven, just to function."

"Well, are you making any progress?"

"On Terry's death?"

"Yes, start with that."

"Look, there's no evidence of foul play. As you suggested, we interviewed Father Michael Nugent. An angry man, and a frightened one. He told us the whole story. Insisted that somebody had tried to kill him to cover it up. Said you believed that as well. It was definitely a hit and run. But we have no leads. The car was stolen from a used car lot in Galway. Forensics turned up nothing. Nobody saw a thing. Or, if they did, they're not talking."

"He told you about Father Roland Cormack."

"Yes. A sorry mess. But there was no evidence of assault on Terry's body. And we only have Father Nugent's story that Father Roland climbed that tower and either pushed or scared young Terry causing him to fall. Father Roland could easily deny that and claim it was an accident. That's not enough for us to issue an arrest warrant. But I'd sure like to pull him in on a charge of molesting. But I can't get a soul to talk. Everybody at that school has clammed up. And the murder of McCafferty has sealed their lips forever. We're sunk, I'm afraid."

Ed decided to tell Tom about his visit with Joe Brosnan in Boston and the story of the *Lavender Mafia*.

"That's why I want Father Roland back."

"Despite what you say, he's committed no crime that we know of. And even if you can get somebody to testify, the church is never going to give him up. And, of course he's a Cormack. There's isn't a judge in the land that would sit on this case."

As Ed contemplated the impossibility of it all, Tom said, "You want to hear the good news?"

"You've got good news?"

"We have a lead, a suspect. In the killings of President McCafferty and Monsignor Fallon. You know we found John Carty's father. Drowned.

166

Couldn't have done it. He was dead the night that President McCafferty died. But we got lucky. The monsignor died in Cong abbey. Gruesome. He was left tied to the old fish house with his body up to the waist in water. Hypothermia, shock, heart gave out. You can say all those things. I say he died of torture. Tortured to death by that mad bastard. We went over every inch of that old abbey. Scoured it for even a matchstick. It was late at night, dark when it happened. So he had to have had a good flashlight to see his way though there. But that's not as good as daylight. And that's where we made the discovery."

Tom had stopped, relishing the story, and Ed said, anxiously, "Go on, what did you find?"

"Some money, fifty euros, two twenties and a ten. In a money clip. That's an American thing, isn't it? I don't believe anybody used them in Ireland. I'll bet they don't use them much in the States these days either, do they? Anyway, it looked like some kind of a souvenir he got when he was in the Marists. Apparently he spent some years in that order after he was ordained. At first we thought it belonged to the monsignor. Until we examined it more closely. It was well used, well worn, but we could still make out the name that was engraved on the back. Father Bernard Flaherty!"

"Isn't he the priest who discovered young Carty hanging from that tree?"

"The very same man."

"My God! You don't think he's the killer, do you?"

"He's our number one suspect. We looked into his background. A brilliant man. Top in his field in math. That's what he teaches. But mentally unstable. Been in and out of mental institutions at least three times that we can find a record for. Who knows, maybe more. You know how the church hides these things. It's a secret organization. But you know that. I'm preaching to the converted here."

"Why would he start killing?"

"We don't know that. We tried to pick him up for questioning. But he's gone. Nobody seems to know where he is. I'm going out to St. Curnan's tomorrow to take a look at his room and his office. Maybe I can learn something. Do you want to come with me?"

"Yes, yes, absolutely."

By now, both exhausted, they called it a day and agreed to meet at ten am. Tom would drive and it'd take them over two hours to reach St. Curnan's. He wanted to be there by early afternoon.

40

Ed Burke slouched in the passenger seat of Tom Buckley's car as they neared St. Curnan's. His internal clock was still running on American time so he dozed off and on during the trip.

Tugging at the neck of his shirt to loosen it, Tom looked at Ed and said, "I'm sure you think I'm breaking all the rules by taking you with me."

"You are! And I'm glad you are."

"When they gave me the keys and the authority to examine Father Flaherty's room, they fully expect me to turn over anything and everything I find."

"But you're not sure you should do that, are you?"

"No, I'm not. I'm afraid that anything I find will wind up in some black hole."

"You mean you're afraid of a cover-up?"

"Exactly! This whole business sucks!"

"Dead on! This is not about perverts. It's all about power. I'm afraid this pursuit of Flaherty is a distraction."

"A distraction?"

"Oh, we must stop him. End the killings. I know that. But that's diverting us from a great opportunity."

"How do you mean?"

"Look, it's about time two things happened in this state. Separation of Church and State. And a demand that the Church clean up its act. Turn over every paedophile to the police. Don't hide them away, make excuses for them, move them around so that they can continue to molest kids. Close all the seminaries under the control of their *Lavender Mafia*. Eliminate the *Lavender Mafia* for ever. Apologize to the faithful."

"But why do you care? You don't believe?"

"You're right. I don't believe. And I shouldn't care. In fact, I should welcome their demise. But that's not happening. The unholy alliance between God and Caesar in this land is a major obstacle."

"Obstacle to ..."

"Obstacle to the future. The church still controls all the schools. The local Bishop is the patron of the schools in his diocese. They own the schools, own the land, dictate the ethos of the school, control the school boards. The Minister of Education should have full jurisdiction over our schools. But she doesn't!"

"You're on a roll this morning!"

"This is something that I'm very passionate about. And this whole business seems to offer an opportunity. But, if we get sidetracked chasing Flaherty it'll be so easy to bury what happened to Terry and those boys. People will cheer Flaherty for carrying out vigilante justice that they know will never come from the courts. And nothing else will change."

170

The time flew, the traffic was light, and soon they reached St. Curnan's and left the car in the staff parking area.

"Do you have to see someone?"

"Since they're without a President at the moment, just the school secretary. It's only a formality."

"OK. I'll hang out. You can pick me up after you sign in."

Ed walked out and stood in front of the school looking down over the sweeping lawn to the big oak trees. A serene picture. Prayer and contemplation came to his mind. And instantly departed when he failed to reconcile that vision with recent events in the College. His reverie was interrupted by Tom: "All set. Let's go."

They climbed the stairs to the second floor and Tom led the way to Father Bernard Flaherty's room. He took a large key from his pocket and inserted it in the lock. He turned it and the lock opened smoothly. The large door opened noiselessly and they entered. Tom closed the door behind them. The midday light forced its way through the closed curtains, giving the room the mood that great cinematographers achieve. For a moment they both stood solemnly, feeling like intruders who'd broken into a private sanctuary. Tom walked across and pulled the curtains open. Sunlight bathed the room, exposing a substantial, but spartan place. Ed let Tom take the lead. Dark wood side-tables sat at either side of the long single bed. A reading lamp protruded from the wall behind the bed and arched over the right side. A Sunday missal lay open on the table beside a half-empty glass of water.

Tom had already pulled out all the drawers on a long sideboard and was now rummaging through the bottom drawer which seemed to be stuffed with newspapers. He pulled them out and spread them on

171

the floor, and said, "My God, would you look at all this!"

Ed had already crossed the room and now stood looking over Tom's shoulder. He saw a collection of page one headlines and stories from Ireland and around the world. It seemed that Father Flaherty had been saving every story on the scandals involving the church. Many of them were the same headlines that lay on the ground beside Joe Brosnan's desk in Boston.

"Seemed to have a fixation on the subject."

"An unhealthy fixation."

"A sick man, our Father Bernard."

As Tom continued to peruse the papers, Ed moved to a large desk that sat beside the window. An open Dell laptop computer, with a separate keyboard and mouse, perched on top of a metal stand, doubling as a desktop. In contrast to the tidiness of the rest of the room, the desk and surrounding area was a mess. Papers, books, correspondence, and other flotsam, all fought for space in the great jumble that surrounded the desk. A small two drawer metal cabinet nestled against the right side of the desk, proving a stand for a printer. The last printed pages protruded from the printer. Ed retrieved them and saw that they seemed to be pages of a manuscript. The footer clearly read © *Creatures of Habit by Bernard Flaherty.* Intriguing title, he thought. In the jumble on the desk he found another hundred or more pages. They were out of sequence so he didn't know the actual number. He turned on the laptop, brought up windows and discovered only one user, called *Avenger.* He felt the hair rise on the back of his neck when he saw that. *Avenger!* So that's how Father Flaherty regards himself!

"Get over here. Take a look."

Tom Buckley pushed up from the floor where he was hunkered down with the newspaper clippings, walked over and looked at the screen.

"*Avenger!* That's exactly what he is."

"And look at this. He's writing a book. I don't know if it's fiction or non-fiction. Maybe the real world and the imagined world have merged in Flaherty's mind. Maybe he doesn't know himself. There're about a hundred pages there but I want to see if there's more on his computer."

With that he clicked on *Avenger* and brought up the desktop. Sure enough, right in the middle of the screen, the folder labelled '*Creatures of Habit*'. He opened the folder to reveal at least a dozen word documents. He pulled a diskette from a box on the desk, inserted it in the computer, and copied the most recent files.

"I'm taking this. I want to read whatever he's written. Maybe it'll explain what's been happening. And, if we're lucky, maybe we'll find out things we don't know. Things that will help us."

"Things that'll help you, you mean. In your crusade."

"Crusade! I'm not on any crusade."

"You been all fired up lately. Preaching about separation of church and state and church control of the schools. This whole mess has you unhinged."

"But what better time to confront all of this?"

"Listen, I only want to do my job. I want to stop Flaherty. But I also want to get Father Roland and all his dirty friends in front of a judge, stop the cover-up, expose the lot of them."

"And you're talking to me about a crusade. Will you listen to yourself, for Christ's sake!"

"OK, OK, let's get out of here. We've seen enough."

173

Ed looked around for a large envelope or something to hold the manuscript pages but saw nothing in sight. He tested the drawers of the filing cabinet and found them unlocked. The top drawer only held some copy paper and little else. But the bottom drawer had books piled on top of each other. He picked up the top book and read the cover, *Sex, Priests and Secret Codes, The Catholic Church's 2,000-Year Paper Trail of Sexual Abuse by Thomas P. Doyle, A.W.R. Sipe and Patrick J. Wall.* The blurb on the back cover said that *'this collection of documents from official and unofficial sources begins its survey in 60 CE and concludes with the contemporary scandal.'* And most of us believe that this is a plague of modern times, of our liberal attitudes, and our breakdown of morals, Ed considered. Not so, not so! He saw that Thomas P. Doyle was a priest, apparently still in good standing, one who has become an expert on the subject and has worked with both victims and those accused of the abuse. The next book, *Goodbye, Good Men by Michael S. Rose* seemed to pursue the same subject. Thinking it to be time that he got an education on the subject, he decided to take both books with him as well.

41

It had been a long day in the west and Ed was glad to get back to Dublin. Tom Buckley dropped him close to his apartment at Ballsbridge Gardens. He'd texted Maria on his mobile earlier and she knew he was tired. They'd planned to go out for dinner but Ed didn't think they had the energy. They compromised and agreed to go out, to the little Italian place around the corner, simple and quick but always excellent. A bottle of red and some spaghetti Bolognese and he'd been nourished for the evening ahead, one that he planned to spend with *The Creatures of Habit*.

At the restaurant Ed filled Maria in on his trip to St. Curnan's and his strange discovery in Father Bernard Flaherty's room.

"I'm going to read as much of it as I can tonight. I need to get inside his head. I need to see what makes him tick."

"I'll help if you want me to. Might be good to get another perspective."

"That's great. But I don't want to impose it on you."

"Are you kidding? Don't you know by this time that we're in this together?"

Ed laughed, "Well, if I don't know by now I must be losing more brain cells than I thought."

They finished the wine, paid the bill, and walked back to the apartment. Ed rummaged through the stuff he'd acquired from Father Flaherty's room. Two books, a folder of documents, and the diskette containing the manuscript of Creatures of Habit.

"Why don't you take these documents and books. See if you can find anything of interest. I'll load this manuscript on my laptop."

Maria brewed a pot of strong Bewleys coffee while Ed inserted the diskette containing the mysterious Father Flaherty manuscript into his laptop. He transferred the file to the documents section and then clicked open. A word document, it appeared on his screen in an instant.

"Coffee. Careful, don't spill it."

"Damn, that's all I need. Destroy the evidence."

Maria retreated to a comfortable place in the living room, under a reading lamp, and placed the documents and books on the coffee table in front of her.

Ed stared at the title page and then moused to the next page. The manuscript opened, starting in the first person. The writer did not identify himself but he was writing a form of memoir, starting at the age of six. Ed wondered if anyone could truly remember what happened to them at six. He decided to browse, knowing he'd go back and read it from the beginning. But he wanted to get a sense of it at first. To his surprise, three pages later, the work changed to the third person and the omniscient writer started his story in the seminary with a tale of deception. Told calmly and dispassionately, it held even more fascination because of that. Browsing ahead, ten pages later, it switched back to the first person and continued the memoir it had commenced. Paging through the hundred and seven pages, he found that the entire work alternated between the first person memoir and the third person storyteller. But he noticed a striking difference about fifty pages into it. Flaherty had started to refer to himself in the memoir as *The Avenger*. It seemed to ramble and become repetitive and the third person storyteller lapsed into rants and rages. It was obvious that this author's mind had deteriorated the further he'd gone into the story. He decided to print it all because he never could read a book from a computer screen. Making sure he had a full load of paper in the printer, he clicked print, got up and went over to join Maria.

She was so deep into the documents that she didn't notice him at first. When she did, she started excitedly, "I can't believe this. I never knew this. You've got to read this. It's unbelievable!"

"Aren't you going to tell me what it is?"

"OK, I thought that all the abuse in the church was something recent, the result of bad priests in a modern world. That's naïve for sure. Listen to this: 'a significant majority of the clergy had been practising such behaviour for decades; a *homosexual collective* within the priesthood viewed it as a *religious rite* and a *rite of passage* for altar boys and young priests.' And it says here that 'this has existed within the church for centuries' and 'it was the topic of Pope Benedict XIV's apostolic constitution, *Sacramentum Poenitentiae* in 1741'"

"I suppose I could do with an education myself. Although what you're reading confirms Joe Brosnan's stories of the *Lavender Mafia*. If it's been around for centuries, it must exist as a secret society within the church. If *Opus Dei* is the church's right wing secret society, then the *Lavender Mafia* must be its left wing secret society."

"But, from my reading here, it goes deeper than that. Much of it is based on paganism. Look at Ireland. Look at even the simplest things here. The holy wells with all the bits and pieces of cloth that people tie on nearby bushes. The water they take home in bottles, believing that it's some kind of cure for all ills. That's all paganism from the days before Christianity. We kept it all and integrated into our Christian practices. The same thing has happened all over the world, especially South America and Africa."

"So what are you saying about these priests ..."

"Here, look at this. I'll read it to you: 'homosexuality, especially boy/man love was practiced among the pagan religions, from the Romans to the Shinto temples of Japan and to the Yucatan in Central America.' And here again, 'it was a common practice among the Gentiles during the time of the Apostles.'

"Are we saying that this behaviour has been practiced for decades and that these people believe that it's some kind of a religious rite?"

"Well, they've certainly used that defense in the past. But it's been hidden, underground for years. It was always there but nobody talked about it. If anyone became a victim, to go public would be a cause of shame. To accuse a priest would be tantamount to heresy. The liberal mores and open sexuality of the sixties has brought it out into the open. Looks like Father Flaherty has steeped himself in this stuff."

"Yeah, you should see the book he's been writing. If you could call it a book. It's seems to be part personal diary and part research paper, and then it seems to drop off into a raging diatribe where he begins to refer to himself as *The Avenger.*"

"A portrait of the killer, then?"

"Looks like it. But I want to go back and read it from the beginning. It's printing out right now."

"It's going to be a long night."

It did indeed become a long night. Ed's eyes couldn't see the page any more and he knew it was time to quit when he found himself reading the same paragraph again and again. He looked at the bedside clock. Two am! Then he looked across at Maria. She was already gone, sleeping peacefully with a book open between her hands. He gently took the book away, turned off the light and called it a day.

42

Ed Burke decided that it was time to pay another visit to Father Michael Nugent. He needed to know more about this Father Bernard Flaherty and he hoped that Father Michael might have some insight into the man. After all, he rationaized, they were colleagues on the teaching staff at St. Curnan's. And he'd be curious to get Father Michael's reaction to *Creatures of Habit*.

Father Michael Nugent stood in civilian clothes outside the main gate of St. Curnan's as Ed Burke pulled up in his car. He rolled down the window and said, jokingly, "I almost didn't recognize you without your uniform."

"Maybe I should dress like this more often," said Father Michael as he climbed into the passenger seat, "now that I'm a target."

"You're looking well. A full recovery?"

"Oh, a twinge here and there and a hip that still bothers me. But I'm bouncing back. The physiotherapist's been doing a good job."

"Thanks for taking the time to see me."

"I've got the time. I'm only on part-time duty yet. Besides, I'm not straddling the fence any more.

I realized after they tried to kill me that I have to take sides."

"Tom Buckley tells me that you submitted a signed witness statement about the events of the night that Terry died. And you named Father Roland Cormack.   That's puts you in conflict with the *pontifical secret*, doesn't it?"

"I see no sign that the church intends to investigate any of this. So I'm going to follow my conscience."

Ed reached behind him with his left hand, grabbed a carrier bag and handed it to Father Nugent, "Take a look.   I found that in Father Flaherty's room."

Father Michael looked at him quizzically, opened the bag and pulled out about twenty pages of the manuscript, *Creatures of Habit*.   As the car cruised along at forty miles an hour on the two-lane country road, he started to read. By the time Ed pulled the car into the lay-by, he'd started to read it for a second time.

"Bring it with you," said Ed, as he pulled a hamper out of the back and carried it across to the benches places strategically for the tourists to view the Irish countryside. No tourists today. The season had only commenced and the place was empty, as they had hoped. They had chosen to meet away from the public eye. Given the hunger for any scrap of news by the media, their meeting would easily have made the front pages of next day's newspapers.

"I've got ham and cheese or cheese and ham. Brown or white bread. Take your pick. Diet coke for me. And sparkling water for you, I think."

"A gourmet meal. And to think that I've been critical of the food at St. Curnan's"

They said nothing for awhile, ate their sandwiches and enjoyed the view. Eventually, Father Michael said, "That manuscript explains a lot."

"How do you mean?"

"The anger. Father Bernard's anger. He was always angry at something. He was manic. Up and down. When he was up, he was angry. When he was down, he was morose."

"And this man was allowed to teach kids!"

"No, no, wait a minute. He was a genius at math. And a fine teacher. He never abused that privilege."

"But the anger ..."

"Most of the time he controlled it with his physical activity. He was a good athlete when he was younger, field, track, long jump, you name it. Here, if he wasn't on the handball court he was out running."

"Was he close to anyone?"

"Nobody. He was a real loner."

"But he was angry enough to kill."

"I can't believe that."

"The guards found evidence that he'd been at Cong Abbey the night that Monsignor Fallon was murdered. And it took a strong man to truss up the monsignor and haul him down to the river. And Bernard Flaherty was strong enough."

"I don't know."

"Well, he's missing. And you've read his manuscript. What do you think?"

"It explains a lot. He was taking his anger out on the church when he wrote that"

"Because he was he abused when he was a kid?"

"I'd say he never got over that. And it seems to have continued in college. And the attempts in the seminary as well. I know he writes some of it in the third person, as thought he wasn't writing about himself.   You can feel the anger simmering under the surface in these stories."

"It's a huge indictment of the Church, isn't it?"

"It's scary.   It shows how anger is festering throughout the church, among my fellow priests. Anger at all the abuse, at the failure to talk about it, at the great silence."

"And it's driven him to kill. We know he was mentally unstable, in and out of psychiatric care over the years. On medication."

"But how can you be 100 percent sure that he's the killer.   The person who killed our President climbed up the outside and came over the wall. Why would Father Bernard do that?   He was already here."

"What if he wanted to point the finger away from himself. What better way? You said he was clever."

"But what about DNA?"

"What about it?   The guards didn't find anything on the rope that McCafferty hung from. And there was nothing special about the footmarks where he climbed the wall. Yeah, they found some of his DNA, hairs in the President's office.   But they found some of yours there as well. And other faculty members. We should expect to find his DNA there!"

Father Michael wiped the mayonnaise from the corner of his mouth, stood up, walked over to the refuse bin and dumped his empty bottle and sandwich wrapper.   When he came back, he said, "You met me to see if I could tell you anything about Father Bernard. It seems to me that you know more about him that I do."

"All I know of him is in that manuscript. We want to find him and stop him. I was hoping you might have some idea where he went. The guards are scouring the country for him but no luck. We need to stop him before he kills again."

"I'm afraid I can't help you. I don't even know if he had a family. As I said, he was a real loner."

"I think maybe the Archbishop and everyone in power are breathing a sigh of relief. The world has discovered a madman to blame. And Terry's death and young Carty's suicide will become yesterday's news."

"That's sounds cynical. They've got a Commission of Investigation underway in Dublin. And a garda detective has been appointed as a 'priest support coordinator'"

"Window dressing! That's all. It'll be as ineffective as the Tribunals that've been investigating corruption for the past ten years. Didn't I hear that the Archbishop is planning to go to court to prevent this Commission from opening what he calls 'sensitive' church files?"

Father Michael had no response. A mist had worked its way down the valley, obscuring their view, and now the first raindrops began to fall. Typical Irish weather, thought Ed, makes me miss the eternal sunshine of Florida. They picked up the last remnants of their lunch, binned it, got in the car and drove back toward St. Curnan's.

Ed parked his car in the staff parking area and walked Father Michael to the front door of the school. They parted and Ed stood for a minute looking out over the sweeping lawns in front and the majestic stand of oak trees fronting the perimeter wall. Boys hurried back and forth between classrooms that were housed in two wings of the school. Gathering his thoughts, he turned around and started to walk towards his car when he saw the boy standing still. Watching him. As he got closer he recognized the boy. Patrick Clarke! Clarke moved suddenly, ran towards him and shoved a brown paper bag in his hand. He didn't speak a word, turned and ran away again.

Ed opened the bag and looked inside. A mobile phone lay on the bottom.

43

Ed Burke was worried. If Monsignor Fallen had been killed because he got Father Roland Cormack to Rome, then maybe anyone associated with Father Roland may be considered a target. He felt that he should warn Lord Desmond Cormack. He knew that Tom Buckley had been to see him but that would probably have been a procedural gardai visit.

So he'd made an appointment to see Lord Desmond and now stood facing him at Castle Cormack.

"Father Roland carries an important family name." Lord Desmond Cormack stood at an angle, so as not to block the light from the nearest window. The painting was old, the kind of portrait one would expect to find in the National Gallery. A tall man graced the canvas, attired in the robes of the Church with his archbishop's hat crowning a face, unmistakably a Cormack one.

"Impressive."

"Yes, Mr. Burke, impressive indeed. That, of

course, is our own St. Roland. I'm sure you must know the history."

"A little. But I must admit I'm sketchy on it."

"Seventeenth century. Three centuries have passed since he was killed."

"He was exceuted, wasn't he?"

"Executed! A fancy word for murder! He was murdered. They took him to London, tried him for treason, then to Tyburn where he was hung, disemboweled, and quartered."

"What were the charges?"

"Lies! Trumped up. That was a time when Catholics were persecuted by England. In the 1670's, King Charles II stepped up the persecution and St. Roland had to flee. He hid out in the mountains, in hovels in the snow and the rain. But they weren't satisfied with that. They wanted him dead. He was still a threat. So they made up these lies that he was in league with the French and that he was planning to overthrow the government. All lies! "

"It's hard to believe a time like that."

"We shouldn't forget. The Church didn't. The Pope canonized him in 1970."

"And Father Roland must feel the burden of inheriting the name?"

"Burden? There's no burden. Only pride. Father Roland knows that he must live up to the name. That's why this whole business is too shocking for words. It can not be countenanced! Never! Do you hear that, Mr. Burke? Never! It's persecution of a more vile and insidious kind. Revisiting us again. Testing us. But we will not fail the test. Cormacks do not fail!"

With that, he turned on his heel and took off down the hall. Uninvited, Ed followed him down the oak-lined hallway hung with more ancestral paintings. He'd left his office door open and Ed followed him through. The room light remained dim, as he remembered from his previous visit. Strong light bothered Lord Desmond so he kept the curtains partially closed.

As though he knew that Ed was right behind him, he swivelled his tall frame around and faced Ed, looking down at him imperiously.

"I want this madman caught. Or killed. That's what I told young Mr. Buckley and his Inspector Flood when they came to see me. Monsignor Fallon did not deserve to die like that. He committed no crime."

"Revenge, that's what I believe it is. If he found out that Monsignor Fallon got Father Roland out of the country, then he killed him to set some kind of example."

"Father Roland is an innocent man."

"Then why don't you ask him to come back. If he's innocent, he'll have no punishment facing him. And no dishonour to the Cormacks."

"And you believe the Cormacks will get justice. You believe we'll be treated fairly. Go out there and ask Bishop Roland if he was guilty. Ask him if he was set-up. Ask him if witnesses lied, perjured themselves. Yes, it was the seventeenth century and this is the twenty-first but nothing has changed. Father Roland will not get justice either. There are those out there willing to perjure themselves to bring him down."

With that he turned away, sat down and looked back at Ed, "You came here to warn me. At least I think that's why you came. Well, you wasted your time. I'm sorry about your cousin's boy but I can't help you. And I will not throw Father Roland to these lions so that they can tear him apart in front of the people. Do you understand that? Now, I'd like

you to leave Mr. Burke. I have nothing further to
say to you."

Ed did not respond. What was the use? He
knew he'd hit an immovable object. So he turned
around and left.

44

"We got lucky. Had a breakthrough in the Father Michael Nugent assault.   Thought you'd like to know."   Even over the phone, Ed Burke could feel the undertone of excitement in Tom Buckley's voice.

"That's great."

"Meet for a pint.   The pub at the Clontarf hotel. In about half an hour. OK?"

"OK. I'll be there."

Ed was already sipping on his pint of Carlsberg when Tom came through the door into the pub. The place was practically empty so they had it almost to themselves. Tom brought a pint of Guinness from the bar, sat down opposite Ed and said, "I didn't want to talk on the phone. You never know who might be listening these days."

"Aw, for Christ's sake, don't keep me in suspense. What's this breakthrough?"

"You know we never quit on the Father Nugent case. Finally, a couple of days ago, we found a witness willing to talk. Seems she saw two kids, well seventeen or eighteen year-olds, running away from that car before it went up in flames. She recognized one of them because he's an altar boy at her local church. Can you believe it? An altar boy!"

"Nothing's what it seems any more."

"Anyway, we brought him in for questioning and he gave up the other lad who was with him. So we picked him up too. They were scared. Never been into any street crime or anything like this before. It didn't take us long to get them to talk. Apparently they work part time in a body shop owned by the uncle of one of them. And this uncle pressured them into putting the fear of God into Father Nugent. They claimed that they hadn't intended to hit him, only frighten him. But the kid who was driving said that he lost control of the car."

"And do you believe that?"

"I don't know. But it doesn't matter. They did the deed and we've got them. The kid who's the altar boy claims that he wanted to get some revenge on the priests, any priest. He dropped one of those glass things they carry, a cruet I think they call it, when he was leaving the sacristy to go on the altar a couple of months ago and it fell and broke at his feet. The priest went ballistic and battered him around the ears. He's been carrying a grudge ever since."

"So they're patsies, that's all. It's the uncle you want."

"Oh, we know that. But we can't touch him. We brought him in for questioning and he denied it. Said the lads were lying. Trying to shift the blame so they could get off easy. Asked us what motive would he have for trying to kill the priest."

"Motive! He's acting for somebody who wants to protect Father Roland Cormack. Or somebody who wants to bury another scandal, especially one involving a Cormack."

"That's what we figured as well. But we have nothing on him. So we had to release him. I'd love to have been able to charge him and send it to the DPP."

"I'm absolutely certain that Lord Desmond Cormack would never do this. It's a tactic that's beneath him. But there're people out there who would sell their souls to protect the church. Who's this uncle anyway? What's his name?"

"Hughie Rogan. That name won't ring a bell with you but George O'Hara will!"

"George O'Hara!"

"Rogan's his cousin, second cousin. He owes much of his living to cousin George, his legal living at any rate. Hughie's been known to cut a few corners making a buck. Not the most scrupulous fella. Cousin George gave him the money to start his body shop operation."

"That's your answer. O'Hara's behind it. Rogan was carrying out his dirty work."

"And why would O'Hara do this?"

"You know the answer. To protect the church. Who comes to their aid on every damn thing. Who's their major benefactor? Who does Archbishop McCready's dirty work?"

"You can't be serious. Now you're accusing the Archbishop of ordering a hit on one of his own priests. That has to be ridiculous!"

"And that's why it stands a good chance of being true. I don't mean that McCready ordered the hit. Maybe he only asked O'Hara if he could make sure that the lid stayed on the events at St. Curnan's. O'Hara is the Archbishop's fixer. And maybe the kids are telling the truth. Maybe Rogan only asked

192

them to scare Father Michael and it went out of control."

"You've been reading too many conspiracy theories. I'll bet you believe that MI5 killed Princess Diana and that the CIA killed Kennedy!"

"I'm not some crazy conspiracy theorist. And you know that O'Hara was up to no good last year. I couldn't prove anything then but you know that he was one of the cabal behind that corrupt bastard, David Manning."

"Yeah, I'm sorry. But damn it, if I thought for a minute that you were right."

"You'd do what? Nothing! You can't prove a thing and you can't do a thing. All you can do is charge these kids with stealing a car and dangerous driving causing serious bodily harm."

"And that's not fucking good enough!"

They looked around. The bar was beginning to fill up and they knew it was time to move on.

As they parted, Ed said, "I'm going to see O'Hara."

"Be careful. Remember, they tried to kill you a year ago!"

45

George O'Hara's secretary returned Ed's call, "Mr. O'Hara will see you at three today.   Is that convenient?"   Ed replied that that would be fine. O'Hara's office sat in the heart of Dublin 4, a most prestigious address, not far from the U.S. Embassy and about a ten minute walk from his own apartment in Ballsbridge Gardens.

All glass, mahogany, with the O'Hara coat of arms in gold on the door, and carpets thick and luscious with a Celtic design all exuded wealth, power, and the image of a fat, well-fed Celtic tiger. Ed didn't know whether to feel soothed or ruffled by it all.   Before he had time to contemplate that, O'Hara materialized in front of him. A large man with a handsome Irish face, friendly and smiling, he almost gushed as he shook Ed's hand.

"Mr. Burke, so glad to meet you. A pleasant surprise. Come in, come in."

And with that, he turned and walked past the reception and the secretaries as Ed followed.   He ushered Ed into his office where Ed was once again surprised. Expecting to be faced with the ostentation that greeted him at the front door, instead he found himself in a working office replete with drawings, models of new developments, plan and elevation of houses, renderings everywhere.   O'Hara's desk doubled as a conference table.   In effect, it was a conference table that abutted a wall credenza supporting his phone and computer.   He guided Ed through the clutter, seated him at the table and then joined him.

"I know. You expected the opulence that met you at the front door. Well, that's image. This is where the rubber meets the road. We build homes and that's what I love. That house you see there, the plans and elevation – that's the most Eco friendly house that's ever been designed. It's green! That's our real image.   But you didn't come to see me about this, did you?"

"You know I didn't."

"Mr. Burke – may I call you Edmond ...?"

"No, call me Ed."

"Well, Ed, I was curious about you. That's why I agreed to see you. I wanted to see the man who was responsible for the death of David Manning, our Tanaiste. Yes, I wanted to meet the man who robbed us of our best and brightest."

"You mean that I helped to get rid of the most corrupt and dangerous politician this country has seen in a long time. And you're being disingenuous. You and your friends eliminated him, like you would cut out a tumour to save your own life. But I didn't come here to talk about the past."

"Why are you here?"

"Don't be coy! You know why I'm here. You must know that the young boy, Terry Joyce, who died at St. Curnan's, was my cousin Emmet's son. I'm sure you and your friends knew that I was back in

Ireland from the very moment I stepped off the plane at Shannon."

"Of course I read the papers. I heard about that tragic accident at the school. Terrible loss of a young life."

"Don't bullshit me. You know damn well that it was no accident. You know that the son of your most important Catholic family, Father Cormack, was responsible for his death. And if that ever saw the light of day, it would open a pandora's box of abuse and scandal that would rock the very foundation of your church. And you couldn't be sure that the only witness, Father Michael Nugent, would keep his mouth shut, could you? You look surprised. You didn't think that Father Michael would confide in anyone about your approach to him. An approach, I might add, that he found insulting."

"Alright, I knew about it. The church has suffered enough. And we've paid millions in compensation."

"Yes, under the most favorable terms. A settlement that you negotiated for them. The Archbishop must love you."

"I serve my church honourably. It does not deserve to be ruined by a few bad apples."

"So you would do anything to protect Mother Church, wouldn't you? That's why you asked you cousin to deal with Father Michael, scare the wits out of him or something like that. But Rogan's not too swift, is he? His thugs almost killed Father Michael. I know we can't prove this. If we could we'd have you both locked up for life."

"You're mad! Those kids were joyriders. Boy racers, that's what they call them. Out for a thrill, lost control of the car. An accident, pure and simple."

With that, he got up, face red and angry, "I am going to ask you to leave, Mr. Burke. You've exhausted my patience. I was curious to meet you and that was a mistake. I'd advise you to end these wild speculations and accusations."

Ed stood up, "Or what? Have me killed again? You tried that once. I don't think you can try that one again. I make you this promise. I am going to get to the bottom of my cousin Terry's death. And if I find that your Church has been burying its sins under the rocks, I'm going to expose them. And you can tell that to Archbishop McCready!"

Ed stormed out of the office, tipping over a table that held a scale model of a new O'Hara Homes development. Bit and pieces scattered everywhere.

46

Minister of Justice Brian Cosgrave knew that Ed Burke was back in Ireland. After Ed's near-death experience at Shannon a year ago, he never expected him to return. But, then again, on second thoughts, he hadn't made allowances for Ed's tenacious spirit. That spirit he remembered well from law school. He laughed to himself as some of those memories returned. He'd taken the phone call from Ed as soon as he got into his office this morning. Luckily he had no appointments and he told Ed to come see him.

The intercom buzzed on his phone, interrupting his reverie "Yes, send him in, Eileen."

Seconds later, the door opened and a tall, bronzed Ed Burke stood facing him. He walked over and reached out. They shook hands, hard. Brian Cosgrave looked appraisingly at Ed, "Damn, you look good. You know you look better now than you did before you were shot!"

Ed laughed deeply, "Thanks, Brian," and nudging Brian gently in the midriff, said, "I see the good life is treating you well too."

"Too much time behind a desk. My wife says I've got to get more exercise," and threw his hands up in the air in a gesture of frustration, "sit down, sit down."

They sat facing each other across the small conference table in the corner of the office. Eileen arrived with coffee.

"I took the liberty," said Brian.

"Thanks, I need my morning fix. All those years in the States, you know. I'm an addict."

"Well, it's the same here now."

Small talk over, Brian looked at Ed, "I never expected to see you back in Ireland again."

"Believe me, I had no such plan. Life was good in Miami. But my cousin Emmet needed me. You're aware of his son Terry's death at St. Curnan's."

"I am indeed. Such a tragedy. I'm sorry."

"Thanks, Brian. Now there's a second boy dead and a killer on the loose. I know the gardai are doing their best but this whole matter stinks!"

"Stay out of it! Leave it to the gardai! Young Terry's death seems to have been a tragic accident. That other boy's suicide and these murders have nothing to do with your cousin's death."

"I don't believe that and Emmet doesn't believe that his son's death was an accident. And he didn't trust the school or the church authorities – same thing – to tell him the truth. And he didn't trust the State either. He trusted me to find the truth. That's why I'm here."

"The gardai have investigated it. They found nothing to suggest that it wasn't an accident."

"And you didn't press the matter very hard, did you? After all, it was the church you were investigating."

"That's not fair. We did a thorough investigation, like we would anywhere. If people choose not to tell us something, we can't force them."

"But somebody knew something. My friend, Father Michael Nugent, knew something. You see, he was there the night Terry died. But you know all that now, don't you? Father Nugent talked. Yeah, after they tried to kill him!"

"And we've arrested the two young men who ran him over in that stolen car. Joyriders!"

"You don't believe that for a minute, do you? Their uncle told them to do it. It was a contract hit. And you know that!"

"No, I don't know that. Their uncle denies it. Claims that those lads would lie through their teeth to cut a deal."

"And you believe him!"

"It's not a matter of belief. It's a matter of proof. We have no proof. We have no evidence against Hugh Rogan. We can not indict him on the say-so of a couple of delinquent kids."

"And, you know, of course that Rogan is a flunky. He owes his life, his business, whatever to his cousin George. George O'Hara, the Archbishop's front man."

"What are you trying to say?"

"I'll spell it out for you. Archbishop McCready uses O'Hara as a fixer, a go between who cuts sweet deals for the church. O'Hara is the supreme lobbyist. I could swear on a stack of bibles that O'Hara's dirty fingers are in this. I believe that the Archbishop is afraid, deadly afraid that the deaths at St. Curnan's will undermine their authority, their freedom to operate without state intervention. So I believe he asked O'Hara to keep a lid on the matter."

"That's wild speculation!"

"Not at all! Did you know that O'Hara approached Father Nugent at the St. Curnan's alumni dinner? Tried to encourage him to keep his mouth shut. Did you know that?"

"No. But that seems to be in character for O'Hara."

"But Father Michael was angry. Gave O'Hara the brush-off. And then O'Hara's cousin hired these two thugs to attack Father Michael. Not too much between their ears, so they overdid it. I suspect that Rogan didn't ask them to kill Father Michael."

"But you have no proof of any of this."

"That's exactly what George O'Hara said to me."

"You went to see him! You accused him of this!"

"I confronted him. I got him to admit that he knew that Father Roland Cormack had something to do with Terry's death. And he readily admitted that a scandal involving the most prestigious Catholic family in the land would bring the people's wrath down on their head. I could see the wheels move in his head: Bad PR! Bad PR! I put it to him that he had his cousin Rogan take care of Father Michael!"

"Are you crazy?"

"I've never been saner in my life. Of course I knew it would rattle O'Hara. I wanted to shake him up. I want the Archbishop to feel the rock of his church tremble beneath him."

"This is a dangerous game you're playing!"

"You mean they might try to kill me again. Like last time."

"Don't joke about it. That's exactly what I mean!"

"So you think they're guilty too?"

"Don't try you child psychology on me. It won't work!"

"I'm sorry. I was out of line with that one. But, damnit, if the Taoiseach can be hauled in front of a tribunal because his friends slipped some pound notes in his pocket when he was hard up years ago,

201

why can't we bring the Archbishop and his cohorts in front of a tribunal for far worse crimes? Why can't we?"

"Hold it!   Seems like you're off on some kind of crusade. This has nothing to do with finding the truth about your cousin's death anymore, does it?"

"Yes it does. And it doesn't. I already know the truth about Terry's death. And I want Father Roland Cormack to face justice for that. And I want the Irish people to ensure that no organization is permitted to exist outside of the law and governance of the people. That's my mission."

"But that's impossible."

"Why is it impossible? Why? All I'm seeking is Separation of Church and State. "

"It takes time. That's what we inherited. The priests were the only ones left to educate us. Under English rule we were denied an education."

"But that's ancient history!   We've moved on. These are not religious schools I'm speaking about. These are state schools, primary and secondary. Schools where the teachers are often appointed or approved by the Church and their salaries paid by the taxpayer. And who is that taxpayer anymore?"

"What do you mean?"

"Look at the last census. Of the four million people in this country, almost half a million are not native Irish.   And close to fifteen percent of our population are not Catholic.   We have Muslims, Hindus, Buddhists, Methodists, you name it.   And you know that biggest chunk are people who say they have no religion whatsoever."

"If you want to fight that battle, go into politics. It's not going to be fought here in Justice."

Ed's passion suddenly subsided and he now sat with his head resting in his hands. He knew that he didn't come here to engage in a diatribe about the

202

state and the church. He had some vague notion that he could engage Brian Cosgrave's support, or at least a benign hands-off for the rough times he thought lay ahead.

"Brian, I'm sorry. I got carried away. I didn't come here to start preaching like this."

"Hey, forget it. I'm worried about you. You're taking on some powerful people. My advice – stay out of it! Leave it alone."

"How can I? That's what I really came to see you about. I'm going to try and get Father Roland Cormack to talk about the night that young Terry died. He's in Rome. I want him back in Ireland. I don't know how to do that yet. But I want you in my corner when I try."

"You know I can only uphold the law. You bring me evidence and I'll see that charges are presented to the DPP."

"They'll try and stop you."

"You mean O'Hara and the Archbishop?"

"And Lord Desmond Cormack as well."

"I promise you this. If Father Roland Cormack has broken any law and you can bring me credible evidence, I don't care who he is or what powerful people are in his corner. I will bring him to justice."

The meeting ended on that note. The Minister of Justice had a busy day ahead. And Ed Burke had had a sympathetic ear from one of the most powerful men in the government. That's all he could expect at this point.

47

George O'Hara sought the counsel of three of his closest allies, TP McGrady, Shane Braddock, and Jack Simpson; men who had bonded together to ensure government support for their enterprises and a playing field tilted in their favour. Their wealth and power depended on that assurance and they were quick to act when threatened.

Tonight they sat together at dinner in TP McGrady's house in the Churchfield estate in the grounds of the K Club in County Kildare.

Dinner over and, with it, talk of golf, the market, the wine list, the good life, they had finally come to their real reason for being there. McGrady got up, retrieved the cognac, poured a healthy measure into their glasses, and said, "George, you've got our attention. Tell us why we're here."

"Slainte!" and as they raised their glasses, George continued, "some of the things I'm going to tell you, you already know from the papers. It's been the number one headline for days. But indulge me for a few minutes while I give you the real story behind all of it."

So George briefed them on the events at St. Curnan's, his meeting with the Archbishop, his confrontation with Ed Burke, the threat to the church and, in a way, to the stability of the power base that they depended upon. Finally, he told them about the botched job his cousin had done on Father Michael Nugent. Then he reached across, refilled his cognac glass, and looked at them. He saw that they were trying to digest what they'd heard.

Jack Simpson piped up with a quirk, "Hell, George, I couldn't care less about your Church. Or any Church for that matter."

Everybody glanced around to see how Simpson's poor attempt at humour was being received. Shane Braddock moved restlessly in his chair. When George O'Hara smiled and shook his head in amusement, they relaxed.

TP McGrady said, "So, what you're telling us is that these killings must end and that this stuff must disappear from page one. Isn't that what you're saying, George?"

"Exactly!   We now know who the killer is. He's a mad priest, name of Flaherty. Can you imagine if he's caught and put on trial? It'll last for months and dominate the headlines. Think of the people who might be called to testify. Everybody from the Cardinal to maybe even the President."

"And you're saying we can't afford to let this happen."

"Yes!"

"Which means that you have to find this priest, Flaherty?"

"And put him out of business!"

"I don't see any other way. That's why you're here. That's why I need your advice."

"You don't need our advice on this. You want to hear us tell you that we think you're right, don't you?"

"In a way, yes."

"OK. Find this mad priest and take care of him. And, if Burke gets in the way, he wouldn't be missed by any of us, would he?"

"Burke is a pain in the ass. And he's already threatened me in my own office."

"Threatened you?"

"Yes, he accused us of trying to kill him last year. And then said that he was sure we wouldn't try that one again. I can remember exactly what he said '. *I am going to get to the bottom of my cousin Terry's death. And if I find that your great Mother Church has been burying its sins under the rocks, I'm going to expose them.* I was so damn angry. I threw him out of my office."

"Look, George, you know that the church has covered all this up, hid all these pedophiles, moved Cormack to Rome. Don't you think that Burke will have the church in his gun sight? It's the kind of target that man would love. He was a damn good criminal lawyer back in New York, you know."

"As usual, you're right. That's why I hang out with all of you."

They started to laugh, quietly at first, then growing loud and raucous, until it sounded like some mad symphony.

48

Hughie Rogan sat in the front seat of George O'Hara's mercedes, parked on a quiet street not far from Hughie's body shop. Hughie had been up early, been through a tough day, and now at eight o'clock, he was dead tired. But George's money kept his business alive so, in a sense, George owned him.

"The Father Michael Nugent thing was a total screw-up! You know that, don't you?"

"I know. Damnit, do you think I'm happy about that?"

"No, but you were responsible. And I hope it's taught you a lesson. You can't screw this one up!"

"I won't."

George pulled a large manilla envelope from under his seat and handed it to Hughie, saying, "There's a lot of info on Father Flaherty in there. Read it, memorize it, then destroy it."

"Where is Flaherty?"

"We don't know. The Gardai lost him. He might even be out of the country. But I don't believe that."

"Maybe this Ed Burke knows where he is?"

"I doubt it."

"Well, maybe if we follow Burke, he'll lead us to him."

"You can follow him if you want to.   But there's no guarantee that he'll lead you to Flaherty. Do your own investigation.   You need to get to Flaherty before anyone else."

"But if the gardai can't find him ..."

"You must be able to torture the information out of somebody! So, go find somebody who knows where Flaherty might be. And torture it out of them, if you have to."

"What about Burke?"

"Yeah, we'd like to see the back of him. For good. He's not our main target but, if he happens to get in your way, you know what to do, don't you?"

Hughie picked up the envelope and, as he reached for the door handle, O'Hara said, "I'm expecting a professional job. No wet-behind-the-ears young punks this time!"

49

Father Roland Cormack sat in front of his laptop in the Irish College in Rome.   He'd led a solitary life since arriving in Rome.   Cardinal Volpe assured him that being out of sight would keep him out of mind until the difficulty in Ireland had blown over.   He wasn't so sure but he had little choice in the matter. He powered up his laptop, connected to the internet and started browsing for any related news.   An *Associated Press* article popped up immediately and he read it with disbelief and increased anxiety:

VATICAN CITY · The Vatican said it has suspended a monsignor from a senior post at the Holy See after an Italian TV programme using a hidden camera recorded him making advances to a young man and asserting that gay sex was not sinful.   Monsignor Silvio Conte confirmed in a telephone interview with the *Associated Press* that he had been suspended from his post at the Vatican's Congregation for Clergy, an office which aims to ensure proper conduct by priests. A Vatican spokesman said the monsignor was suspended while the case was under investigation.   Milan daily *Corriere della Sera* had previously reported that a young man had contacted *La7* and said he had been in contact with several priests on chat lines popular with gay men. *Corriere* said *La7* then filmed encounters between the man and priests with a hidden camera.

Stunned, Father Cormack knew he had to get to Cardinal Volpe immediately. *They're closing in*, he thinks. Monsignor Conte has been a close ally in a critically important position.

He phoned Cardinal Volpe's office, and learned that the Cardinal was attending a board meeting at the Vatican Bank.

The Vatican Bank, despite its notoriety, is completely unpretentious. Housed in a medieval tower that was once a dungeon, it has no branches and very few employees.

The board meeting had commenced early that morning and was still in progress five hours later. Of all the difficult matters that had faced the bank over the years, today's was causing great debate among the board members. A San Francisco attorney was attempting to have an audit performed. His case involved about three hundred plaintiffs who were seeking restitution of assets allegedly stolen during World War II by the Ustasha dictatorship, Hitler's Croatian puppet regime. The Ustashi had stolen millions from their victims and moved it to the Croat treasury. The plaintiffs claimed that the Vatican Bank laundered these stolen millions after the war to several destinations in South America. A US State Department report implicated the Vatican Bank in the laundering of Nazi money, stating that about $47 million was moved to Spain and Argentina.

This raised the spectre of earlier scandals where the Vatican Bank had been involved in the collapse of both the financial empire headed by Michele Sindona and the Banco Ambrosiano, chaired by Roberto Calvi. Sindona later died in jail from a cyanide laced cup of coffee and Calvi was found hanging from a London bridge. Called a suicide at the time, since then his death has been classified a homicide by the Italian courts. In the midst of this, millions of dollars belonging to the Vatican Bank disappeared and was traced to Latin America. Banco Ambrosiano had also been making hundred million dollar loans to companies registered in Nicaragua, Panama, and Peru, companies owned by the Vatican, many of them having only an address. There was much speculation that these funds were used for a variety of purposes from paying political bribes to funding right-wing propaganda movements throughout the region.

After considerable discussion the board decided unanimously to file a request with the US State Department to have the case dismissed on the grounds of sovereign immunity. The Vatican Bank – the Instituto Per Le Opera di Religione (IOR), or the Office of Religious Works - formally established in 1942 as the official bank of the Vatican state, was granted sovereign immunity under the terms of a pact signed between Pope Pius XII and Benito Mussolini in 1929.

Despite these matters dominating the meeting, it ended to the satisfaction of Cardinal Volpe. Although he and two of his *Lavender Mafia* colleagues had strong influence on the board, they could never risk becoming complacent.

They'd convinced the board to invest heavily in their seminaries and recruitment programs in the third world. They'd also ensured that sizeable contingent funds were reserved to fight mounting worldwide legal battles. Today had been a good day.

But the day was about to turn bad. The Cardinal knew that when he saw Father Cormack waiting outside in his car. As he approached, Father Roland opened the door and got out.

"I didn't expect you to meet me. What's the matter?"

"I have some bad news and I wanted you to hear it from me first."

Father Cormack, words tripping over each other, described the Associated Press release about Monsignor Conte. Cardinal Volpe steeled himself.

"Bad! Very bad! We do not need this now. Not when there are several law suits being brought against us for cover-up. And the world media are salivating over it all."

"That's why I thought I should see you immediately. I know you'd have found out very soon but I need your advice."

"What's bothering you?"

"I think this will only keep the matter alive back home in Ireland. I don't know if I should stay here much longer. I'm very worried."

"We will take care of this. Trust me. I will talk with Monsignor Conte and we will find a way out of it. If the Monsignor has to sacrifice himself for the common good, then so be it. You should not be concerned."

"But it's not that. I can't stay here. It's the deaths in Ireland. Especially Monsignor Fallon. He was like a father to me. I feel responsible."

"Listen to me, you are not responsible for the actions of a madman."

"But I know Father Bernard Flaherty.   I taught beside him at St. Curnan's. If that boy hadn't died, and the other boy had not killed himself, then Father Flaherty might still only be the eccentric maths professor.   Instead of the murderer he's become. I feel responsible.   I started it.   I have to end it."

"Father Roland, you're not thinking straight. You're under too much stress.   I'm afraid this Monsignor Conte matter has caused you to lose your common sense."

"No, it's brought me to my senses. I am not a killer. My uncle, Lord Desmond, called. He told me that the Gardai have dropped the investigation. They could find no evidence against me. That boy's death was an accident. "

"So you can stay here. You don't need to hide any more. I need you here. And you need to be here. For your future."

"But what is my future now?"

"It's still the same. The church needs you. We need you. I believe your Uncle Desmond wants to see you become a prince of this church one day, maybe even greater."

"I know all about the Cormack ambition for me. But I don't share that ambition."

"Have you told that to your uncle?"

"No. It would break his heart."

"Well, I don't believe you either. You need to take time to get over all of this. And going back to Ireland at this time would be a terrible mistake."

"But I know Father Bernard Flaherty. Maybe I can find him, talk to him, get him to stop."

"Leave it to the police."

"But they can't find him. I don't think they will either. Father Bernard might be crazy but he is

213

very resourceful. If he knows I'm back in Ireland, maybe I can find him."

"But why wouldn't he want to kill you too?"

"Maybe he does. Yes, maybe he does. But I have to confront him. I have to talk with him. I have to try and stop him before he kills again. Don't you understand? I started all of this. I have to finish it."

Cardinal Volpe's car slowed down in front of his residence before coming to a stop. The Cardinal reached out and held Father Roland Cormack firmly by the arm, "Archbishop McCready will be here next week to get his red hat. The newest Irish Cardinal. It's important that you are seen in attendance. Promise me that you will stay for that. And afterwards we'll talk. I am hopeful that you will see things differently by then. Promise me?" And, Father Roland knew that the 'promise me' was an order, not a request, so he nodded his head in assent.

50

Father Bernard Flaherty prayed, for over two hours, on his bare knees on the cold wooden floor in Peter McDaid's house in Rathgar. Then he rose, put on his jeans, a fleece top, his best walking socks, a pair of hiking boots, and finally a soft woolen cap that he pulled down over his ears. He slung his backpack over his shoulder and left the house.

He took a bus to O'Connell Street and walked east for about ten minutes until he reached Amiens Street, which connected him to Store Street and *Bus Aras* at Connolly Street Station. He expected that the Gardai had broadcast information about him so he couldn't afford to use his driving licence to rent a car. He bought a bus ticket to Letterkenny, seeing that it would connect him to the 5:30 Lough Swilly bus which would get him into Fanad about 7 that evening. The right time, he thought.

Father Aloysius Smith thought that he might as well be a hermit. Stripped of his right to say mass or perform any of his priestly duties, he had been sent to this bare-walled, cold and unwelcoming old cottage in the wilds of Donegal. After he'd been expelled from the USA, the church in Ireland wanted to exorcise him from their midst, hoping that the multi-million dollar lawsuits that might follow would never materialize. So they stripped him of everything, short of laicizing him, and banished him to this forlorn place. Oh yes, they provided him with a meager monthly stipend, just enough to maintain himself. And they did leave the phone connected, probably an oversight on their part. Not that he had anyone to call, or that anyone wanted to call him. The phone sat there, dead. It might as well have been disconnected.

He'd been there for two months. Seemed like two years to him. Every other morning he had one boiled egg and one slice of toast for breakfast. On the in-between mornings, he enjoyed a bowl of porridge, the kind his mother used to make. Pinhead oatmeal soaked overnight and boiled the next morning. None of those tasteless oat flakes for him. This morning was a porridge day. He had lifted a large spoon of hot porridge to his mouth when the phone rang, startling him. He lost control of the spoon and the porridge fell onto the front of his woolen sweater, seeping into the threads. Angry at himself and alarmed at the phone which continued to ring, he got up and answered it.

"Hello."

"Father Aloysius Smith?"

"Yes?"

"My name is Ed Burke. You don't know me but I need to talk to you."

Unaccustomed to the phone and wary of everyone, he hesitated for some time, so Ed decided to speak again.

216

"Father Smith. This is very important. To you and to me. Some terrible things have happened here in Ireland. My cousin's little boy, Terry, was killed at his boarding school, St. Curnan's and then another boy there committed suicide. Since then, the school President has been murdered and now a monsignor too. I want to stop all of this. And I want to get justice for my cousin. I know all about you and the charges against you in the States. That's why I need to talk with you. I think you have information that could help."

"I know very little about anything you've said. I've been in isolation up here for most of the past two months. No TV, no radio, no news of any kind. And you're the first human being I've spoken to in weeks. So I don't know if you're telling me the truth – or if this is some kind of a trick."

"Believe me Father, it's no trick. It's very serious. And I think your life may be in danger."

"I think you're testing my patience."

"No, Father, listen to me! Please! The person who killed President McCafferty and Monsignor Fallon ..."

"Did you say Monsignor Fallon?"

"Yes. Did you know him?"

"Oh, God, he was a mentor at the seminary. A wonderful person. I loved him. He can't be dead!"

"Well, he is! Murdered by the same man who murdered President McCafferty. And your monsignor was murdered because he loved. Loved the wrong people. The same love that brought you to where you are today. They haven't caught this murderer. You must be on his list. For the same crimes as the monsignor. I need to talk to you. And you need protection."

Father Aloysius Smith felt as though he was suffocating. His heart was racing and his breathing came in short gasps. He sat down and tried to breathe deeply and regularly. He rubbed his carotid artery to try and override the tachycardia he was experiencing. Ed could sense, with the irregular breathing and gasps that came across the phone, that Father Smith was experiencing some difficulty. So he waited.

Finally, Ed heard Father Smith's voice, distant and low, "Alright, Mr. Burke. I'll see you. Let me give you directions."

Father Smith's laborious breathing and halting speech meant that Ed had to ask him to repeat some of the directions more than once. Finally he thought he'd got enough to help him find his way. He thanked Father Smith and told him to expect him tomorrow.

Father Bernard Flaherty's Lough Swilly bus was running a little late and he didn't reach Fanad until 7:30 pm. He had a good sense of where the house was located. After all, he'd spent many summer holidays, when he was a young boy, in Buncrana and Moville. Donegal held a special place in his memory.

It was a fine evening and, once off the bus, he relished the walk. He reckoned that he'd have about four or five miles to cover so he picked up the pace, estimating that he could cover it in forty-five minutes.

He was right. Exactly forty-five minutes later he saw the outline of the cottage up ahead. The road was bordered by a dry stone wall on one side and clumps of untended hedgerows on the other side. Finding a break in the wall, he stepped behind it, took off his backpack and opened it. A few minutes

later he emerged, in full clerical uniform, as Father
Bernard Flaherty.

Father Aloysius Smith had fallen asleep, with his
book open on his lap, in front of the turf fire that
blazed in the open hearth, when he opened his eyes to
a sound he thought he'd heard. There was only
silence here so he told himself that he'd imagined it,
as usual. Then he heard it again. Unmistakeable
this time. Definitely a knock on the door. Somebody
lost, he thought. Nobody visits me. He forced
himself to his feet, went to the front door, and opened
it. To his amazement, a priest stood there.

"Father Smith?"

"Yes," he answered, tentatively.

"I'm Father Bernard Flaherty. Archbishop
McCready asked me to see you. May I come in?"

Father Smith hesitated. Then, knowing that
he had little choice and now curious, he stood aside
and let his visitor enter. Father Flaherty crossed the
floor to the fireplace and looked up at the two very
prominent wrought-iron hooks over the mantle,
hooks that had once held a shotgun. Then he turned
around and stood with his back to the fire. Father
Smith looked lost in his own house. Finally he pulled
out one of the wooded chairs from the small table in
the corner and sat down.

"I can't imagine what the Archbishop wants
with me."

"So you think he abandoned you up here. And
forgot about you."

"He hoped I'd go away. Disappear for ever.
That's the message I got when I returned. I never
saw him myself. But there's no doubt that he made
all the decisions about me."

"And now he's faced with a multi-million dollar lawsuit from the boys in California that you defiled." Father Flaherty's voice had changed, become deeper and harsher. His face now seemed transformed into something that almost seemed non-human. A fire had commenced in his eyes.

Father Smith saw this transformation illuminated in the flames from the fire and a shiver ran through him. There's something wrong here, he sensed. He stood, prepared to ask this Father Flaherty to leave when it happened. An arm swung out in a wide arc, holding the poker it had lifted from the fireplace, and connected with the side of Father Smith's head. He fell, unconscious, to the flagstone floor.

Father Aloysius Smith felt the pain first. Still semi-conscious, he tried to move his hands and couldn't. Something cut into his shoulder blades sending shafts of pain through him. He tried to scream but only choked. His head had fallen forward onto his chest and he realized that he was standing up. No, hanging up! His feet barely touched the ground and he couldn't move his legs. Something that cut into his ankles held them together. As he became more conscious he could feel great burning pain in the soles of his feet. Finally forcing his eyes open, he saw the flames leap around his legs. He was hanging directly over the fire. Forcing his head up, he looked across the room and saw the figure of Father Flaherty silhouetted in the light of the flames and the paraffin-oil lamps behind him.

"Came in handy, those shot-gun hooks. The Lord moves in mysterious ways. Preparing the ground ahead of me. Do you know who I am?"

Father Smith couldn't speak. He tried but the words got lost in the pain. Only a growl of pain escaped.

"The Archbishop didn't send me. The Lord sent me to avenge him, to cleanse his temple of the defilers. And you are a defiler! You will die here tonight. You can burn to death, slowly and painfully. Or you can go quickly."

As he said that, he held a large carving knife over his head. The only one in the cottage, one that Father Smith had never used. Light glinted off the edge.

"Tell me who heads your secret society of defilers in the church. Give me a name!"

But Father Smith's head had sunk into his chest again. It wasn't certain that he even heard the demand. In fact, he seemed to once again be in a state of semi-consciousness.

"Ah, ha! Suit yourself! Be a martyr then!" screamed Father Bernard Flaherty as he piled more and more turf and logs on the fire that now raged well beyond the fireplace. He opened a large can of paraffin and threw the contents over the fire, igniting it into a massive bonfire whose flames now licked the face of Father Smith.

Laughing maniacally, he fled the cottage, shouting, "You'll burn in hell! Burn in hell! Forever!"

It was easy hitching a ride into Letterkenny. Even though he hadn't done anything like it since his college days, Father Bernard Flaherty knew that the fear of strangers had not reached Irish shores. People were still open, some still left their cars unlocked in the parking lots, and some would even

221

leave the keys in their door to make it easy for someone to enter the house. That was especially true in very rural areas like this part of Donegal.

Traffic was sparse but he got lucky almost immediately. The second car he thumbed down stopped at the roadside and waited for him. Driven by a friendly middle-aged local man who only talked about the weather and the price of petrol, he reached Letterkenny without incident, in time to catch the last Lough Swilly bus into Derry where he checked into a Bed and Breakfast near the train station.

Ed Burke reached Letterkenny by noontime next day, unaware that Father Bernard Flaherty was at that very moment sitting on a train on its way from Derry to Belfast.

Ed had had a pleasant and uneventful drive up from Dublin. The weather'd been good, the traffic sparse, and the scenery magnificent, especially when he got to Donegal. He stopped at the edge of town, picked up a coffee and a copy of *The Irish News.* No surprise there. The death of Monsignor Fallon and the hunt for his killer still dominated. Sean Coyne had full command of page one. No international event or crisis had occurred to deflect attention. So Sean had a captive readership. And he was using his platform to turn it all into a wider story: the authority of the church and its moral decline. He had started a whole new dialogue on separation of church and state. *It's an ill wind that blows no good*, thought Ed, remembering those as words often used by his mother.

He finished his coffee, put aside the newspaper, glanced again at the directions he'd scribbled in his phone conversation with Father

Aloysius Smith, started his car and headed for Fanad. Forty minutes later, as he rounded a bend on the narrow winding road, he could see the cottage straight ahead. But as he neared it, something didn't seem right. It now looked like an abandoned, derelict place. The window glass was broken as though it had been blown out in places, dark streaks discoloured walls that used to be white. Parts of the roof seemed to have been burned at some time. *Maybe I've got the wrong place*, he thought. He pulled his car into the verge of the road and got out. Immediately a strong burnt smell, almost putrid, hit his nostrils. He could now see that wisps of smoke still emanated from the roof space. The outside of the front door seemed untouched and he lifted the latch and pulled. The door had stuck but it wasn't locked. He pulled and jerked it open. Covering his mouth and nose with a handkerchief, he eased himself inside. The putrid smell forced its way though the handerchief as his eyes took in the carnage. The entire interior had been burned. Walls were blackened, ceiling and rafters gone, the sky showing through near the chimney, debris all over the floor. But it wasn't that that held him transfixed. It was the grotesque remains of something that had once been human hanging, like a horror film scarecrow, from the hooks that protruded from the chimney wall.

Ed Burke sat in a trance-like state in his car with the windows closed to keep out the stench. He'd been sitting like that for at least twenty minutes. Ever since he saw the burned remains of Father Aloysius Smith. At least he assumed that it was Father Smith.

Finally he got a grip on himself and picked up his mobile phone. Realizing that it was off, he turned it on, saw that he had messages waiting, bypassed that and dialled Tom Buckey.

Tom answered immediately, "Where are you? I've been trying to reach you all day. I need to see you."

"Sorry, I forgot to turn on my mobile. I really shouldn't own one of these things. I'm in Donegal."

"What're you doin' up there?"

"I came to see Father Aloysius Smith, you know, the priest who was deported from California a couple of months ago."

"Are you never going to learn? You're going to get yourself killed. And you won't make it back this time!"

"He's dead!"

"What?"

"Well, if you'd stop your rant and listen. Father Smith is dead.   Murdered. Burned at the stake, you might say!"

"Holy Christ! Not another one!"

"Nothing holy about it.   A real mess. The cottage is gutted and Father Smith – or what remains of him – hangs from hooks over the fireplace."

"He's done it again!"

"That's a good guess, I'd say."

"Well, you better get your people here as soon as you can.   And you'll need to notify Dr. Mona Kennedy."

"You'd better stay there till we take a statement."

"No bloody way!   I'm not hanging around. Right now I need a stiff whiskey. Or two. Or three. What did you want to see me about?"

224

"Oh, hell, it can wait.   Where are you going to be?   You're not driving back to Dublin tonight, are you?   Where can I find you?"

"I'll be up in Derry.   Probably book into DaVinci's for the night.   I've stayed there before. They take good care of me."

"Maybe I'll see you there."

An hour and a half later, Ed Burke drove across the border separating the Irish Republic from Northern Ireland although there was absolutely no evidence of any border.   Since the peace process had commenced and the IRA had given up its armed resistance, the border posts and armed patrols had gradually disappeared.   The army had been taken off the streets and moved to barracks.   Now they were gone entirely and all evidence had been pulled down.   *At least one of the intimidating presences in the island had been neutralized*, he thought, *if only we could get the church to 'withdraw within its own barracks.'* Twenty minutes later he left the Strand road and pulled into the parking lot at The DaVinci hotel.   He checked in at reception and, even though he had no reservation, they found a room for him.   Minutes later he exited off the elevator on the third floor, walked down the aisle, found his room number, inserted the electronic key, and entered.   As usual, the room was spacious, two double beds American style and the nice touch of tea, coffee, biscuits, a kettle and cups all ready.   *Something stronger I need tonight*, he said out loud, to no-one but himself.   He looked at his watch.   Five o'clock.   Time to soak in a hot shower and then pop downstairs for dinner in the pub and those whiskeys.   *But, damnit, you're losing it,* he said to himself, *you almost forgot, you must call*

Maria! He called her immediately, told her about Father Smith, and said he was staying over in Derry for the night. When he hung up, he could still feel the worry in her voice running through his head like a tuning fork.

Father Bernard Flaherty stood on the upper deck of the ferry as it pulled out of Larne and headed into the Irish Sea, bound for Cairnryan in Scotland. The sea was calm with a gentle breeze. The ferry was filled with people; truck drivers who commuted regularly between Ireland and Scotland; and families with young children crowded the lounges, their accents neither Irish nor Scottish and yet containing both. Young continental backpackers and a few ubiquitous Americans made up the rest of Father Flaherty's fellow travellers.

Alone with the seagulls on the upper deck, he watched the Irish coastline disappear and imagined that that was exactly what Columba would have seen as he left Ireland to establish his mission on Iona and commence a ministry that would bring his Celtic Christianity to Britain and the Continent. A Prince of the O'Neills who never ran away from a physical fight, Father Flaherty felt sure that St. Columba would understand his mission to purge the Church of the defilers.

51

No sooner had Maria Lane put down the phone after the call from Ed in Derry when it rang again. Assuming it to be Ed, she picked it up and said, "OK, I know you miss me but ..."

"I'll always miss you."

She stood transfixed and embarrassed. It wasn't Ed on the phone and, although she hadn't spoken to him in a year, she couldn't mistake the voice, "Oh, my God, Tom! I thought it was Ed calling again. I'd just got off the phone with him."

Tom Flanagan's name was synonymous with *FlanAir,* the aggressive and highly successful young airline he owned, one that, in its first three years of existence, had captured twenty-five percent of the market of its competitor, *RyanAir.* *FlanAir's* headquarters sat in Custom House Docks, adjacent to the IFSC, the International Financial Services Centre, the hub of international banking and finance in Ireland.

"Don't be embarrassed. And I do miss you. I wanted you in *FlanAir*. But you had to run off to the States and play nursemaid to Burke!"

Maria remembered. At the time she'd been the Administrative Assistant to TP McGrady and had been working closely with Tom and Ed to bring down a very corrupt Minister and his powerful cronies. *But that's all in the past, I've got to leave it there.*

She was brought back to consciousness by the sound of a voice calling her name. She realized it was coming from the phone in her hand.

"I'm sorry. I got lost for a minute."

"I'm worried about you. And about Ed. A year and a half ago we knew what the game was and we knew who the players were. Even then Ed almost got himself killed and the country lost you too."

"What are you talking about?"

"Ed's up to his ears in this whole scandal. The boys who died at St. Curnan's and now these killings."

"One of those boys was Terry Joyce, Ed's cousin. And Ed wants justice, that's all."

"No, that's not all. This thing has gotten out of hand and I called to warn you."

"I don't understand."

"You know I move in the same social circles as O'Hara. And apparently he hasn't been that discreet lately. I think he's drinking more than he should. And last night he was so tipsy at the club that he confided in a friend of mine, a person that he misguidedly thinks holds the same right-wing religious views as himself. Well, he was crying into his drink about the scandals and about how these latest events at St. Curnan's threatened to undermine the church. And that the two greatest dangers were this murdering priest on the loose. And this bastard Edmund Burke. His exact words. And he intended to get both of them!"

"That's crazy!"

"No, when somebody like him gets pissed, it's usually the truth that comes out. That's why I called to warn you."

"But Ed won't quit. You know him. He's up in Derry tonight. There's been another killing."

"Who was it this time?"

"That priest, the paedophile, the one who was kicked out of California a few months ago. What was his name? Smith, that's it, Father Aloysius Smith."

"Yeah, I remember the name. But he disappeared off the news as fast as he appeared."

"Exactly what Archbishop McCready wanted. They hid him away in some old remote cottage up in Donegal. Ed found out where he was and went up there to see him. But when he got there, the cottage had been burned and Father Smith was dead. Murdered. Hanging like a roasted animal, Ed's words, over the fireplace."

She could hear Tom Flanagan swear at the other end of the phone and then say, "Is this the same killer? Who killed that monsignor over in Cong?"

"Ed doesn't know. But he'd bet it was him."

"The 'murdering priest' that O'Hara intends to get!"

"*The Avenger.* Father Bernard Flaherty."

"Well, they don't ever want him to be caught or come to trial. This is someone that they want to disappear permanently. Clean. No long trial. No front page display of the church's dirty laundry."

"You mean they'll kill him!"

"Yes. And they'll take Ed out for good measure. Two birds with one stone. If they can get away with it."

229

"But this is the Church, Tom. They don't go around murdering people!"

"Oh, no! Tell that to the thousands they killed during the crusades. And the people they murdered during the Spanish inquisition. Tell me that that wasn't murder."

Maria had no answer.

"You get to Ed right away. Tell him what I told you. Tell him I want to see him when he gets back from Derry."

As soon as Tom Flanagan was off the phone, Maria called DaVinci's in Derry but Ed didn't answer. She tried his mobile phone but the call was diverted to his answering service but she did not leave any message. She knew he was probably in the pub anaesthetizing himself. She really couldn't blame him and headed for the cognac herself.

52

Ed was standing on Derry's walls, overlooking the Guildhall, when his phone rang.

"I called you again last night but you had turned off your mobile?"

"Oh God, Maria, I'm sorry! It was a helluva day and I didn't want to talk to anyone, especially Tom Buckley. I called him after I found the body and he asked me to stay there. But I refused."

"Don't you need to give them a statement?"

"Yes. But I'll stop with the gardai in Letterkenny today and give them one. To keep the record straight. Anyway, you've got me now."

"Well, I think it's important. Tom Flanagan called, a couple of minutes after you called me last night. He thinks you're in danger."

"Tom! You know I should have called him when we came back. Still owe him a lot from last year. If he hadn't airlifted me to the hospital from Omey Island, I might not be around today."

"Well, you know that Tom isn't spooked very easily. Someone overheard O'Hara when he had too much to drink. In the club. Threatening to get

Father Flaherty. And mouthing off that you were a troublemaker too. He's a dangerous man. What did you do to set him off?"

"I didn't tell you. I went to see him about the attempt on Father Nugent."

"You didn't accuse him of that, did you?"

"Well, not at first. But it sorta got out of hand."

"So you did accuse him?"

"Yes, damnit!"

"That wasn't very bright! He and his 'friends' tried to kill you a year ago. I know what they're capable of. Where are you now?"

"I'm standing on Derry's walls. Overlooking the Guildhall."

"What are you doing there?"

"Nothing! Absolutely nothing! After last night I needed to clear my head before I drove back. Besides, this wall stands as a symbol of the great struggle between Catholics and Protestants on this island. Between the Catholic supporters of James and the Protestant supporters of William of Orange. Fighting over an English crown on Irish soil. Kinda perverse, don't you think?"

"You don't have to give me a history lesson. I know all about the Siege of Derry."

"But it's so peaceful up here. I suppose the Good Friday agreement actually worked. I would never have believed it."

"OK, that's great. But what point are you making?"

"A very simple one. Ever since Patrick landed on these shores, our destiny's been driven by Christianity of one form or another. We blamed the English for subjugating us. Well, the English are long gone from most of this island but the people are still dominated by these churches."

232

"You're stating the obvious, aren't you?"

"Yes. But maybe it has to be stated. Every day. Over and over. You know that what's happening is more about power and control than it is about paedophilia. They've already paid out over $2 Billion dollars in damages to victims in the US alone and they've started to lose the faithful there. That's a huge crack in this wall I'm standing on."

"So what are you saying?"

"I'm saying that they will fight to protect themselves here in Ireland. They'll cover-up, hide priests, transfer them out of the country, start propaganda, try and destroy the integrity and credibility of anyone who opposes them."

"And you're saying they'll resort to violence."

"If necessary. Yes, I'm saying that. This mad priest, Flaherty, is a huge danger to them. They don't want him to be caught. He's smart and they don't want him to sell his story to the papers. They're deadly afraid of that."

"And you think they'll try to kill him?"

"I do."

"And they'll kill you too if you get in their way. You know that, don't you? Oh, why don't you walk away from all of this. You can't bring your cousin's boy back. And you can't defeat these people."

"Listen. I've been thinking. This whole business is not fair to you. And we need to get away for a while. There's one last thing I need to do before I can say that I tried to get justice for young Terry. I need to speak to Father Roland Cormack in Rome. But I thought that would give us an opportunity to spend a weekend in one of the most wonderful places I know."

"Where?" In that one word Ed could feel the anticipation in Maria's voice.

"The Villa D'Este. On Lake Como. I've made reservations for next weekend. Google it. You'll see what I mean."

When Ed left the walls and walked back down the Strand Road to DaVinci's he could still hear the throaty laughter that Maria made when she was happy.

53

Sam McDevitt walked around his office alternately rubbing his chin and scratching hios unruly white hair.   Sean Coyne sat waiting.   He'd finished outlining his proposal for the series of articles suggested by Ed Burke.

McDevitt stopped and returned to his high-backed comfortable chair behind his big oak desk. Fishing a large pencil out of the ceramic container on his desk, he proceeded to *tap, tap, tap* the end of it on the desk-top.

Finally, having considered Sean's proposal, he said, "I am not a crusader.   I do not want to start a crusade against the Church. If such a series were not seen as valid investigative journalism, it could be depicted as a propaganda onslaught against the Church.   And, despite today's secular Ireland, the people would not stand for a wiitch-hunt, perceived or otherwise, against the Church.   And they'd boycott this paper.   We'd be bankrupt in no time. Do you understand my concerns?"

"Yes, I understand. But I'd never write something like that. And you'd never publish it."

"It's perception, perception!"

"I still say that I can write a story that will have the presses at this paper working over-time to meet the demand. Don't you like that?"

McDevitt smiled. *The fire has returned to Sean Coyne's belly*, he thought. *Good, that's where I want him!*

"Where is Burke now?"

"He's on his way to Rome."

"But there's no guarantee that he can persuade this Father Cormack to come back here and talk to you?"

"He thinks he stands a good chance. He thinks he can convince Father Cormack that his life is in danger. He also thinks that he can make him feel guilty over the death of young Terry Joyce. Make him feel responsible for all these killings."

"That's a tall order!"

"I know. But this is Ed Burke we're talking about."

"And you're a believer!"

"Yes, I am. If anybody can pull this off, Ed Burke can."

"OK. Let's say you're right. What about this mad priest who's running around killing people? Doesn't Father Cormack run a big risk coming back here. Isn't he a target of this madman?"

"That's right."

"Well, isn't he safer staying in Rome?"

"Probably."

"So how can Burke overcome that. Surely Father Roland is not a fool."

"The gardai are looking for this crazy priest. It's their top priority. He can't evade them much longer."

236

"That's wishful thinking! He's gotten away so far. He may be crazy but he's crazy like a fox."

"But we can't let him take control. Stop us from acting. If we do, he wins, we lose. Look, Father Cormack's not stupid. He'll know the risk involved. And, if Ed Burke can succeed in making him feel responsible for all of this, then he'll talk. And I'll have a story to write. Maybe the best story in years! Do you want to pass that up?"

"No! You outline this proposal to me. In writing. By the weekend so that I can take it home and think about it. OK."

"I'll have it on you desk in twenty-four hours."

"And tell me Burke succeeds in getting this Father Cormack to tell his story to you. Tell me the minute that happens!"

The meeting was over. McDevitt never ended a meeting. He returned to whatever he was working on before the meeting started. Everyone experienced with his style knew when to get up and leave. Sean Coyne did that, with a smile on his face. He knew that he'd hooked McDevitt.

54

Ed Burke pushed open the wooden shutters on his bedroom window at the Villa D'Este and looked out at the placid blue water of Lake Como. He had slept like a baby. It was ten a.m. and people were already lounging around the pool. It whetted his appetite for an early morning swim. He looked back at Maria, out like a light on the bed. The duvet had slipped off her, and she was lying face-down with her body pressed into the mattress. Totally relaxed, like a puppy. They had slept in the nude, like they always did in the warmth of Miami. He walked over to the bed and gently pulled the duvet up around her. But her legs twitched, she shifted on her side, opened her eyes and looked at him.

"Oops! I didn't mean to wake you. Thought I'd go for a dip in the pool."

"Later. Then I'll go with you."

She tossed the duvet from the bed, sat up and pulled him towards her.

An hour later they sat poolside watching the haze lift from Lake Como. The waiter arrived with two large glasses of fresh orange juice, coffee, and croissants.

"This is the life," said Ed as he raised his orange glass and clinked Maria's.

"We could have this in Miami now," chided Maria.

"We promised that we'd leave all that behind while we're here this weekend."

"I know. I love you so much I want this to go on forever. I don't want to lose you."

"Look at me," said Ed as he put down his glass and took her face in his hands, "I am not going anywhere. You're going to have to put up with me when I'm a doddering old fool!"

Maria started laughing, a happy and relaxed sound . For now he had taken her mind away from Ireland, from the abuse, from the killings, from her fears. He knew that that would be short-lived. He did not know what awaited him in Rome on Monday.

On Monday the yellow taxi took them from the airport to The Atlante Garden hotel right in the heart of Rome. A good four star hotel, Maria had chosen it for its Jacuzzi bath tubs and because it was only two blocks from the Vatican where Ed had arranged to meet Father Roland Cormack that same day.

It hadn't been difficult to reach Father Roland by phone from the Villa D'Este. Ed had anticipated that it would take a lot of persuasion on his part to get Father Roland to meet him. But he was surprised when Father Roland agreed to meet him right away.

Maria said she'd get acquainted with ancient Rome in his absence. She'd never been to Rome and now, in her mind, the images of toga clad senators in the Roman Forum competed with more modern images of Gucci and Versace. And, of course, the hotel brochure informed her that the main shopping area lay nearby. *That's dangerous*, she thought, given her love of Italian designed shoes and bags.

An hour later Ed set out to walk to St. Peter's Square and the Vatican. He had instructions on where to go when he got there. The dome of St. Peter's stood majestically in the sky, reminding him of the supreme authority of the church.

Even though he had never met Father Roland Cormack, he recognized him immediately. Not from the photographs he had which showed a handsome fair-haired, blue-eyed young man who would look at home in Esquire Magazine or in one of the Hollywood fan sites. No, he recognized him by the body language, the language of the aristocracy, the language of superiority: shoulders squared, eyes looking directly ahead, feet planted confidently. He had shed his clerical garb and wore an open necked white shirt, black trousers and black shoes. Not exactly the street attire one would expect from a man of God. But, of course, Ed had to keep reminding himself that firstly, he was looking at a Cormack and, only secondly, a man of God.

"Ah, Mr. Burke." He acknowledged Ed's approach and walked towards him. As he got closer, Ed could see that he was not quite as tall as his own six foot one. Probably around five ten and a half. *Strange that my mind should be focusing on such triviality,* he thought, *maybe it's because I feel I'm entering unknown territory here.*

"Father Cormack, I suppose we can go somewhere where we won't be disturbed."

"Yes, it's best that we meet somewhere away from the Vatican."

At that moment Father Roland gestured with his hand and a taxi that had been parked nearby started its engine and pulled up beside them. The driver got out and held the door open. They both climbed in. As the taxi drove off, Father Roland confirmed their destination to the driver.

They sat sipping cappuccinos in a little quiet café, in a little quiet street, far removed from the eyes of those who frequented the Vatican. Father Cormack was speaking.

"I had to leave Ireland. I had no choice. Monsignor Fallon arranged it. They were afraid of another scandal."

"So you were all protecting the Church. Another cover-up, Father. But you weren't another priest, were you? No, you're a Cormack!"

"We can't choose the family we're born into, Mr. Burke."

"I don't give a damn what family you were born into! I'm here because you killed my cousin's boy. You killed Terry Joyce! And I want you to face justice for that."

"Believe me, I'd give anything to rewind the clock and undo Terry's death. It was an accident. A terrible accident! You know the gardai have investigated it and have reached the same conclusion."

"You're the only person who says it was an accident. The gardai have no evidence to prove otherwise. That's all. Even Father Michael Nugent who was with you that night blames you for Terry's death. You chased him up into that old round tower

241

on a terrible night when it was lashing rain and the wind was howling. Young Terry was terrified. But all you wanted was his phone. His god-damned phone! He died over a god-damned phone. It might have been an accident that he fell off that old tower but I blame you. It's as much your fault as it would be if you'd pushed him off yourself. Can't you see that?"

"I have never forgiven myself for Terry's death. I know you think I ran away. But I didn't. It was decided for me. But I'm not going to run away any more. I'm going back."

Ed had not expected this. On reflection, he didn't know what he had expected to accomplish with this meeting. He only knew that he'd never reach any kind of closure himself over Terry's death unless he met Father Roland Cormack face-to-face and looked him in the eye.

So he repeated what he thought he'd heard Father Cormack say, "You're going back?   To Ireland?"

"Yes, I blame myself not just for Terry's death but for all the killings since then. If it hadn't been for my actions, Monsignor Fallon and President McCafferty would still be alive. And Father Flaherty would still only be a very eccentric maths teacher at St. Curnan's."

"You said it, Father!"

"You haven't been able to stop Father Bernard, have you? And you can't find him either."

"Right on both counts. We believe he's hiding out somewhere. There's a lot of sympathy for what he's doing. Don't you understand that?"

"Yes, unfortunately many people live with very narrow unbending views of the world. They don't have the courage to do anything about it themselves but I can see that they might secretly cheer on someone like Father Bernard."

"He calls himself *The Avenger*. Did you know that?"

"No. But it seems appropriate. I suppose he thinks he's acting on behalf of the Lord. Poor Bernard. I knew he had very extreme views. But I never expected that he'd do anything like this. I thought that I knew him better than anyone at St. Curnan's. That's if anyone could really know Bernard at all."

"He's a sick man. And a very intelligent one. That makes him doubly dangerous. Did you know he was writing a book, something called *Creatures of Habit?*

"No. That's news to me. But the title fits. *Creatures of Habit, Creatures of Obsession.* Fits Father Bernard. Maybe it fits all of us."

Ed didn't comment on that so they sat, wordlessly, for a minute until Father Roland said, "Did you know he has a sister?"

"No. Are you sure? I thought he had no family. None still living, that is."

"Oh, he has. She's a nun. In the Benedictines. "

"Have you met her? Do you know where she is?"

"No, I never met her. And I don't know where she is. In Ireland somewhere, I believe."

"Maybe she's protecting him."

"No. Even if she wanted to, it would be impossible. She's most likely in a closed convent where anyone, other than a nun, would stick out like a sore thumb."

"So she can't help us even if we do find her."

"I don't know. I have to try and stop Father Bernard. Maybe I can find out where she is, get her to talk to me. I've made my decision. I'm going back

243

after Friday's ceremony."

"After Archbishop McCready gets his red hat from the Pope."

"Won't you attend?"

"Yes, I'll be there.   But I'm no fan of McCready. I think he's guiltier than sin. He's behind all the cover-ups in the Church in Ireland. And I think he'd go to any length to preserve his power. Being a 'prince' of the church will seem to him to be official sanction of his conduct."

"That's bleak and unkind. You're a bitter man. I will pray for you."

"Don't! I certainly don't want your prayers. I didn't come here for your understanding. I only want one thing from you. I want you to explain to Terry's mother and father why their son is dead. And I want you to tell your story to the Irish people. I don't want you to hide behind the church. Or behind the Cormack name for that matter. I have a friend, an excellent journalist, and a man of total integrity, who will put your story on the front page of his newspaper. He will not exploit you. The page will be yours and the words will be yours."

Father Roland Cormack sat in silence. Ed could see him reflecting on his suggestion so he prompted him some more.

"Maybe if you do this you can end the cover-up and bring some kind of peace to Terry's parents."

"You know you are asking me to commit suicide. I might as well leave the priesthood after doing that. And I'll be disowned by Uncle Desmond. And he wanted me to fulfill the Cormack legacy. To maybe one day realize the dream of a Cormack Pope."

"I'm afraid you'll never fulfill that dream. Even if you don't tell your story. It's over for you. It'll have to be pursued by the next Cormack generation."

244

Ed realized that they had exhausted all they had to say to each other. Still he felt unfulfilled. Empty inside. He had hoped for some kind of contrition, some kind of sorrow from Father Roland Cormack. But he hadn't got that. Still, it was some compensation to know that Father Cormack was coming back to Ireland. If he does decide to tell his story to Sean, then that's more than he could possibly have hoped for before he came here.

55

Ed Burke and Maria Lane arrived on time for the mass inside Saint Peter's Basilica where Pope Benedict would name the new cardinals. Father Roland Cormack had ensured that they would be part of the congregation for the event.

The mass was crowded but Ed and Maria had been ushered close to the altar where they had a vantage point during the entire service. Ed could easily see Father Roland Cormack off to his right, close to a tall stately looking Cardinal, whom he assumed to be Cardinal Volpe. A man that Ed would have taken to be an American had he been wearing any attire. Something about Americans, he thought, their posture, their body language, even when immobile, stamped them indelibly.

The Pope, resplendent in an embroidered gold vestment and a 19th century gilded mitre, or Bishop's hat, once worn by Pope Pius IX, sat on a gilded papal throne set on an altar decorated with crimson roses. The vestment was a long, golden silk mantle embroidered with scenes from the life of the saints. It was held up by two altar servers as he proceeded up and down the main aisle.

As the cardinals knelt in turn before him, he placed a three-pointed red hat, the 'biretta', on their heads; the red colour meant to remind them that they may one day be called upon to spill their blood for the faith and the church. The crowd applauded and cheered as he pronounced each new cardinal's name and the cardinals greeted well-wishers as they proceeded down the aisle of the basilica.

Outside in St. Peter's Square, groups from the cardinals' respective countries celebrated with native dancing and flag waving. Cardinal McCready greeted people from Ireland, saying, "I am honoured that Pope Benedict XVI has created me a cardinal."

The formal ceremony would be held later in the day at the *Pontificio Collegio Irlandese*, The Irish College. As they moved away from the clusters of people greeting the cardinals, Maria said, "Do we have to go to The Irish College?"

"We don't have to. You can see some more of Rome instead. But I think I should go. I want confirmation that Father Cormack intends to come back and face the music. And I'd sure like to talk to Cardinal Volpe. I want to see what makes him tick!"

"You're dreaming! He'll never talk with you. Why would he? And what does he have to gain?"

"I'll have to convince him that he'll have something to lose if he doesn't talk with me."

"I'm sure he doesn't want Father Cormack to leave his safe haven here in Rome. He'll see you as a threat."

"Then that may motivate him to talk with me."

247

"I don't see what you'll get out of this."

"Look, we need to fight these people back home. And we can't do that unless we understand them. Volpe might show me where they're vulnerable. It's worth a try. What have I got to lose?"

"You're a stubborn man, Edmund Burke! Well, I'm coming with you then."

The taxi dropped them in the Piazzo San Giovanni in Laterno, near Via dei Santi Quattro where The Irish College stood. Leaving the Piazzo, they walked towards the Irish College. Two large palm trees dominated the grounds in front and iron gates at the entrance read: 'Collegio Irlandese' and 'Colaiste na nGaedheal'.

Ed looked at Maria as he rang the bell on the gate at the right, "A lot of history here. This college was founded in 1628."

"So it's been running for almost four hundred years."

"Well, not quite. It closed for about twenty-eight years during the French Invasion and the Napoleonic Wars. The French entered Rome in June 1798."

"Thanks for the history lesson."

"But you haven't heard the most important part."

"And you're going to tell me, aren't you."

"During the seventeenth century a very notable seminarian was educated at the College. Roland Cormack, the martyred Archbishop."

"Wow! So Father Roland Cormack should feel the hand of history on him here."

"And the hand of destiny. That's why I want

248

to make sure he intends to come back."

People congregated around the front entrance as they approached and they saw faces that carried household names back in Ireland, notable politicians from north and south, and other dignitaries. Priests and religious clustered in the doorway and filled the inner hallway. Ed and Maria smiled and nodded, presented their invitations, and squeezed their way through the throng.

Father Roland was easy to spot. He looked uncomfortable when he saw Ed and moved towards them, almost as though intending to head them off. Ignoring Maria entirely, he said to Ed, "I did not expect to see you here."

"I'm not here for the cardinal's speech. Before I leave, I wanted to hear you tell me again that you're coming home."

"Yes, I have decided."

"And I wanted you to arrange a meeting for me with Cardinal Volpe."

Now Father Roland's face took on a look of consternation. He fumbled for words, finally managing, "Cardinal Volpe. Why?"

"You must know why. I want to understand. I want to talk with the man who left such an impact on the Church in America. Maybe he can defend himself. And you! He's got a lot of explaining to do and he might as well start with me."

"He will not see you."

"How can you be so sure?"

Father Roland contemplated that but he had no time to respond. The President of Ireland had finally arrived and the crowd was ushered into position for the speech from Ireland's new cardinal.

As Cardinal McCready entered the room and moved to the podium, loud applause broke out. He raised his hand to say 'enough' but the clapping continued, only dying out reluctantly as the cardinal commenced.

"Ladies and Gentlemen, Today has been a very joyful day. I am very honoured and humbled that Pope Benedict XVI has created me a Cardinal. I am delighted to be joined today by so many of my family and friends, and by brother Cardinals, Bishops and Priests from Ireland. I am also very grateful to the President and all the other representatives of Government, North and South, who have joined us for this occasion. These have been difficult and traumatic years for the Church in Ireland ...

He found himself tuning out and, looking at Maria, he could tell that she was somewhere far from here in her head. Glancing around, he thought he saw Father Roland trying to signal him but convinced himself that he was mistaken, probably only the priest's hand brushing back his hair. He watched and saw it again. No, there was no mistake. Father Roland's face seemed highly agitated and he was indeed trying to make contact.

Ed raised his hand in acknowledgement, whispered in Maria's ear, and moved past all the people on his right until he reached Father Cormack who tugged at his sleeve and spoke into his right ear, "He's here! Look! Over there!"

Ed followed Father Roland's gesture and saw a tall priest with head bowed, almost attempting to merge into the clergy on either side. He couldn't see his face so he asked, "Who is it?"

"Father Flaherty! It's Father Bernard!"

"No, it can't be. You must be mistaken."

"I'm not. It's him!"

Almost as though he'd heard, the tall priest lifted his head and looked directly at them. Yes, it *is* him, thought Ed. Even though he'd never met him, he'd seen photos of him.

Forced into action, he said to Father Roland, "I have to get you out of here. Can you get the police? Have them surround the place. I'm going after him."

"The Italian police! That won't be easy. But there's usually a police car in the Piazzo. And there are more today outside because the President is here. Maybe I can slip out and contact them. What are you going to do? I should try and talk with Father Flaherty?"

"Are you crazy? Why do you think he's here? He came to kill you!"

People around them were slowly getting annoyed at them, even though they had kept their voices low. But the cardinal's speech was ending and people were clapping again.

Father Roland started to squeeze through the crowd towards the door and Ed made a direct line towards Father Flaherty. But it was obvious that he'd spotted their moves because he elbowed the person next to him, tumbling him into an overweight older priest who immediately fell on the floor. People rushed to give him first aid and Father Flaherty disappeared in the commotion. Ed dived through the throng, catching a glance of Flaherty as he left through the front door.

Outside he could see Father Roland talking feverishly with a Chief of Police and then pointing excitedly at Father Flaherty as he emerged from the College.   Two policemen tried to stop Father Flaherty but he threw a punch at one and kicked the other ferociously on the shin. Dodging the police car, he ran out on to the street with Ed in pursuit.

The police weren't accustomed to chasing a priest but Father Roland had been joined by Cardinal Volpe and his presence convinced them. But valuable time had been lost. One police car was dispatched but Father Flaherty now had a good head start.

Ed stayed close in pursuit, thankful for his days spent in the fitness clubs in Miami. Still, he could see that Father Flaherty was very fit and sure of himself. He ran with great assurance as though he knew where he was going. Ed could only hope to keep him in sight because he did not know Rome.

They ran past the *Ospedale Militare del Celio*, people staring with concern at the running priest and with puzzlement at Ed as he followed. As they passed in front of the church of SS. Giovanni e Paolo, the police car had caught up and it veered into the kerb in front of Father Flaherty. One policeman got out and started towards him, boxing him between himself and Ed who was now moving in.

But Father Flaherty suddenly dodged into the side entrance to the *Villa Celimontana* and ran across a green lawn that the locals call *"praticello all'Inglese."* The policeman had joined the chase and was now running abreast of Ed. But Father Flaherty had not slowed down. In fact, like a marathon runner, he seemed to be pacing himself. Ed was breathless and the policeman had moved ahead of him. They crossed a dusty playground as a woman grabbed her young daughter and pulled her out of the way. An Egyptian obelisk stood ahead and Father Flaherty rounded it with ease before running out of the villa's front entrance.

Ed had begun to feel the strain as they ran through winding streets that seemed to be getting narrower and narrower. As the police car caught up with them, Father Flaherty dashed into a street so narrow that only a bicycle or a scooter could pass. When they reached the entrance to that street there was no sign of Father Flaherty. They had lost him. The police car could go no further and the policeman who'd shared the race came back to Ed who was sitting on the ground with his back against the wall.

In remarkably good English, he suggested that they had to call it off and offered to take Ed back to the Irish College.   Ed nodded as the sweat poured down the side of his face.

Back at the Irish College, everyone had gone.   Ed found Maria waiting anxiously inside. She rushed to meet him, clasped him in a hug and held on, her heart thumping and her eyes red.   He kissed her gently and said, "We lost him."

"I was worried about losing you. Why did you do that?"

"I thought I could catch him."

"Oh, God, your body was really damaged when they shot you last year.   And now you want to risk it all again."

"I'm fine. I'm in great shape. You shouldn't worry."

"That's easy to say."

"Look, I need to see Father Roland. We need to get him out of here.   I'm certain that Flaherty came here to kill him."

"But you know it doesn't make sense to me."

"What do you mean?"

"If Father Flaherty came here to kill Father Cormack, why did he attend the cardinal's reception? Didn't he know that he risked being seen? After all Father Cormack would know him, seeing that they worked together at St. Curnan's."

"That's a good question. But all I can say is that Father Flaherty is not operating on all cylinders. After all he believes that he's an emissary from the Lord, that he's doing God's work.   He probably felt that he was entitled to be a guest at the reception. And maybe he thought that the news about him

253

might not have reached Father Cormack here at the Irish College. Let's face it. He's delusional. And the success of his killings have probably made him feel that he's protected by God. What do I know? He's crazy!"

"Where is he now?"

"We don't know. He got away from us in some old city neighbourhood. He knows this city well. He could be anywhere. You stay here. I've got to see Father Roland. Convince him to come back with us. I believe he's in danger and I have to convince him of that."

It wasn't difficult finding Father Roland. He had an office, a cubicle, not far from the Vice-Rector whom he was assisting at the college. He agreed to book a seat on the same Aer Lingus flight that Ed and Maria were on. Being mid-week he wouldn't have any problem getting a reservation.

As Ed put it to him, "The way I see it is, you're between a rock and a hard place. Stay here and you'll die. And it won't be as a martyr. That will sully the name of your illustrious ancestor, a real martyr, who hangs on these walls. Come back with me, come clean, help us open up the church closets in Ireland and let the fresh air in. That may not seem like much of a choice to you now but, if I were you, I'd come home with me and face the music. Personally I should be leaving you here to meet your fate, to rot in hell after what you did to young Terry Joyce."

56

At Rome's Citavecchia airport, Ed and Maria checked in for their flight and then waited for Father Roland Cormack. After fifteen minutes had passed, Maria looked at Ed:

"Maybe he changed his mind."

"I don't think so."

"What makes you so sure?"

"Because he's got nowhere to go."

"He could stay here. I know that that's what Cardinal Volpe wants."

"Yes, that's right. But I'm convinced that Father Roland's coming back with us. Look, he's still responsible for Terry's death. I came here to bring him back and I'm not leaving without him. If he doesn't make the flight, you go on without me. I'll go after him."

"You don't think that something happened to him?"

"You mean, from Father Flaherty?"

"Why was he at the Irish College?   You said yourself that he must have come to kill Father Roland, didn't you?"

"Yes, I believe that's why he's here.   And Father Roland's been under police protection since. So if they haven't found Flaherty, he's probably lying low somewhere.   When he finds out that Father Roland has come back to Ireland, he'll probably follow him back.   Hopefully the police will catch him before then."

"You don't believe they will, do you?"

"No, I don't.   He's avoided everybody so far. And it won't surprise me to find out that he's given them the slip here as well."

At that moment a very red faced Father Roland rushed, breathless, into the terminal. He saw them immediately and ran towards them but they pointed to the check-in desk and urged him to go there instead. He had barely time to check in and get through departures to the gate.   As they walked together toward the gate, he blamed the traffic snarls in Rome for almost causing him to miss the plane. He also said that there was no news about Father Flaherty. Apparently no-one knew where he was.

"But I still think I can talk with him."

"Look, he came to Rome to kill you.   How do you think you can talk to a crazy man who's on a mission from the Lord?"

"I have to try.   I owe it to Monsignor Fallon and to President McCafferty."

"But you owe me first.   You owe justice to young Terry.   Even more than that, it's time to tell the whole story.   You agreed.   I'm going to arrange that with Sean Coyne as soon as we get back.   Where can I reach you?"

"I'm going to stay with Uncle Desmond.   For the next four weeks."

"Then what?"

"I don't know. I'll probably be assigned to the Archdiocesan office until all this is cleared up."

The plane had started boarding and they parted as they climbed the stairs to the cabin. With a last minute reservation, Father Roland Cormack was seated toward the rear of the plane, whereas Ed and Maria were close to the front. So they had no opportunity to talk on the flight.

Cardinal Volpe had accumulated much power and prestige within the Church hierarchy, much of it based on his political acumen and managerial ability. In addition to his degrees of divinity, he held a *magna cum laude* MBA from Harvard, and a Ph. D in political science.

The Pope had discovered that the Holy See had few religious or lay people on its payroll with such expertise and ability. And the Holy See was struggling to match its income to its growing expense base. In recent years, spending had doubled or tripled, income had failed to meet expenditures, reserves had been depleted to cover shortfalls, and the decline in the dollar's exchange rate had reduced the value of much of the annual Peter's Pence collection that was sourced in the US. So the Holy See needed some urgent and vital strategic planning and fiscal management, as well as a top to bottom policy review and departmental restructuring.

The Pope was relying on Cardinal Volpe to deliver. He had assigned him a special project, *Renewal for the New Century*, and funded him for a staff of ten of his own selection. He'd also assigned first class office space in the sprawling Palazzo San Calisto apartment and office complex in the trendy,

257

high-rent neighborhood of Trastevere.   And he'd given Cardinal Volpe a sumptuous, 3,000-square-foot penthouse apartment on the top floor, at a rent less than ten percent of the cost on the open market. The cardinal had undertaken the project with great diligence, had hired his first three staff members, and had prepared a weekly 'one-pager' for the Pope. 'One-pagers' had become his classic method of distilling the hard facts of a management report, complete with risks   and   opportunities,   into   a   succinct communication.

Being an American, the cardinal expected to have the latest creature comforts in his apartment. Being an Italian-American who grew up in his immigrant mother's kitchen in Brooklyn, watching her teach him how to prepare her matchless sauces, his love of cooking stayed with him.   So the kitchen would be the most important place in his apartment.

Fortuitously, he had discovered that Pope Benedict had found that the Papal Apartments had been in disrepair and had commenced refurbishment. The project, carried out over three months while Benedict was in summer residence at   Castel Gandolfo, included the building of the new library to accommodate Benedict's 20,000 books, upgrading for electrical wiring and plumbing.   The heating system was repaired and the kitchen was refurbished with new ovens, ranges, and other appliances donated by a German company.   Cardinal Volpe chose the same contractor to redesign the kitchen at his new San Calisto apartment.   But he chose the appliances himself.   He chose cutlery made by *Wilkins*, an old Bremen company, and he settled for nothing less than fine *Solingen* for his cleevers and other working knives.

He took a small tray holding his freshly brewed pot of morning coffee over to the kitchen table that faced out of the window to the city below. He looked at his watch. Eleven a.m.   Father Roland would be at the airport now, checking in, preparing to leave. Going back to Ireland to 'face the music', the term he'd used. He'd tried hard to dissuade him. He knew that Father Roland was making a terrible mistake.   Yet his years of political know-how had failed to persuade Father Roland not to go. He had failed.   And he seldom failed at anything.   He also thought about *this mad, murderous priest* who had come here to kill Father Roland. The police had not found him. No-one seemed to know where he'd gone. And no-one seemed to know how he'd managed to travel unnoticed from Ireland to Rome. *He may be crazy but he's also very clever,* thought the cardinal, *probably knows that Father Roland's on his way back today, so he'll most likely go back after him. Well, at least Father Roland has that guy, Burke, in his corner.*   He drained his coffee mug and said a silent prayer for Father Roland.

Father Bernard Flaherty knew Rome intimately and he had become fluent in the language during his time in the city. *A lifetime ago, and yet just yesterday,* he contemplated, as he emerged, totally sated, from the little family run trattoria,   near the Piazza San Calisto, where he had had lunch of home made gnocchi and gorgonzola cheese.   He laughed to himself as he remembered the day, when he was only fifteen, that he had brought home some gorgonzola cheese. An exotic and unheard of thing in his home. He could still see his sister crunching up her nose in disgust.   But he'd loved gorgonzola ever since. Dressed in his priestly attire, they had treated him with great deference and respect in the little

259

restaurant.

He'd had already been to the Palazzo San Calisto.   Housing many of the congregations of the Holy See, it hadn't changed since his time in Rome with the Marists.   Using a false name, he had arranged an interview for a position with the *Renewal for the New Century* project.   The interview had gone well and he'd arranged an appointment with Cardinal Volpe, in his private apartment on the top floor.   He had not expected to fail the interview because he knew that he was the Lord's emissary and the Lord would prepare the way for him. With time to spare before his appointment, he sought out a small shop that sold hardware and other household items, where he bought three rolls of duct tape and one of those ankle length plastic raincoats that tourists use.

Cardinal Volpe looked at himself in the full length mirror in his bathroom. Red piping ran down the borders of his long black robe and red buttons adorned the front.   He adjusted the red silk cummerbund around his waist, then hung the heavy silver cross around his neck.   He was due at the Vatican within the hour but he'd made time to talk with the priest who had interviewed for one of the positions on his project.

All his books had arrived and he felt comforted by the floor to ceiling shelves that lined his study. He crossed softly over the fine oriental rugs to his large antique desk and sat down. Looking at his watch he could see that his interviewee was due in ten minutes. Time to catch up on some correspondence.

Absorbed in his work, he had not heard the priest he was expecting being ushered into his study until he heard the rustle of pages. He looked up to see a tall priest, with his back to him, browsing the books on one of his shelves. Taken aback by the audacity, he said, sternly, "Excuse me! May I help you?"

The priest turned around and, said, disarmingly in a soft Irish accent, "Oh, I beg your pardon. I didn't want to disturb you. And I'm addicted to books."

"Are you Father Carmody who interviewed for the position on my project?"

"Yes, I am."

"Well, come into the light where I can see you better. Sit down here."

Father Bernard Flaherty knew that this moment could be crucial. He wasn't sure if the Cardinal had seen him at the Irish College or if Father Roland had given him a description, or even a photograph. As luck would have it, neither had occurred. Cardinal Volpe had not seen Father Flaherty that day. He'd only seen the commotion caused by the chase. And Father Roland had not given him a description, or photo, of Father Flaherty. Father Flaherty saw no recognition in the Cardinal's eyes as he sat down in the chair positioned at the side of the desk.

The Cardinal reached across to his in-box and retrieved a curriculum vitae on Father Carmody that he'd received earlier in the day from his project team. He noted the words they'd scribbled on the edge. *Good candidate! Hire him!* He'd take their word for that so he wouldn't need to probe Father Carmody's expertise. In the twenty minutes he'd allocated for the meeting, he would probe his personality instead.

"I see that you have spent the last few years teaching mathematics. Tell me what you learned that you could use as a member of my team."

261

"I learned that numbers can lie. And they can be manipulated by those who lie."

"And you think that insight can help us."

"Yes. Obviously the Vatican's numbers lied. Or somebody used them to present a rosy, but false, picture of the health of the church's finances."

"Are you suggesting that some church leaders are liars?"

"Yes. Or, if not, then they're incompetent."

"Maybe it's because they're only human ..."

"No. They thought that they were infallible. In matters other than faith."

Cardinal Volpe was beginning to feel uneasy. Even though this Father Carmody was speaking with great assurance, he detected an undertone of threat. He paused to take stock and change tack on the interview.

As he did so, Father Carmody asked, "Tell me, is it true that you head the secret society of defilers in our church?   In your USA it's been called *The Lavender Mafia.*"

Cardinal Volpe's heart jumped in his chest. Always in command in every situation, he now felt very vulnerable.   But his shock quickly turned to anger.

"How dare you! Who are you? You're not a priest. What do you want?"

"Oh, I think you know what I want. I do the work of the Lord. I am His *Avenger!*"

As recognition spread across the cardinal's face, Father Flaherty looked again at the golden chalice he'd admired when he sat down. A replica, at least twice the size of a normal chalice, It sat on the corner of the desk, facing him. Now he understood. The Lord moves in mysterious ways. And the Lord provides.   A vessel that held the body of Christ. Placed there for him.   He jumped up abruptly.   And

Cardinal Volpe, startled by his rapid movement, was unable to deflect the blow from the chalice and he fell unconscious to the floor.

Cardinal Volpe woke up to a splitting headache, his first feeling of consciousness. He didn't know where he was or what was happening to him. Thinking for a moment that he was in bed having a nightmare, he felt the urge to urinate and attempted to swing his legs out of bed. But he couldn't move. And the bed felt hard as iron. Suddenly his memory cut through the pain in his head like a lightning flash and he remembered trying to deflect the blow from the chalice. Gradually he opened his eyes and saw the light hanging from the ceiling overhead. It was either turned down low or the blow to his head had affected his vision. As his senses returned, he knew that he was lying on his back on the dining room table. He seemed to be tied down and he felt like Gulliver. Something had been taped across his mouth so he couldn't speak. He tested each arm and felt restrained by something that bound his wrists. Then he tried each leg and got the same feeling that something was holding his ankles firmly to the table. He couldn't move his upper body and his waist and stomach seemed to be constrained, as though he was wearing a belt much too small.

"Duct tape. A great invention, don't you think?"

The voice, loud and clear, and unmistakeably Father Carmody's whom he now realized was the mad Irish priest, Father Flaherty, who'd come to Rome to kill Father Roland.

The man behind the voice moved closer so that he could bend his head to see. The priestly clothes

263

were gone and he seemed to be dressed in black inside a long transparent plastic raincoat.

"The plastic raincoat. Another great invention. Keeps out all rain and other liquids."

He could see that Father Flaherty held a book in his hands. He watched as he opened it.

"My dear Cardinal Volpe, are you ready to listen to the words of the Lord? They were written for you. The Lord finds you guilty, Cardinal Volpe! And what did the Lord say about the punishment that must be meted out for such crimes. He was very clear about that. You must know what he said ..."

" *From Matthew 5:29 If your right eye makes you do wrong, take it out and throw it away. It is better to lose a part of your body, than for your whole body to be thrown into hell."*

Father Flaherty put down the book and approached Cardinal Volpe whose eyes showed absolute terror and tears flowed freely down his cheeks. He could see that the cardinal was trying to speak but the duct tape across his mouth prevented that. Father Flaherty walked behind the cardinal, held his head firmly with his left hand and ruthlessly gouged out the cardinal's right eye with his right thumb. At some point the cardinal's body ceased its thrashing and twitching and went still.

It seemed ages later when he regained consciousness. The pain in his head was now no match for the excruciating pain coming from the empty socket of his right eye. He could hear Flaherty's voice again.

"You'll have to look to your left to see me now. I'm afraid the Lord has thrown away that right eye that made you do wrong. I have moved to this side to accommodate you."

He waited until he saw that the cardinal had forced himself to turn his head to the left.

"Are we ready? The Lord is getting impatient, I'm afraid. Do you remember what he said in Matthew? Well, I'll read it for you."

"From Matthew 18:8   If your hand or your foot makes you do wrong, cut it off and throw it away! It is better for you to enter into life without hands or feet than to have two hands and two feet and be thrown into the fire that burns for ever."

"And you don't want to be thrown into that fire that burns forever, do you?"

Father Flaherty's voice seemed to have changed, to have deepened, to now sound animal-like, deranged. Even through the pain he was suffering, Cardinal Volpe could hear the change. And he knew he was about to die. He said a prayer asking that his death be swift. He looked blearily out of his one good eye to see that Father Flaherty was now holding his *Solingen* cleever in his right hand and feeling the edge with the thumb of his left hand. Suddenly Father Flaherty swung it over his head and brought it down with a thump on the table. Cardinal Volpe's right arm swung free of its restraint but he knew that his wrist and hand remained bound. Strangely, he felt no pain this time. He could see the cleever swinging overhead once more as he began to lose consciousness for the very last time.

57

At Dublin Airport, Father Roland climbed into the large black limousine waiting to take him to Castle Cormack and Ed and Maria caught the next taxi to Ballsbridge.

They dumped their bags inside the door of their apartment, kicked off their shoes, and hung their coats in the closet. Maria disappeared for a moment and returned with two glasses, a corkscrew, and a chilled bottle of McGuigan's Black Label Australian chardonnay. Ed opened the bottle and poured. They clinked glasses, kissed, and sank deep into the living room couch. They could feel the weight of Rome beginning to lift. But just as quickly the phone rang, jarring them back into the real world.

"Don't answer it. Let it ring. If it's important, they'll leave a message, "said Ed. But Maria was halfway to the phone when he said that.

Ignoring him, she said, "Hello," and listened, uttering "Oh, My God!" and "When did it happen?" and "Yes, he's right here."

Turning the phone over to Ed, she said, "It's Tom Buckley."

"Tom, what's up?"

"It seems you don't know."

"Don't know what? We just got in from the airport."

"There's been another killing!"

"Who?"

"Cardinal Volpe. In Rome."

"Oh, no! When?"

"A few hours ago. You were probably in the air when he was killed. Butchered!"

"Where?"

"In his apartment. In broad, god-damned daylight!"

"Father Flaherty?"

"Who else?"

"How did he die?"

"Horrible death. He was tortured and, like I said, butchered. His right eye was gouged out of his head. Both hands and both feet were chopped off with a cleaver. He bled to death. Pages of the bible were ripped out, you know those parts from Matthew where it says 'if your hand scandalize you, cut it off'. The hands and feet were stacked on top of the pages. That's his signature. *The Avenger.* He's telling us he's doing God's work."

"I suppose he got away."

"Yeah, he was long gone when the cardinal was discovered. Apparently Cardinal Volpe was due at some important meeting at the Vatican and, when he didn't show, they sent somebody to check on him. Otherwise we wouldn't have known a thing until tomorrow."

"Has this hit the news yet?"

"Damn right. Turn on your TV. It's on every network. There was another bombing in Iraq today. About a hundred people died. And the green zone was attacked. But the cardinal's murder pushed all that off the headlines. Look at the BBC, CNN, Fox, Sky. Half their top reporters are on their way to Rome. This will dominate the news for a long time. Even RTE are sending Charlie Crowe. And it's big when they send Charlie. Watch the evening newspapers."

"I have to get to Father Cormack. Warn him. The paparazzi will be on his tail."

"Is he back?"

"Yes, he came back with me."

"How the hell did you manage that?"

"It's a long story."

"You know we need to interview him. The case on Terry Joyce is still open. We have nothing to indict him. But we want a statement from him."

"He knows that. And he'll give it to you. Let him settle for a couple of days."

"What's the matter with you? I thought you have throttled him if you'd got your hands on him. Now it sounds like you're protecting him."

"I'm not. I'll explain. Can we meet somewhere?"

"I need to see you now. Something I can't talk about over the phone. Can I come over?"

"Sure."

"OK. In about an hour's time."

As Tom Buckley walked through the door into Ed Burke's apartment an hour and a half later, the enticing aroma of something cooking filled his nostrils and set his appetite raging.

"We're eating. You're welcome to join us," said Ed as he ushered Tom inside.

They turned the corner into the open plan kitchen and living space and found flames licking the side of a large wok as Maria stirred.

Smiling, she said to Tom, "Grab a bowl and take a seat."

Maria set the wok in the center of the table, announcing, "I hope you like Chinese.   Noodles, vegetables, shrimp, chicken."

"Hey, this is gourmet dining for me, Maria," said Tom, as Ed filled his glass with the chardonnay, "You know, I don't know why I came over here. You've knocked it totally out of my head."

Dinner over, they retreated to the living room. It was difficult to focus on matters of life and death so Ed broke the silence.

"You're right about the news.   It's on every network, every minute.   They're hardly taking time for commercials.   And they've gathered every pundit and opinion maker for instant analysis.   And the conspiracy theorists are out of the closet again."

"Hey, you've got to expect that.   This is the biggest story in some time."

"And they seem to have found out about Father Flaherty.   They're even calling him *The Avenger.*"

"That was bound to happen."

"Unfortunately!   And you know what comes after Rome, don't you?"

"Here!"

"Well, this is where it started.   And this is where they'll come.   Every damn network will be crawling over the place in the coming weeks."

"I've been told that the Japanese are here already!"

"Well, I called Father Cormack.   Told him to keep his head low.   He's completely distraught over Cardinal Volpe.   The cardinal was his mentor, even more than that. Tom, there's a deep dark story behind all of this. It's centuries old. Started long before the church took shape. I'm hoping that I can get Father Cormack to tell the story."

"Where is he?"

"He's staying at Castle Cormack."

"That figures."

"You will leave him alone for a few days."

"Hell, we'll be distracted enough with all these news reporters crawling all over us. But you can tell him that we want him in soon to make a statement. Anyway, none of this is why I came here."

Ed sat back and let that sink in for a minute, then said, "You mean, whatever you couldn't talk to me about over the phone."

"That's right. It's about Father Flaherty. We know where he's been hiding out."

"Great! How did you find out?"

"Nothing magical. Good old slogging detective work, that's all.   We've traced him to a house in Rathgar. Peter McDaid, a fellow he went to the seminary with. Left before ordination. A loner, real odd. Shares much of the same right wing extreme religious views as Father Flaherty. But very successful. He's an architect."

"So McDaid let him hide out at his place."

"Yeah, McDaid is a sympathizer. If he was crazy like Flaherty, I'm sure he'd have done the same."

"What are you planning to do?"

"Nothing!"

"I don't understand."

"OK. We've staked out McDaid's house. He doesn't know that we've discovered him. So he can't alert Father Flaherty. We're hoping he'll come back there after Rome."

"You want him back?"

"That's right! Look, there's little chance of him being tried in Italy if he claims refuge in the Vatican. Since the Lateran treaty of 1929, Italy has recognized the Vatican as a sovereign state. No extradition treaty exists between them. This has happened before and it ended in a stalemate. Italy wanted the Vatican to turn over someone for crimes committed in the Italian state and the Vatican refused, citing in its defense Article 11 of the Lateran treaty which says "central bodies of the Catholic Church are free from every interference on the part of the Italian state." So we don't stand a chance if he hides out over there."

"How are you certain they won't arrest him in Rome anyway?"

"Because we know that he boarded a plane an hour ago!"

"What!"

"We found out how he got to Rome. Don't ask."

"I know, just good old slogging detective work."

"Father Flaherty used to be in a religious order, the Marists. Remember that money clip we found in Cong, some kind of souvenir he got when he was overseas with the order. He spent a few years in Rome and he had a special Vatican passport when he was there. That's why he knows the place and why he's been able to go to ground there."

"So that's how he got to Rome."

"The Vatican passport. Show it at any customs and they'll wave you though. It's magic. They don't even look at it. Flaherty kept that passport when he had the mental breakdown. They should have taken it away but they didn't. Another administrative screw-up."

"So he flew from here to Rome."

271

"No, he was more cautious than that. He didn't want to be risked being recognized by someone at Dublin Airport. So he went north and took the ferry from Larne to Cairnryan in Scotland. Once there he flew from Glasgow to Rome."

"And is he returning the same way?"

"Exactly. He's on a flight to Glasgow as we speak."

"And you're going to let him through."

"We've got McDaid's house staked out. We're pretty sure that's where he's headed. We'll take him there."

"Incidentally, not that it matters now, I found out that he has a sister."

"We know. We found out too. She's a nun, Sister Brigid. Out in the west. In Connemara. He's had no contact with her for years, as far as we know. She may not know a thing about all of this."

"So you haven't contacted her?"

"We haven't seen the need."

"I'd like to be there when you take him."

"Ed, I can't do that. I'm not even supposed to be briefing you like this. But, dammit, we owe you and I won't let the system screw you like it did the last time. But, I honestly can't have you there at the stakeout."

"OK. But I want to talk with him."

"Well, maybe there's a way we can work that out. But not right away."

"When do you think he'll get to McDaid's? That's if you've called it right."

"He'll be in Glasgow this evening. Probably B&B it overnight. Get the ferry tomorrow morning. So he'll be in Larne about three or four o'clock. I figure he'll take his time, stay over in the north for the night, and get here sometime day after tomorrow. And we'll be waiting for him."

With that, he stood up, "Look, I've overstayed my welcome. I gotta go," and he gave Maria a huge hug, "Best meal I've had in a long time.   I'll be expecting an invite soon again," and laughed loudly as Ed let him out the door.

58

As Tom Buckley opened the bottle of Ballygowan still water and took a slug, his mobile phone rang.

"Buckley."

It was Chief Superintendent Flood, head of the Special Detective Unit and his boss, checking in.

"No, it's all quiet here. McDaid came home about eight o'clock."

"I hope you're right about this. This is a political hot-seat we're in. Flaherty's not just any criminal. He's a priest for Christ's sake, and a serial killer as well. Had a call from the Taoiseach. Apparently he got a call from our brand new cardinal. So they're breathing down our necks!"

"I don't think he'll show up to-night. But we'll keep a car here all night, just in case. The PSNI confirmed that he came in on the ferry to Larne and then caught a bus to Derry. They lost him after that. I guess he wasn't their top priority."

"I want this man caught!"

"I'll have the full team in place by five am. We'll get him."

"Take him alive. I don't want him dead. Some people might prefer that and I want to disappoint them. Do you understand?"

"My feelings exactly. No one will use a weapon unless it's to save a life. And there's no evidence that Flaherty uses any. His weapons of choice have been ropes and knives. And fire!"

"Call me as soon as he shows up and keep me informed all the way."

The call ended and Tom checked his watch. Eleven fifteen pm. He called his two men in the car parked diagonally across the street from McDaid's.

"I'm outa here. I'll be back at five with the rest of the team. Anything develops in the meantime, call me. And you know the drill: *stay invisible*! "

At exactly five am, Tom Buckley's team of six arrived. The night before they had parked two unmarked cars on McDaid's street and one on the matching street behind where McDaid's garden abutted his neighbours; so as not to arouse attention with the unusual movement of cars into the street at that early hour. Two of the team relieved the men who'd completed the all night stake-out. Tom and his team had familiarized themselves with the traffic movement on this street. Some cars would leave early, taking people to work. Others would begin to come and go during late morning and throughout the day as mothers took kids to school and other activities. A few cars never moved; they were only used for weekend getaways. The team realized that they must blend into this flow. They'd brought their own tea and sandwiches, assuming that this could be a long one. Most stake-outs were.

275

By early afternoon even the most patient of the team were getting restless. Tom Buckley sat in the car nearest to McDaid's and he had to provide encouragement. He reckoned that if Father Flaherty had stayed overnight and caught an early bus, maybe even hitched a ride, it would be late afternoon before they'd see him.

He was right. At exactly twenty minutes to four, Joe Breen elbowed him in the ribs. Tom looked across at McDaid's in time to see the back of a man as he opened the front gate and walked up to the front door. He removed a backpack, laid it on the ground beside him, and fished in his pockets. Finding what he wanted, obviously the house key, he reached up and inserted it in the lock, turned the doorknob and opened the door. Without a glance over his shoulder, he picked up the backpack, entered the house and closed the door behind him. The actions of a man who felt completely secure.

"That's him!"   Elated that his judgement was right, Tom contacted the team, confirmed the sighting, and asked them to stand by for his instructions. They already had a game plan, worked out as soon as they had discovered that McDaid's was the priest's safe house. Then he called the Chief to update him.

In the middle of his call to the Chief, Breen nudged him again and Tom looked where Breen was pointing. A car had pulled into the empty parking place in front of McDaid's and a man got out. He looked around and they saw that it was McDaid.

"Looks like we've got a complication, Chief. McDaid's home. He doesn't usually make it home till seven or eight in the evening."

"You have planned for this possibility, haven't you?"

"We have. But it would have been simpler if he hadn't shown up. I'll keep you updated. We'll be going in there in about fifteen minutes."

At ten minutes past four, Tom and four of his team approached the front of McDaid's house. The other two got out of their car and stationed themselves outside the entrance to the house that abutted McDaid's on the street to his rear. Confirming that everyone was in place and ready, they moved. They knew that this was not a 'ring the bell and ask permission' exercise. They had to get in to McDaid's, and move fast to subdue and take Flaherty so they had came with the equipment needed to break down the door.

When they reached the front door, they saw that McDaid had made it easy for them. He'd left the heavy outer door open and the inner vestibule door, half glass on the top half, was locked. A large bay window looked out of the red brick to the right of the door.

Tom directed one of his team to bust in through the bay window and the other two to break the vestibule door. He called the team guarding the rear and told them to stand by, that he was moving on a count of ten.

Peter McDaid and Father Flaherty were downstairs in the kitchen at the back when they heard the breaking glass and the smashing front door and the shouts.

"This is the gardai! Stay where you are. Do not move!"

McDaid had talked with Father Flaherty about what to do if this ever happened. He would block the gardai while Father Flaherty would escape out the back and over the fence into his neighbour's garden. He'd placed a ladder against the fence, in case the unthinkable happened. He always knew the risk he was taking giving shelter to Father Flaherty when he knew the gardai were scouring the country for him.

"Go! Go! Go!" he yelled as Father Flaherty hesitated.

He opened the utility closet in the kitchen and grabbed the shotgun he'd acquired recently and stashed there. He was no expert with a gun but he knew that the gardai couldn't be sure of that. He could hear some of them thump up the stairs and then footsteps heading his way. He pushed Father Flaherty through the back door of the kitchen and turned to face the guard who'd rushed in from the drawing room, fully kitted with an Uzi sub-machine gun, assault gear, bullet–proof vest, the works.

"Drop the gun!"

But McDaid raised the gun to his shoulder, aiming directly at the guard's face. The garda knew he was in a stand-off and held his ground. He was only supposed to shoot if his life was in danger.

So he gave the order again, "Drop the shotgun on the floor and stand back!"

But McDaid sensed that, given the culture within the Gardai and the fact that they'd screwed up and shot dead one of their own in a recent exercise, he had the advantage. At least the time to give Father Bernard a head start.

Father Bernard Flaherty had fled across the back lawn, picked up the ladder where it had fallen, leant it against the fence separating the two properties, climbed fast, reached the top and jumped. But he lost his balance, hit the ground hard and came down with full force on his left arm. Biting his lip to prevent his own screams, he had barely enough time to push himself into the old garden shed as the two guards who were manning the rear burst though the outer door that led from the street to the garden, and leaped over the fence into McDaid's garden. Father Flaherty, holding his arm, ran out into the street, and walked fast in the opposite direction. The streets were busy now with people coming home from work and others heading out for the evening. Luckily he'd taken his backpack as he left and he stopped briefly, found a scarf and made a sling for his left arm. He could see it swelling already and he feared that he'd broken it. As he blended into the crowd sirens pierced the air. Reinforcements on the way. *A case of locking the stable door after the horse had gone.* He decided he needed to go north and west, cross the canal, reach the south side of the Liffey and try to get a ride west from some kind traveller. At the next corner he took a chance and went into the little corner grocery store, almost extinct in the land of the Celtic Tiger. He bought a pack of paracetamol and, once outside, popped four of them in his mouth. Then, head down and covered with his woollen cap, he headed west.

The clatter of feet descended the stairs as McDaid and the Garda faced each other. Tom Buckley moved past the Garda and faced McDaid,

"I'm Detective Tom Buckley," and he flashed his identification at him, "now, put down the shotgun,

Mr. McDaid. You're only making things worse for yourself."

Peter McDaid realized that he couldn't maintain the standoff much longer and he'd given Father Flaherty his head start. So he lowered the gun. Two Gardai rushed him, one took away the shotgun and the other hand-cuffed him.

"Where's Father Flaherty?" asked Tom.

"I don't know," lied McDaid.

"Did he get past you?" Buckley asked the two gardai who'd entered the house from the back garden.

"No, we didn't see him."

"OK. Search this house again. Top to bottom, every closet, every cupboard. Check the attic as well. And take him out of here," pointing to McDaid.

Then he called Chief Inspector Flood.

"You lost him!"

"We're searching the house again but he seems to have gotten away. I don't know what to say. We played this one right by the book. If he got past us, then it must have been within the last half-hour. Can you send out an alert to all the gardai in the Dublin area, with his picture. Of course, he could look like anyone, the way he changes back and forth from civvies to clerical garb."

"Goddamn it, Tom! We're going to look like fucking idiots!" This was one of those rare times when Tom Buckley heard his chief's language hit the gutter. It would get worse. He knew it. So he listened, painfully, to the stream of invectives that poured down the phone line. Until, the Chief, spluttering, ran out of steam, saying, "You think he's got away, don't you?"

"Sorry, Chief, yes I do. Flaherty is very resourceful. And determined. And we have no idea where he might go. And he might have other friends like McDaid who admire what he's doing."

280

They tore McDaid's house apart and found nothing. Father Flaherty had escaped. Buckley and his team withdrew and took McDaid with them. They'd question him at length but Tom didn't believe he'd be able to tell them anything.

59

Ed Burke and Maria Lane were halfway out the door to dinner when Ed's mobile phone rang.   Ed answered, "Burke."

"Tom Buckey.   I've got bad news.   He got away."

"Flaherty?"

"We had him surrounded and he still slipped the noose. Sure hasn't helped my career."

"Where did he go?"

"Hah! That's the sixty-four thousand dollar question!   He disappeared into the city.   We've alerted every garda on duty but there hasn't been one sighting. Well, a couple of false ones but that's to be expected. We haven't a clue where he's gone."

"He's not finished."

"With his killing, you mean?"

"That's what drives him now. I think he didn't try for Father Cormack in Rome because he had a more important target in the cardinal. But he's back here now and he might try for him."

"You don't really know, do you?"

"No, I don't. I could make a long list of the people in this country whom the *Avenger* would add to his punishment list."

"But who do you think might be at the top of such a list?"

"I'd put Father Roland Cormack there. And our new Cardinal McCready too. And then there're the names that have hit the headlines here in all those scandals, from Ferns to Belfast."

"If you throw them in, you'll have a huge list."

"And don't you think that Father Flaherty believes that all of them deserve the Lord's vengeance?"

"So you think he's going to keep on killing?"

"I do. Until somebody stops him."

"Well, we failed today."

"You may not be the only people out to get him."

"What do you mean?"

"Those in power in the church must be terrified of this man?"

"Afraid for their lives. Of course."

"No, no. Afraid for their Church. Afraid to lose its influence, its power. In a strange way, this is all about power over others. I've been thinking about this whole mess ever since I got the call in Florida about Terry's death. This is not about his death. He was a victim alright. But he was a victim of the system."

"And what does this all mean for Flaherty? You're losing me."

"Look, the last thing those in power in the church want is for you to catch him. Because you'll put him on trial for months. And he'll defend himself. In order to do that, his legal team would call anyone that matters to the stand, even Cardinal McCready. And O'Hara!"

"George O'Hara!"

"Damn right! He's the public face of the Archdiocese. He does the political dirty work on their behalf. And you know only too well that he and his buddies have done worse than that. You haven't been able to mount a case against him."

"So you think they want Flaherty dead?"

"Absolutely! They want these killings to stop. They're keeping this whole business on the front page. But they don't want him caught and put on trial. They've got ways. They probably have a contract out on him now. And on anyone who gets in their way."

"That means you."

"No, they don't want me this time. I know O'Hara hates my guts and wouldn't shed a tear if I got hit by a truck. But they're not wasting their time on me."

"Don't be too sure."

"I'm never too sure. Once I start operating on assumptions, I'm going to fail. I know that."

"So what are you going to do?"

"I need to see Father Cormack. Two reasons. He needs to be warned that he may be on Flaherty's list. And I need to set him up with Sean Coyne. He's made me a promise that he'll go public with his story. That could be the best thing to come out of this mess."

"OK. But keep in touch with me. I'll make sure that Father Cormack gets special protection immediately. I'll get gardai out to Castle Cormack."

"Good. Be aware, though. Lord Desmond won't like it."

60

Father Roland Cormack paced, restlessly, around his room at Castle Cormack. His Uncle Desmond had greeted him profusely when he came back from Rome. They mourned the loss of Monsignor Fallon and his uncle unleashed his rage over the killings, blaming the Minister of Justice, the gardai, the Taoiseach, the Cardinal, and every person in authority in the State for the failure to capture Father Bernard Flaherty. But his uncle had not confronted him about the allegations over the death of young Terry Joyce. It wasn't part of the Cormack culture, certainly not the Cormack male culture, to speak openly about things that ran counter to their way of life. He knew that his uncle wanted to talk about it but probably found it too painful so he was probably waiting for the right time. Father Roland had thought long and hard about the future since Rome. And since his encounter with Ed Burke.

His pacing brought him to the window again. He stopped and looked out over the sweeping front lawn, the flowerbeds, the plants, the statuary, the six-foot high walls that bordered the lough, the shimmering water, the islands dotted here and there in the distance, and a lone boat with two men fishing in the mid-distance. A grandeur of landscape that might only be captured by a great artist. People with their ubiquitous digital cameras will always be disappointed with the result. For a moment these thoughts crossed his mind and lifted him away from the trauma that had enveloped him. But only for a moment ...

He realized that the ringing sound that had seemed so far away was coming from his own body: his mobile phone. A necessity that he hated.

"Father Roland," he answered.

"Roland, come down to the drawing room immediately. News from Rome," said Lord Desmond and hung up.

Taking the stairs two at a time, Father Roland bounded into the drawing room to see his uncle standing before the TV screen. A little hard of hearing, he'd turned the sound up high. He could see that it was a special bulletin from CNN News...

Cardinal Volpe had been expected at the Vatican and when he didn't appear, someone went to his apartment to see if he was OK ⋯ and that's when the gruesome discovery was made ...

Father Roland stood in shock as Cardinal Volpe's brutal murder dominated the news. A priest, an Irish priest, a Father Carmody, was the last person to see him. Apparently this Father Carmody had disappeared and there seemed to be no record of anyone called Father Carmody. So they were assuming it to be an alias and they were speculating that this missing priest and the one who had disrupted the Cardinal McCready celebration at the Irish College were one and the same.

Lord Desmond turned down the volume and turning to Father Roland, said, "It's Flaherty, isn't it?"

Father Roland was choking on his own tears as he said, "Oh dear God, it must be."

"And Cardinal Volpe was your friend, a man with great influence. Why would he kill him? Why?"

"I don't know," he lied.

Lord Desmond straightened his back, tightened his jaw, and said, "Roland, you're not telling the truth. All these events are connected. From the boy they accuse you of killing to the murder of Cardinal Volpe. They're all connected. Do you think I'm a fool? I've avoided mentioning all this unpleasantness before. Out of a misguided hope that it would all go away. That they'd find this murderer and put an end to it. But now I know. It's not going away, is it? It's never going away, is it?"

Father Roland couldn't speak. He was still in tears over the loss of Cardinal Volpe. His world, his vocation, his future, his ambition, the great hope of the Cormacks that one day there would be a Cormack Pope, all crumbling around him now. He wiped his eyes and ran from the room.

Back in his own room, he had gained some composure. He called Ed Burke's number but there was no answer. So he left a message and asked Ed to return his call.

Then he packed an overnight bag and picked up the keys to the car his uncle had loaned him during his stay.

His phone rang as he was about to leave. It was Ed Burke returning his call. Ed asked him if he'd heard the news about Cardinal Volpe.

"That's why I called you. I can't believe it!"

"Listen to me, Father Flaherty is here. He took a flight back."

"I don't understand. If you knew that, why didn't you have the Italian police, Interpol, somebody pick him up?"

"Because we wanted to arrest him and put on trial here. We want to hear his story. You know we want your story. But we want his as well. Without hearing what he has to say, the people of this country will not understand. They have a right to know. A right to know everything. No more secrets. No more hiding behind the confessional. Do you understand what I'm saying Father Roland. I'm angry now. All of this must be dragged out of the closet. Out into the light of day where we can all look at it. And only then can we make our judgements."

"So, have the gardai arrested him?"

"Unfortunately, he got away. We knew where he'd been staying in Dublin. And that's exactly where he went when he came back. But the gardai screwed up."

"And what if you don't catch him?"

"Then he'll claim his next victim. And it might be you!"

"I'm not afraid."

"Don't give me that! You're like the rest of us. Or maybe being a Cormack deludes you into thinking that you can rise above it all."

"I'll forgive you for that. Because you really don't believe that. You're angry. There's no point in taking it out on me."

"Listen to me, Father Roland, I believe that little Terry Joyce would still be alive if it weren't for you. And this whole murderous chain of events might never have been triggered. So I shouldn't care if you become the next victim!"

"But I feel responsible. You know that."

"And that's why you're more important alive than dead. You're going to tell your story to Sean

Coyne. Set the record straight. If you do that, you'll make amends for Terry's death."

"But, if you don't catch Father Bernard, I must do something about it."

"What can you do? Do you think you can stop him?"

"He might listen to me. I was the only one who connected with him at St. Curnan's."

"Listen, Father, I think you're kidding yourself. If we fail to get him I want you where we can protect you. I've arranged to have the gardai assign a unit to you. They'll be there within the hour."

"Sorry. I won't be here."

"Where are you going?"

"I'm going to see Sister Brigid. Father Bernard's sister. I've discovered that she's at Dunfergal Abbey. Maybe she can help."

Father Roland ended the conversation abruptly. Ed Burke thought that Father Roland was wasting his time chasing after Father Bernard's sister. According to Tom Buckley, Father Bernard had kept up no communication with his sister at all. It's as though he was an only child. Nevertheless, Ed knew that one should never assume anything.

So he called Tom Buckley and asked him to re-assign protection to Father Roland while he was at Dunfergal Abbey. Then he packed an overnight bag, drove his car to the nearest petrol station, filled her up and headed west.

61

Father Bernard Flaherty got lucky.   He'd been thumbing a ride for about half an hour with no success and a light drizzle had started.   He took shelter in a doorway and watched the traffic as it approached.   He knew he didn't stand a chance with the Mercedes and BMW drivers.   He'd already tried. So he waited and watched.   He saw a battered looking dark blue van in the distance, and, as it neared he could read the license plate and saw that it was a 1993.   Fifteen years old and a Mayo registration.   Exactly where he wanted to go.   So he stood out and thumbed for a lift.   The van passed and then braked and pulled into the side of the street.   He ran up and the driver rolled down the window.

"Lousy evenin', where ye goin'," the driver asked in a strong west of Ireland brogue.

"Mayo, Dunfergal actually."

"Man, ye jest got lucky.   Goin' all the way to Dunfergal meself.   Hop in.   Ye can keep me company."

"Thank you, thank you!"

"Hurt yer arm?"

"Ach, didn't watch where I was going and took a bad tumble."

"Maybe ye need a doctor?"

"No, it's only bruised."

"Ye're not a Mayo man, are ye?" the driver probed as he merged into the traffic.

"No, I'm not. How can you tell?"

"Ah, Jaysus, ye're right ye know. Ye can't tell anymore. Sure there's more Poles and Nigerians in Dunfergal than locals."

"It's the same everywhere."

"On holiday, are ye?" the driver persisted. He was a rough and ready type who looked to be a jack of all trades. Late thirties, early forties, unshaven, dirty tousled fair hair, crooked teeth that had never seen an orthodontist, and a beer belly pushing over his belt.

"That's right. Want to walk around Mayo for about ten days. No car, no bike. I only want to walk about the place."

"As the Germans say. 'ye want to see the nature'.

Father Flaherty forced himself to laugh at that, then he said he was tired and he'd like to try and take a nap. The driver, who hadn't even introduced himself, reached behind him and handed over a big rough dirty blanket. Father Flaherty rolled it up and bolstered his bad arm. Then he closed his eyes and tried to block out the pain, a technique he'd practised over the years.

62

Father Bernard Flaherty reached Dunfergal about four hours later. He snoozed, or at least kept his eyes closed most of the way. He didn't want a continued stream of small talk with the driver. And he wanted to avoid the man's nosy nature. As soon as they reached Dunfergal, he stirred himself, picked up his back pack, thanked the man for helping him, and got out at the square in the middle of town. He adjusted the sling on his arm and clenched his teeth. He'd become accustomed to the pain.

Kehoe's Bar and Restaurant commanded the corner and he decided to stop and have some food. At the bar, he settled for fish and chips and a coke. When it arrived he popped three more paracetamol into his mouth, knowing that it wouldn't kill the pain but would take the edge off it. The bar was empty, except for a couple of tourists and a local sitting alone in the corner, sipping his pint of Guinness. The place wouldn't fill up until about ten at night, when the music started. He chatted with the bartender and found out that a bus that passed Dunfergal Abbey would leave within the hour. So he hurried his meal and left.

The bus left on time and reached Dunfergal Abbey about twenty minutes later. He sat up front near the driver to make it easy to get off. The bus pulled in to the main gate, let him off, and then immediately continued its route.

Sister Brigid knew that it was a bit late to be on her way to the little cemetary. Dusk had already set in and the light was dying. But it promised to be a fine evening with a full moon and a star-studded sky. She never tired of looking at the heavens on nights like these. Since the terrible news about Father Bernard she now came here to pray once, sometimes twice, a day. It was the only place where she felt that she could talk directly to the Lord. She blessed herself, held her head in her hands, then looked up and started to pray.

Our father who art in heaven, hallowed be thy name, thy Kingdom come, thy will be done on earth as it is in heaven. Give us this day our daily bread and forgive us our trespasses as we forgive those who trespass against us. Lead us not into temptation and deliver us from evil ...

Dear Jesus, please deliver Father Bernard from evil, please free him from the hands of the devil...dear Jesus, please save his soul, please hear my prayers, I beg of you...I never ask You for anything but now I am asking, begging You to save Father Bernard...they say he thinks he is Your avenging spirit, that he believes he's doing Your work...but he is not well, please make him see that

293

what he's doing is not Your work, please help him,
dear God.

She thought she heard something behind her
so she stopped and looked around but saw nothing.
Convinced that her imagination had filled her with
sounds and echoes, she rested her head on her
clasped hands and focused her mind on her
conversation with God. Until she heard the voice.

"Sister Brigid." Her name, uttered in a
gravelly voice, a voice that seemed familiar, startled
her. She stood up, now a little scared, looked back
and saw no-one.

"Who's there?" she pleaded.

A deep spluttering cough drew her eyes firmly
to to her left. Deep in shadows, she saw a figure
emerge into the dim light and move closer. She
stood, transfixed. The figure moved out into the light
and she could see a tall man with his arm in a sling.
He lifted his left hand and removed the cloth cap
from his head, letting the light shine fully on his face.
She gasped in shock, her hands flew to her mouth
and she dropped to her knees on the ground.
Silently, she thanked Jesus for hearing her prayers.

"Father Bernard. Oh, thank God!" She rose
from the floor, held her arms out wide, crossed the
space between them, wrapped her arms around him,
and held him tightly. Tears flowed down her cheeks
and her breast heaved with sobs. He didn't speak,
just held her with his good arm until her sobs
subsided.

She wiped the tears from her eyes, pulled
back from him and said, "You're hurt."

"My arm, I fell," he said, explaining nothing,
"Can I stay here for a while?"

"Bernard, I think that the Lord sent you to
me. I've been praying and praying for you. Praying

294

that He would intervene, ask you to stop. And my prayers have been answered."

Father Bernard didn't argue with her. He felt that the Lord moved in strange ways and if He had used that approach to get Sister Brigid to help, why should he argue with it. So he decided that it would be best to play along with it.

"You're right, Sister Brigid. The Lord did send me here. He told me that you would take care of me, that I could rest here. And pray here. Pray for guidance."

Sister Brigid's orderly life had not prepared her for a situation like this. In fact, her sheltered life had assured her that she would not face the trials and traumas of the lay world around her. And her life was bounded by strict rules. She had to get Mother Abbess's permission to even leave Dunfergal for a few hours. All of this flashed through her mind as she now knew she was about to break all those rules.

"Most of the nuns have retired so much of the residence here is unoccupied. I will take you there and you can stay until the Lord guides us."

Father Bernard thanked his sister and they walked away from the graveyard, side by side. Sister Brigid had a new jaunt to her step and Father Bernard began to relax. He knew that the Lord would provide for him. After all, he was about His Father's work.

High on the side of Dunfergal mountain, the watcher adjusted the focus on his infra red binoculars as the two figures emerged from the road that led from the little cemetery to the front entrance of Dunfergal Abbey. The stooped figure on the left with the nun's habit easily stood out. But it was the man on the right that interested him. Looked about the right height, carrying his arm in a sling. But he couldn't see the face. Nevertheless, he'd be willing to put a bet on it. They'd found their man. He scrambled down and ran to the rear of the administrative offices where he'd already jimmied open a window. The office staff had left for the day so he climbed in and picked up the phone. Mobile phones had no coverage at Dunfergal, access blocked by the hills.

Hugh Rogan was in his car near Athlone, on the road to Dublin, when the call came through on his mobile. He swung off at the upcoming roundabout and pulled up to the petrol pump. He needed a fill-up anyway so he gave a thumbs up sign to the Polish kid who was manning the pumps. Then he pulled his mobile off the dashboard, left the car and walked around the back of the shopping area before talking.

"You're sure it's him."

"I'd swear to it. He must have hurt himself when he got away in Rathgar. Got his arm in a sling."

"That's good. It'll give us an advantage. He's a dangerous bastard. Don't underestimate him."

"I won't. What do you want me to do?"

"Nothing, absolutely nothing. Keep him in your sights. We don't want to lose him. If he leaves, follow him. If you see anything odd goin' on, call me."

"I have seen somethin' strange."

"What is it?"

"Maybe nothin' but there's been another priest hangin' out with this Sister Brigid since yesterday.

Might mean nothin' but it seems odd to me. And around about the time I seen him, the gardai pulled in to the Abbey."

"The gardai? That's definitely odd."

"It's even odder. They're still here. Two of them. Almost looks like a stakeout to me."

"Maybe they're watching for Flaherty, just like you."

"Well, if they are they haven't seen him. Otherwise this place would be surrounded now."

"You're right. We don't know why they're there but it sure as hell complicates things."

"How long do I have to hold out here?"

"Not very long. I want to take out this bastard before he's arrested."

He called Dublin and cancelled his business appointment. Then he called O'Hara and updated him. Finally he called his two specialists and asked them to meet him in three hours time. Finished, he walked back to his car.

€45 euros to fill his goddamned tank. Fucking oil at $125 dollars a barrel. He swore under his breath as he gave the Polish kid a euro tip. The kid looked surprised. *Probably only gets a tip from the yanks. .* He backed out, turned left, entered the roundabout and took the exit to Mayo.

63

When Sister Brigid had taken the call from Father Roland Cormack, she had listened to him explain why he wanted to talk with her, why he wanted to contact Father Bernard, why he thought he could convince him to stop. He was most persuasive. She told him that she did not know where Father Bernard was, that she had not heard from him in years. But despite that, Father Roland insisted in coming to see her. So she had agreed. She never expected that Father Bernard would arrive first.

Now, she sat facing Father Roland Cormack, worried. She had informed him that Father Bernard had arrived at Dunfergal unexpectedly and that she had given him refuge. He insisted on seeing Father Bernard. Despite her reservations, Sister Brigid decided that she'd agree to Father Roland's request and take him to see her brother. Maybe he'd succeed where everyone had failed. She didn't really believe that. She only believed it would happen if it was God's will. And, after all, Father Roland was God's priest, his disciple.

So she prayed silently that he would succeed as he followed her through the empty residence

298

building until they reached a closed door with light seeping out from under it.

She knocked, waited, knocked again, and when she heard nothing, she turned the handle and opened the door. At first the room seemed to be empty. Then as their eyes adjusted to the dim light they saw him: in the corner, in the lotus position, right arm now free of the sling, hands clasped together, eyes closed and lips moving without sound.

"Bernard, Bernard," she said, and when he didn't respond, she tapped him on the shoulder and said his name louder.

Slowly he opened his eyes and his lips stopped moving as he looked up and saw both of them. His eyes registered no surprise at the sight of Father Roland. He uncoiled himself from the lotus position, stretched out his legs and pushed himself to his feet.

"You know Father Roland Cormack. He wants to talk to you. I think you should listen to him," she said and turned to leave.

"Father Roland, the Lord sent you to me. I know he did."

"Bernard, I've been your friend for a long time. I'm the only person you could talk to at St. Curnan's. That's why I'm here."

Sister Brigid thought that it seemed to be going well so she quietly slipped out of the room, closed the door behind her, and left the building.

Father Bernard pulled out a straight backed chair and invited Father Roland to sit down. Then he began to pace back and forth as he said, "Maybe we should pray together."

"Maybe we can do that. But I want to talk. That's why I came to see you Bernard. I want you to stop the killing."

"Why? Are you afraid of me, Roland?"

"No, I'm not."

"Maybe you should be. Are you afraid of hell then?"

"Everyone should be afraid of hell. If that's what it takes to lead a good life."

"Do you think I'm not leading a good life?"

"God will judge you. Only he can forgive you, Bernard. I am very sad. You killed Monsignor Fallon. A good man and a member of my family. And you ended the life of Cardinal Volpe, a man whom I admired and loved. So I can't forgive you. Only God can. But I want you to stop. Turn yourself in. Spend the rest of your days asking God to forgive you, asking Him to save your immortal soul."

"I brought you a gift from Rome, Father Roland."

Disconcerted and distracted by the unexpected change in conversation, he watched as Father Bernard took something from a back-back lying against the wall and walked behind his chair. He decided to get up. Too late. Suddenly a grip like a vice encircled his wrists and he felt them being bound to the chair. He kicked out his feet and the chair overturned, sending him on his back.

Father Bernard stood over him, laughing maniacally, "Duct tape. Your gift from Rome. Has so many uses." Then he held each ankle and bound Father Roland's legs to the chair, leaving him well trussed up. He lifted the chair and stood it upright.

"So you think I went to Rome for Cardinal Volpe?"

Father Roland sat terrified. *I was wrong, I was wrong, Burke was right, I am his next victim,* the silent words reverberated around his skull as he sought a way out of this. He could see only one way. Talk Father Bernard out of it.

"No answer. Why do you think I didn't tape up your mouth? Because I want you to talk to me. That's why. You can scream if you want to but there's nobody here. Nobody will hear you."

"Why did you go to Rome?" Father Roland didn't recognize his own voice.

"Why? You know why? I came for you and you got away. I had to settle for my second choice. Poor Cardinal Volpe. He didn't know that the Lord sent me to avenge Him. I'm afraid he didn't study the bible, the warnings that God left for those who defiled. And he defiled, didn't he? Just like you, Roland."

"Bernard, you are wrong to believe that God sent you to avenge him. This is not the God we follow. Our God is a loving God, a forgiving God. He would never send you on a mission like this."

"No? And why did He send you to me?"

"Maybe He sent me to talk you out of this. Why don't we pray?"

Father Bernard realized that he was actually enjoying this. With time to spare and no need to run, he decided to let Father Roland think that he could save himself.

"Prayer? Is prayer your last meal, your last supper?"

"Why don't we pray together and ask God for direction, ask Him to show you the way?"

"Alright, then. Your last wish. We'll say a decade of the rosary. Like we did every night when I was a little boy," and he went to a bureau against the wall, pulled out the center drawer and reached in. Then he held up a most beautiful mother-of-pearl rosary.

"Found it here earlier. The nun who used to live here left it for us. She must have sensed that it would be needed. Ach, sure with your hands like

301

that, you won't be able to use these beautiful beads. I'll have to hold them for both of us."

He knelt down on the rug that covered the middle of the floor, looked up to heaven, and began to say the rosary.

New black wrought-iron gates framed the main entrance to Dunfergal Abbey. Ed Burke had been here once before, a long time ago, and he still remembered. He drove left into the car park, designed for the brisk tourist business.

As he walked out of the car park, he paused on the little bridge and looked at the Abbey sitting majestically on the far side of the lough, at the foot of Dunfergal mountain. The air was fresh, the skies clear, and the sun shone; a perfect day to showcase Dunfergal Abbey. He lifted his eyes to see the imposing white statue of Christ standing high up the sheer side of the mountain. A path, not discernable by the naked eye from his position, carved out of the side of the mountain, led up to the statue. Dangerous due to slippage and erosion, it was closed. A shame, he thought, what a marvellous view one would have up there.

Walked briskly through the front entrance of Dunfergal Abbey, he almost bowled over two elderly nuns. He asked them where he could find Sister Brigid, and they pointed to the main staircase and told him to go to the music room.

He found her there, at the piano.   Startled, she stopped playing and looked up at him.

"Sister Brigid, my name is Ed Burke. I need to see Father Roland Cormack now. I know he's here."

She dismissed the student and then asked Ed to follow here into the small changing room at the

302

rear. Finding two old metal chairs in the corner, she sat down and invited Ed to take the other. He thanked her but remained standing. Then he introduced himself again, explained who he was, talked briefly about the death of young Terry Joyce and the killings carried out by her brother.

"Father Roland is naïve enough to think he can talk Father Bernard into giving himself up. But I think he's in danger. I think he plans to kill Father Roland."

She buried her face in her hands, saying, "Oh, dear God!"

"Father Bernard escaped from the gardai in Dublin. We think he might be coming here to see you. You may be his last resort."

"I've prayed for Bernard every day. I asked Jesus to intercede. To stop him. Even to send him to me. I thought that I could reason with him. Sometimes our prayers are answered. And sometimes they are not. The Lord moves in mysterious ways. We have to be patient."

"But we have no time for patience. I need to talk with Father Roland. I need to get him out of here in case your brother does come here."

Her face changed at that very moment, almost like the sun moving across a meadow and leaving a dark shadow behind. She didn't have to say anything. He knew.

"Your brother's already here, isn't he?"

"Yes, he's here. And he's hurt. He came here looking for sanctuary. How could I turn him away? I asked Jesus to send him to me and he did. My prayers were answered."

"But he doesn't think he's been doing anything wrong, does he?"

"No, he thinks he's on a mission from God, that he's an avenger. I'm afraid it's his mind, you know. He had a mental breakdown when he was a schoolboy and then, later, he had to leave the Marists. He was in hospital for over a year. But they said he was cured, that he was better. Sure, if he hadn't been, how could he have taught at St. Curnan's for all of those years?"

"You can't protect him. He's dangerous now. And deluded. You need to turn him over to the gardai. The sooner we have him in custody, the safer he'll be. Can't you understand that?"

"I'm afraid it's not that simple any more."

"What do you mean?"

"Father Roland went to see him."

"You mean they're together! Now!"

"Yes."

Ed thought, *I'm too late, too late*, and said, "You've got to get me there now. I might be too late already. There's a garda car parked out in front. Go to them. Get them to follow me. Now, show me where I can find Father Roland and your brother."

Sister Brigid led him out of the music room and out through the front door of the Abbey until they reached a small wrought-iron gate. She fished around in her habit for a key, opened the lock, and led the way towards a long grey, almost foreboding, two storey extension to the Abbey that once housed the many nuns who'd made this place their home. Then she gave him directions to Father Bernard's room and turned back to talk with the gardai.

As Ed approached the room, he could hear voices, almost chant like. He stood outside the door and listened. Now he could discern it better. They were praying together, saying the rosary. *Maybe Father Roland's been right. Then I've been wrong. I've read it all wrong. But I was so sure that Father Roland was in danger.*

He decided to wait until there was a break in their prayers. It happened almost immediately. Silence. Then a shout, a cry. *This isn't right. Something's wrong.*

He opened the door, stepped inside and froze. He could see Father Roland bound to the chair and Father Bernard hovering over him. Father Roland's eyes showed fear and anguish. But Father Bernard stood, almost triumphantly.

"Back away! Now!" yelled Ed.

"It's no use!" the words came out of Father Roland's mouth in a hoarse growl.

Father Bernard moved towards him, swinging a length of rope like a lasso. But Ed ducked, moved sideways, and closed the distance between them, catching Father Bernard momentarily off-balance.

Ed moved quickly on the balls of his feet, never taking his eyes off Father Bernard. He aimed a high kick, thrusting forward and pivoting the heel of his supporting leg in the direction of the kick. He kicked upwards, aiming for the right arm, the one that Sister Brigid had told him was injured.

But Flaherty was swift and he countered the blow, sending Ed sprawling in the corner and rushed forward to kick him in the head. Ed rolled aside, came up behind him. He knew his opponent was stronger and that's why he must avoid him. But he had an advantage. Father Bernard Flaherty was not skilled in karate or in how to fight such an opponent. So he rushed Ed in classic street fighter manner.

Ed jumped to meet him, grabbed him behind the head and knee kicked him, making him move his hands to his face. But Ed knee kicked him again

305

bruising Father Bernard's hands and forearms. Stumbling and in pain, Ed punched him hard in his right arm.

Hurting now and holding his right arm, Father Flaherty backed out of the room and ran. Ed picked himself off the floor and told Father Roland that Sister Brigid had gone for the gardai and he'd soon be free. Then he turned and ran after Father Flaherty. He could not let him escape this time.

He heard the clang of the little wrought-iron gate and knew that he was right behind. No sign of the gardai. He hadn't time to think about that so he kept going. As he rounded the side of the Abbey he could see Father Flaherty disappear upwards, towards the school itself. He got there a minute later to see Father Flaherty fail to get into the school. Spotting Ed he fled upwards again, through the gate that led to the mountain path to the statue of Christ.

Ed followed. As he passed through the gate he noticed the sign warning people of the danger and telling them to stay off the path. But he rushed ahead because this part of the path was not steep. He could see that he was gaining and he kept up the pace.

Soon the path turned and meandered straight up the face of the mountain. No place for vertigo. The ground beneath, filled with gravel and stones, made the footing unsafe. He stumbled and fell and picked himself up again. As the path became steeper and he became breathless, he began to slow. But Father Flaherty was slowing down too.

He could hear Father Flaherty somewhere close ahead of him. Looking up, he could see that they were nearing the statue of Christ. As he turned a corner, grabbing the metal railing for support, a large rock missed him by inches and a second one grazed his shoulder. Father Flaherty had taken a stand directly in front of him.

He had no choice. He had to rush him. The skilled moves of karate wouldn't help him here on this rubble strewn path. As more rocks rained down on him, he rushed Father Flaherty and head butted him in the midriff. But Flaherty was still stronger and withstood the attack. Catching Ed off-balance he shoved him over the side, turned and headed upward towards the statue.

Ed struggled to climb back onto the path. He hung on to the metal railing, feeling it sway and bend. Worried that it would give way and send him tumbling down the mountain to be either gravely injured or killed, he tried to gain traction with his feet.

Suddenly the sound of a rifle shot shattered the stillness and then a second came in quick succession. Spurring himself on, Ed climbed over the railing as a third shot hit the side of the mountain only feet away from him. He threw himself flat to the ground as another shot hit the exact spot where he'd been. Realizing that he was a target, he crawled upward, now afraid.

But the shooting had stopped as quickly as it had started. *Maybe they think they got me,* he thought and then immediately thought, *Flaherty! Oh, my God!*

He crept to his knees, looked up and saw the statue of Christ, a few yards ahead. Head down, he clambered up the rest of the path until he reached the statue. Convinced that the sniper had gone, he stood up and saw a slumped figure on the bench in front of the statue. Knowing that it could only be Father Flaherty, he braced himself and walked over.

Then he saw it. Blood and brains splattered the foot of the statue and dripped to the ground. Flaherty was dead.

He heard people on the path below him. He couldn't see who if they were enemies or friends. Nowhere to hide, he'd reached the end of the road and prepared to fight to the end, if necessary.

Then he saw them: three gardai. Friends, not enemies. He let the air out of his lungs and slumped down, now feeling every ache in his body. His trousers were torn and he could see the abrasions on both knees, bloody and pockmarked with tiny bits of gravel.

64

At 10.30 pm Maria Lane caught *Aer Arann's Flight 239* from Dublin to Galway, arriving on time at 11.15 pm. Fifteen minutes after landing at Galway Airport she sat in a taxi on her way to Ed's cottage at Claddaghduff. Tom Buckley had called to tell her what happened at Dunfergal Abbey and to assure her that Ed was fine. *A little bruised, that's all*, he had said. But she had failed to take comfort in that. The nightmare of a year ago had never gone away.

At one am she stepped out of the taxi and walked into Ed's arms in the doorway of his cottage. Smiling and happy, she suddenly turned to tears.

"But I'm OK," Ed said as he hugged her close.

"But I'm not. I can't take this."

"Well, you won't have to any more," said Ed, holding her hand as he closed the door behind them, and offering her a hot whiskey, already waiting, "For medicinal purposes. Slainte!"

"Just what the doctor ordered. Let me look at you. Tom said that you were a little bruised, that's all."

"Tom's right. Some scratched knees. Maybe some bruises but that'll show up later and I'll be expecting some tender loving care."

The combination of the hot whiskey and Ed's comforting words made Maria relax and she asked, "What do you mean, I won't have to take this any more?"

"We're leaving. Back to the States. I don't want to live here any more."

"But Ireland owes you."

"Oh, yeah! The powers-that-be in this country would love to see the back of me. And I want nothing more to do with them."

He walked to the window and looked out over the beach to Omey Island, feeling the hypnotic pull of the place. *But I won't let it capture me again.*

Maria didn't press him on the matter. She knew when Ed went into one of these deep moods that he was inaccessible. So she waited and sipped her whiskey. Finally, he turned around, walked across the room, reached up and took a brown paper bag down from a shelf. He looked inside and then tossed the bag into the blazing peat fire.

"Destroying the evidence?"

"Very perceptive. You're right. That's Terry's phone, the thing that started all of this. Patrick Clarke, the boy who had it, finally gave it to me. I didn't know what to do with it until now. I never even looked at the photos."

She said nothing. He refilled his whiskey glass and turned towards her.

"They got them. Did Tom Buckley tell you?"

"He may have said something but it went in one ear and out the other."

"They shot one of them dead. Wounded and captured another. And he's talking. They've already arrested Hugh Rogan."

"So you were right. O'Hara's behind this killing."

310

"But they'll never prove it. Rogan won't talk and they have absolutely no evidence against O'Hara."

"So he'll get away with it?"

"Yes.   And everybody, from the Garda Commissioner to the Taoiseach, will be happy about that."

"So they think it all ends with one crazy priest and some assassin."

"Right! And they won't find a jury in this country to convict Rogan. The people will think he's a hero for killing Flaherty. They'll treat him the same way as that man who shot an intruder in the back as he left his house. Another hero!"

"So it's over then."

"Oh, no!   There's a time bomb ticking. And it'll go off slowly."

"What do you mean?"

"Father Roland Cormack."

"Didn't you save his life at Dunfergal?"

"Yes. That's ironic, isn't it? I saved the life of the man responsible for the death of young Terry Joyce. But he's going to tell his story to Sean Coyne and it'll be serialized for weeks to come. Cardinal McCready will wish he'd chosen another vocation!"

"So that's why you're in a hurry to leave."

"Right. I'm leaving anyway. But that's a big motivator. I do not plan to be around when, as the man says, 'the shit hits the fan'!"

By now the hot whiskeys had mellowed them and the tiredness had fully overcome Ed. So Maria took his hand and led him to the bedroom.

65

The flowers were still fresh on Terry's grave and his name, etched on his new headstone, looked sharp and clean.   Emmet and Claire knelt down beside the grave.   They prayed and Claire fidgeted with the small stones that adorned the gravesite.   Ed Burke knelt too.   But he did not pray.   He hadn't prayed in years and realized that he'd lost the habit.   And the belief.   He stared at the headstone and down at the grave and saw no sense in the death, saw no continuation.   Only the end.   *What a waste*, is all that he could think.   But he knew that it was comforting to believe as he looked at the solace it brought to Emmet and Claire.   Especially Claire.

66

Miami, Florida, USA.

Ed Burke jerked awake, in alarm. Disoriented, he sat up in the midday sun to find that he'd been lying on his lounger on the patio of his Miami home. He'd fallen asleep and had been reliving the nightmare of his shooting in Ireland.

Almost two years ago now, he reminded himself, *I guess this latest madness in Ireland has resurrected it again.*

The events of recent days seem to have happened in some other parallel universe, he thought. The last two editions of *The Irish Daily News* lay on the ground beside him. He'd received them by special delivery that morning from Sean Coyne.

He got up, adjusted the lounger to the sitting position, picked up the papers and sorted them back in order.

The front page stared back at him: *Creatures of Habit. A Story of a dark world, centuries old. As told to Sean Coyne by Father Roland Cormack.* A note from the editor stated that the story would be serialized weekly and that he expected it to run for the next four to five months. That means anywhere from sixteen to twenty episodes, Ed calculated. In the middle page of the second edition, letters to the editor divided into two groups: those who praised it and those who damned it. Strangely, there was no comment from the Archdiocese. Ireland's new Cardinal McCready was unavailable for comment. But not Lord Desmond Cormack. He had exploded in anger across all media, dominating RTE's evening television news programmes.

Ed had started to read when he heard the front door open. The sliding glass doors to the patio parted and he looked up to see Maria standing there, face glowing from the Florida sunshine.

"I love Publix! Supermarket shopping is worth it to have one of their young men carry everything out to my car. And then refuse to take a tip!"

"So you agree. We did the right thing to come back."

"But I suppose I'll always be a bit homesick."

"That's a small price to pay for spending summers in New York and winters here."

Maria laughed happily and, as she turned back inside, she said over her shoulder:

"Strawberry daiquiris coming up!

67

Dublin, Ireland

Father Roland Cormack pulled the collar of his coat up around his neck and stepped out of his residence. He looked at his watch. Seven pm. In half an hour's time he was due at the offices of *The Irish Daily News* for another session with Sean Coyne. This would be the third episode in his story and he'd already set Ireland on fire with the first two episodes.

He had underestimated the consequence. He'd become famous. The Paparazzi had begun to follow him. So he'd changed his residence again only two days ago. The gardai weren't interested in the matter so he was seriously considering hiring his own security. But that would be a last resort.

He walked down the front path to the little black-iron gate set in the low wall bordering the front of the property. He leaned over the wall and looked up and down the street. Seeing nothing unusual, he opened the gate, stepped out onto the sidewalk, closed the gate behind him, and walked down the street to the place where he'd parked his car.

When he reached his car, his heart sank. The front right wheel, the one close to the kerb, was flat as a pancake. Being a priest failed to prevent him from swearing under his breath. *Must have picked up a nail somewhere*, he thought. Had he examined the tyre more closely, he might have seen the neat hole left by the very sharp implement that had been used to puncture it.

He opened the car, threw his overcoat and jacket inside, and rolled up his sleeves. Then he unbolted the spare wheel inside the boot and hoisted it onto the ground. Next he started to loosen the nuts on the right front wheel. That done, he placed the jack under the side of the car and knelt down to lever it upwards.

As he did so, he glanced sideways, in time to see a man walk straight towards him.

He swore under his breath again. *Damn them, they've found me again!* He rose to confront the man, now only feet away from him. Startled, he could see no face, only a black balaclava. *Well, he's picked the wrong person to rob! I've only a few pounds on me.* He decided to try and talk his way out of it.

"I'm a priest. Doesn't that mean anything to you?"

But the man said nothing. Instead he moved fast. Too late, Father Roland tried to dodge the assault and failed. The man struck him and he suddenly felt a sharp pain in his left arm. Looking down, he saw the gash that ran from his wrist to his elbow and his blood flowing feeely.

In total shock, he fell back against the car, unable to defend himself. His attacker moved swiftly, shoving the blade under Father Roland's ribcage and forcing it directly upwards into the heart.

Father Roland Cormack died on the ground beside his car.

AUTHOR'S NOTES

This novel draws much from the recent headlines of abuse, especially in Ireland and the USA. According to Fred Martinez ,a widely published Catholic writer and former TV broadcaster , the existence of a gay culture in the priesthood has been well documented and the *Lavender Mafia* is a term coined by novelist and Catholic priest Andrew Greeley which refers to a purported underground faction within the leadership and clergy of the Roman Catholic Church that protects and advocates rights for homosexuals. The *Lavender Mafia* has been blamed by some members of the Church's orthodoxy as enabling or exacerbating the recent sex-abuse scandal in the United States. These critics allege that the *Lavender Mafia* has managed to dominate many of the Church's seminaries, and that whistleblowers are treated as criminals, while active homosexual priests are protected and promoted by their allies. Father Donald B. Cozzens' book, 'The Changing Face of the Priesthood,' alleges that there has been "a heterosexual exodus from the priesthood" because of the unabashed gay subcultures in some seminaries, and that potential heterosexual candidates for the priesthood are intimidated from joining an institution that fosters a gay culture.

The crisis between Ireland and the Vatican over the protection of children saw it's zenith in the words of the Prime Minister of Ireland, Taoiseach Enda Kenny, in his speech on the Cloyne Report, on 20 July 2011 where he said *"the Cloyne Report excavates the dysfunction, disconnection, elitism....the narcissism that dominate the culture of the Vatican to this day."*

319

Extracts from that speech follow as well as links to the CLOYNE, MURPHY, RYAN, FERNS reports into clerical sex abuse in Ireland.

The town of Dunfergal, Dunfergal Abbey and Dunfergal Mountain do not exist. I must reiterate: this book is a work of fiction. Any reference to historical events, real people, or real locales is used fictitiously. Other names, characters, places and incidents are either products of the author's imagination or used fictitiously. Any resemblance to actual events, locales, or persons, living or dead, is entirely coincidental.

St. Curnan's is completely fictional. I know of no school, current or historical, that housed within it a *Lavender Mafia* subculure or such exploitation of students. But the sense of order and discipline is real. It comes from my own experience as a boarder at such a school in the days when corporal punishment was *de rigeur,* where priests carried leather straps under their soutanes, and where some seemed to get a sadistic pleasure out of their use. However, those days have ended. No corporal punishment is used today to force students to learn.

I think that this excerpt from a previous work of mine describes my experience best:

He'd won a scholarship to college when he was eleven and spent four years there as a boarding student. The college was run by priests although half the teachers were lay. It was there that MacDara's reverence for priests and awe for the institution they represented had ended. Maybe it was there that the seeds of agnosticism, or even atheism, had been sown. *MacDara preferred to think of himself as a secular humanist these days. Eccentric priests had dominated the classrooms. Father Toner, who taught mathematics, would often pick up the heavy bound Hall's algebra and whack an unsuspecting student across the side of the head. MacDara remembered one of many incidents.*

"MacDara, where's Doolan today?"

Father Toner purposely mispronounced Dolan's name. Dolan was not a boarder. He was a day boy and lived at home in the city.

"He's sick, Father."

"How do you know that, MacDara?"

"Well, he said he wasn't feeling well in class yesterday, Father. So I assumed he was sick today."

"You assumed, MacDara! You have no proof!"

"No, Father."

"Q.E.D., quod erat demonstrandum.   Proof, MacDara! In other words, you don't know and you lied to me."

"Isn't that correct, MacDara?"

"No, Father!"

"I said, isn't that correct, MacDara?"

"Yes, Father."

"Come up here!"

MacDara could still feel the sting in the palm of his hands from the six slaps that he received for lying from the leather strap that always hung threateningly inside the side pocket of Father Toner's long, dark soutane. The college was Catholic to the core. Its original role had been to prepare boys for the priesthood and that was still a principal mission. The church controlled the education system. Newspapers and radios were banned at the College. Outside influences and distractions were to be avoided at all costs. All evidence of civil authority was absent.   The authority of the Church was

321

paramount. Small rebellions preserved the sanity of the few who refused to become brainwashed by the system. MacDara was one of those few. They used to draw lots to choose a volunteer who would risk scaling the high walls that surrounded the grounds and making it to a local shot to buy a packet of Woodbine cigarettes, the cheapest available. They had a special hideout behind the walls where they smoked while someone kept a lookout for the prefects. They also made radio receivers, crystal sets they called them, MacDara recalled. He remembered the night that the Dean had entered his dormitory after lights out and tripped over a crystal set earthing wire he had tied to the metal leg of the adjoining bed. That got him twelve, six on each hand with a leather strap, outside the Dean's office the next morning. His hands had swollen to double their size after that; couldn't hold a pencil in class that day.

Prime Minister of Ireland, Taoiseach Enda Kenny speech on Cloyne Report

Wednesday, 20 July 2011

http://www.rte.ie/news/2011/0720/cloyne1.html

Excerpts from the Statement by the Taoiseach on the Dáil Motion on the report of the Commission of Investigation into the Catholic Diocese of Cloyne, in Dáil Éireann

The revelations of the Cloyne report have brought the Government, Irish Catholics and the Vatican to an unprecedented juncture. It's fair to say that after the Ryan and Murphy Reports Ireland is, perhaps, unshockable when it comes to the abuse of children. But Cloyne has proved to be of a different order. Because for the first time in Ireland, a report into child sexual-abuse exposes an attempt by the Holy See, to frustrate an Inquiry in a sovereign, democratic republic.as little as three years ago, not three decades ago.

And in doing so, the Cloyne Report excavates the dysfunction, disconnection, elitism....the narcissism that dominate the culture of the Vatican to this day.

The rape and torture of children were downplayed or 'managed' to uphold instead, the primacy of the institution, its power, standing and 'reputation'. Far from listening to evidence of humiliation and betrayal with St Benedict's 'ear of the heart'......the Vatican's reaction was to parse and analyse it with the gimlet eye of a canon lawyer. This calculated, withering position being the polar opposite of the radicalism, humility and compassion upon which the Roman Church was founded. The radicalism, humility and compassion which are the very essence of its foundation and purpose. The behaviour being a case of Roma locuta est: causa finita est. Except in this instance, nothing could be further from the truth.

A day post-publication, the Tánaiste and Minister for Foreign Affairs and Trade met with the Papal Nuncio to Ireland, Archbishop Giuseppe Leanza.   The Tánaiste left the Archbishop clear on two things: The gravity of the actions and attitude of the Holy See.
And Ireland's complete rejection and abhorrence of same. The Papal Nuncio undertook to present the Cloyne Report to the Vatican. The Government awaits the considered response of the Holy See.

I believe that the Irish people, including the very many faithful Catholics who - like me - have been shocked and dismayed by the repeated failings of Church authorities to face up to what is required, deserve and require confirmation from the Vatican that they do accept, endorse and require compliance by all Church authorities here with, the obligations to report all cases of suspected abuse, whether current or historical, to the State's authorities in line with the Children First National Guidance which will have the force of law.

Clericalism has rendered some of Ireland's brightest, most privileged and powerful men, either unwilling or unable to address the horrors cited in the Ryan and Murphy Reports. This Roman Clericalism must be devastating for good priests.... some of them old... others struggling to keep their humanity....even their sanity........as they work so hard.....to be the keepers of the Church's light and goodness within their parishes...... communities... the human heart.

But thankfully for them, and for us, this is not Rome. Nor is it industrial-school or Magdalene Ireland, where the swish of a soutane smothered conscience and humanity and the swing of a thurible ruled the Irish-Catholic world. This is the 'Republic' of Ireland 2011. A Republic of laws.....of rights and responsibilities....of proper civic order..... where the delinquency and arrogance of a particular version..... of a particular kind of 'morality'..... will no longer be tolerated or ignored.

Cardinal Josef Ratzinger said: 'Standards of conduct appropriate to civil society or the workings of a democracy cannot be purely and simply applied to the Church.' As the Holy See prepares its considered response to the Cloyne Report, as Taoiseach, I am making it absolutely clear, that when it comes to the protection of the children of this State, the standards of conduct which the Church deems appropriate to itself, cannot and will not, be applied to the workings of democracy and civil society in this republic. Not purely, or simply or otherwise.

THE CLOYNE, MURPHY, RYAN, FERNS REPORTS

THE CLOYNE REPORT (2011)
http://www.rte.ie/news/2011/0713/cloyne.html
Thursday, 14 July 2011

The Cloyne Report has found that former Bishop John Magee falsely told the Government and the HSE that the Catholic Diocese was reporting all allegations of clerical child sexual abuse to the civil authorities. It also found the Bishop deliberately misled another inquiry and his own advisors by creating two different accounts, one for the Vatican and the other for diocesan files. Running to 400 pages and detailing findings on 19 priests who faced abuse allegations over a 13-year period, the report deals with how the Cloyne Diocese handled abuse allegations as recently as 2009. The report criticised Bishop Magee for showing little or no interest in the management of clerical child sexual abuse until just three years ago. In the opening pages, the report claims that the Bishop had 'detached himself' from the management of child sexual abuse cases. It declares that his response was 'totally inadequate'. The Commission states that the greatest failure by the diocese was its failure to report all cases to gardaí.

THE MURPHY REPORT (2009)
http://www.rte.ie/news/2009/1126/abuse.html
Thursday, 26 November 2009

The three-volume report, covering a period of abuse from the period 1975 to 2004, was published this afternoon by Minister for Justice Dermot Ahern. The report details a litany of abuse perpetrated by priests against more than 300 victims. It says that Archbishop Desmond Connell's strategies in refusing to admit liability often added to the hurt and grief of many victims of abuse. The Commission of Investigation cost a total of €3.6m up to April of this year.The report rubbishes the view put forward by the church that the abuse was hidden from view and somehow took church authorities by surprise. It states that the vast majority of priests turned a blind eye to abuse. The report states that the Commission has no doubt that clerical child abuse was covered up by the Archdiocese of Dublin and other church authorities. It states that the structures and rules of the church facilitated that cover-up. It also says that State authorities facilitated the cover up by allowing the church to be beyond the reach of the law. It claims that the welfare of children, which should have been the first priority, was not even a factor considered in the early days by State and church authorities. The preservation of the good name, status and assets of church institutions was the first priority, according to the report, which states that priests were seen as the most important members of the institution. The Commission says that it has identified 320 people who complained of child sexual abuse during the period 1975-2004. It also states that since May 2004 130 complaints against priests operating in the Dublin Arch Diocese have been made. The report details the cases of 46 priests guilty of abuse, as a representative sample of 102 priests within its remit.

THE RYAN REPORT (2009)

http://www.rte.ie/news/2009/0520/abuse.html

Wednesday, 20 May 2009

This new report says sexual abuse was endemic in boys' institutions and a chronic problem in some residential institutions. The report has strongly criticised the Department of Education for its handling of complaints about residential institutions. The Department of Education generally dismissed or ignored complaints of child sexual abuse and dealt inadequately with them according to the report. The report states that the safety of children was not a priority for the Christian Brothers who ran the institutions. The report follows ten years of work by the commission which dealt with thousands of complaints from former residents of predominantly Catholic institutions. The report says that the Christian Brothers Order was defensive in the way it responded to complaints and claims the order fails to accept any congregational responsibility for such abuse. More allegations were made against the Christian Brothers than all of the other male orders combined. The commission received thousands of complaints of emotional, physical and sexual trauma inflicted on children by Catholic priests, brothers and nuns. More than 100 institutions, chiefly run by religious orders, including industrial schools, institutions for children with disabilities and ordinary day schools, were examined by the commission chaired by Mr Justice Seán Ryan.

THE FERNS REPORT (2005)

http://www.rte.ie/news/2005/1025/ferns.html

Tuesday, 25 October 2005

The report of the Ferns Inquiry says that it identified more than 100 allegations of child sexual abuse, made between 1962 and 2002, against 21 priests.Six of the priests had died before any allegations of abuse were made against them. The report concludes that 'both Bishop Herlihy and Bishop Comiskey placed the interests of individual priests ahead of those of the community in which they served'. It says the nature of the response by the Church authorities in the Diocese of Ferns to allegations of child sexual abuse by priests operating under the aegis of that diocese has varied over the past 40 years. The report says that between 1960 and 1980, it would appear that Bishop Donal Herlihy treated child sexual abuse by priests of his diocese exclusively as a moral problem.

He penalised the priest against whom the allegation was made by transferring him to a different post or different diocese for a time, but then returned him to his former position. It says that by 1980, Bishop Herlihy recognised that there was a psychological or medical dimension to the issue of child sexual abuse. His decision in 1980 to send priests in respect of whom allegations of abuse were made to a psychologist was 'appropriate'. But 'what was wholly inappropriate and totally inexplicable' was the decision to appoint to curacies priests against whom allegations had been made and in respect of whom a respected clerical psychologist had expressed his concerns in unambiguous terms as to their suitability to interact with young people. The report criticises Bishop Herlihy's decision to ordain 'clearly unsuitable men' into the priesthood when he knew or ought to have known that they had a propensity to abuse children.   In   the   case   of   Bishop Brendan Comiskey, the report says that 'in almost every case significant periods elapsed' before the Bishop could persuade the priest in question to vacate his position and undergo assessment and treatment. The report says that in no case did Bishop Comiskey persuade or compel the priest concerned to stand aside from his priestly ministry. The Ferns Inquiry also highlighted major failures in St Peter's College where all the priests investigated by the inquiry were ordained. Over a random five-year period selected by the inquiry, ten priests who were in St Peter's have come to the attention of the inquiry over allegations of child sexual abuse. Fr Donal Collins who was a teacher and then a principal, consistently abused boys over a 21-period, it says. A member of a religious order, who spoke to the inquiry, recalled a high level of sexual activity in the college but did not recall child sexual abuse as being a problem.

CREATURES OF HABIT

Pat Mullan

Pat Mullan was born in Ireland and has lived in England, Canada and the USA. He now lives in Ireland. He has published articles, poetry and short stories in magazines such as *Crannóg, Buffalo Spree, Tales of the Talisman, Writers Post Journal.* His short story, *Galway Girl,* was short-listed for the WOW Awards and was published in the new WOW Magazine in Galway in April 2010.

Recent work has appeared in the anthologies, DUBLIN NOIR (published in the USA by *Akashic Books* and in Ireland and the UK by *Brandon Books)* , *City-Pick DUBLIN* (published by *Oxygen Books* in 2010 to mark Dublin being chosen as UNESCO'S City of Culture for 2010), and *NOIR by NOIR West* (from Arlen House) in 2014.

His first novel, *The Circle of Sodom,* received two nominations, one for Best First Novel and one for Best Suspense Thriller, at the 2005 ***Love Is Murder*** conference in **Chicago.** His second novel, *Blood Red Square,* was published in the US in 2005 and a new edition, published in 2011, is now available on-line as a paperback and as an ebook. His latest novels, *Last Days of the Tiger* and *Creatures of Habit* are now available on-line as ebooks on Amazon Kindle, Barnes & Noble's Nook, Kobo, and elsewhere; they are also available in paperback.

He is a member of *International Thriller Writers, Inc.* and *Mystery Writers of America.*

Visit him at: www.patmullan.com

CREATURES OF HABIT

Pat Mullan